A L I E N

P R O T O T Y P E

A L I E N
P R O T O T Y P E

A NOVEL BY TIM WAGGONER

TITAN BOOKS

A L I E N ™ : P R O T O T Y P E

Print edition ISBN: 9781789090918
E-book edition ISBN: 9781789092202

Published by Titan Books
A division of Titan Publishing Group Ltd
144 Southwark Street, London SE1 0UP

First edition: October 2019
10 9 8 7 6 5 4 3 2 1

A CIP catalogue record for this title is available from
the British Library.

Printed and bound in the United States.

Did you enjoy this book?
We love to hear from our readers. Please email us at readerfeedback@
titanemail.com or write to us at Reader Feedback at the above address.
www.titanbooks.com

DEDICATION
This one's for Lance Henriksen, science fiction and horror's MVP.

Chronology note: This novel takes place between the novel *Alien: Isolation* and the comic book series *Aliens: Resistance*.

1

"Holy shit."

Tamar Prather said the words so softly, someone would've had to be crouching alongside her to think she'd done more than exhale. Normally, her self-control was so complete that this slight lapse was the equivalent of screaming at the top of her lungs. Given the cause, she decided she could forgive herself this once.

The stasis pod had no identifying marks—no manufacturer's symbol, no serial number—but it was top-of-the-line tech. Likely a Weyland-Yutani product. The container was three feet high and just as wide, basically square, although its edges were rounded. *Probably for aesthetic effect*, Tamar guessed. The company's designers were big on extra touches like that, thought it set their products apart from their competitors.

She'd found the pod hidden in a storage compartment built into the floor of the captain's quarters. Although "hidden" was a misnomer. She'd spotted the seams in the floor the moment she'd walked into the cabin, hadn't even needed to use the omniscanner she held in her left hand. Employing the tool to unlock the compartment, she removed the top panel and then scanned the pod to determine what lay inside. The shielding prevented a detailed readout, but the result, though woefully incomplete, displayed on the screen.

One word: *biomatter*.

This could be it, she thought. *The holy fucking grail*.

"How's it going, Tamar? You find anything—"

Jumping a bit, she turned her head to see Juan Verela standing in the open doorway. He was tall and muscular, with a shaved head and a black mustache and goatee that were badly in need of trimming. He wore black pants and boots, but his pride was an ancient brown leather jacket held together with generous applications of insta-seal and prayer.

The big man's eyes fixed on the storage pod still resting in the open floor compartment, and his mouth stretched into a wide grin.

"I *love* stasis pods," he said. "Especially when they're hidden like that. Means there's something important inside, and *that* means credits. Lots and lots of—"

Tamar's body acted on its own, with no input from her conscious mind. She jumped to her feet and spun, drawing the Fournier 350 from her side holster. No need to disengage the weapon's safety; she never left it on. The pistol was set to silent mode—a must in her line of work—and the weapon emitted two soft *chuffs* as she put a pair of bullets into Juan's forehead.

The man stiffened, a look of confusion on his face, which seemed only natural since he'd just had his brains turned into slurry, and then he crumpled as if he were a synthetic experiencing a complete system shutdown. Prather was strong, but Juan was too massive for her to catch. Instead, she dashed forward, rammed him with her shoulder, and directed his falling body onto the bunk. He hit the thin mattress with a thud, but the impact was muffled, and she doubted anyone else on the ship could hear it.

She gazed down at Juan's corpse. He'd landed face down and hung halfway off the side. Not the most dignified of deaths, but Tamar had seen—and caused—worse in her career. She had acted on instinct, but if she'd taken the time to consider her actions, the result would have been the same. There was no way she could let her companions know what was—what *might be*—inside the stasis pod.

Still holding her gun, Tamar crouched next to the open storage compartment and touched the omniscanner to the pod's surface again. The pod's control system was locked, of course, but the scanner—while not as good, perhaps, as a Weyland-Yutani product—was more than capable of granting her access.

After several seconds she was in, and she used the scanner's touch screen to send the pod a command. Servomotors engaged, small black wheels emerged from the pod's bottom and sides, and the pod began to climb out of the compartment. Stasis pods this size were too heavy to lift, so they came equipped with movement-assist tech. Tamar stood and faced the open doorway as the pod made its way up and onto the cabin floor. Tucking the omniscanner into a loop next to the comm on the side of her belt, she kept her gun trained on the door in case any more of her crewmates decided to make an appearance.

Tamar was six and a half feet tall, lean and muscular. She had sharp, hawkish features that were striking, if not especially pleasing, and wore her blond hair cut short— long hair gave an opponent something to grab. A sleeveless khaki T-shirt covered a nusteel undergarment, along with tan slacks and knee-high black boots. She looked more like an athlete than she did a pirate, and while her crewmates wouldn't have been surprised to learn that she was a competition-level martial artist, they would've been *very* surprised to learn she'd just killed their captain.

When the stasis pod finished climbing out of the storage compartment, Tamar stepped out into the corridor and looked both ways to make sure it was empty. It was. She jogged down the corridor, pistol in her right hand raised and ready to fire, the stasis pod whirring along behind her like an obedient pet. She wished she could speed up the damn thing, but it was designed to be sturdy, not fast. She had to force herself to keep from running full-out.

This had started as another routine smash-and-grab job. The *Manticore* was a pirate vessel, and the crew had thievery down to a science. They frequented well-known intersystem trade routes, constantly broadcasting a false distress signal. Eventually a ship responded—only the most cold-hearted people would abandon a crew out here in the cold, dark vastness of space.

The *Manticore* waited until the *Proximo* was in range, and then fired its rail gun. The weapon used electromagnetic force to send multiple projectiles at great speeds, with devastating effect. They'd targeted the ship's engines and communications array, and once the boat was dead in the water, they'd docked and boarded. The crew of the defending ship had been ready to put up resistance, but the pirates of the *Manticore* were prepared for that. They came wearing breathing masks and throwing gas grenades.

There was an exchange of gunfire, but it didn't last long, and the *Manticore*'s crew were able to round up their wheezing, red-eyed victims and escort them to the ship's brig. After that, it was a simple matter to ransack the ship, searching for anything that could be sold on the black market. Tamar had served on the *Manticore* for the last seventeen months, and during that time the crew had raided a dozen different ships, but none of them had ever presented such a prize as what she suspected lay inside the stasis pod.

This was the reason she'd joined the *Manticore*'s crew in the first place. She wasn't a pirate, and preferred to think of herself as a professional in the field of "freelance information acquisition."

Put simply, she was a spy.

The galaxy—at least, the small portion of it that humans had settled—was in a state of constant upheaval, but the nature of large-scale conflict was different now. No longer did nations strive against one another for control of territory and resources or to increase their global status. Out here, there were no countries, no governments, no rulers. There were only the mega-corporations, constantly struggling to outcompete each other and increase their wealth and power. Tamar had been hired by one of the mega-corps—Venture—and tasked with infiltrating a pirate crew to keep an eye out for any stolen items which the corporation might turn to its advantage. It was boring work, but it paid well enough, and she'd only signed on to two years with the *Manticore* and its crew.

There were nine months left before Venture gave her a new assignment—hopefully, a more exciting one. During her time on the pirate vessel she hadn't discovered a single thing that might be of even minor interest to her employers, and she'd all but given up hope.

Until today.

She needed to get the stasis pod off this ship without any of her surviving companions stopping her. Tamar preferred not to hurt any of them, though. Several of them had been her lovers at one time or another. There was a lot of downtime on a spaceship, and if you weren't passing a trip in cryo-sleep, you had to find some way of occupying yourself. She was too much of a professional to allow herself to become emotionally attached, but she'd prefer to avoid killing any more of them.

Doing a quick mental rundown of the surviving *Manticore* crewmembers, she guessed where they were most likely to be. Lia Holcombe was guarding the *Proximo*'s crew in the brig, and Tamar wouldn't pass near there on her way to the docking port. Kenyatta Lehman might still be busy with the ship's computer system, reviewing the official cargo manifest and searching for an unofficial one, an encrypted list of off-the-books cargo. If she'd finished with that, though, she might have joined Sid Chun in the cargo bay so they could start assessing which of the *Proximo*'s goodies they should take and which—due to size and weight constraints—they would be forced to leave behind.

The cargo bay was located near the docking port, though Tamar could avoid it by taking a more circuitous route through the ship. Doing so would mean adding time to her journey, and she didn't know if she should risk it. If one of the surviving pirates tried to contact Juan, they'd receive no reply. They wouldn't be too concerned at first—comms malfunctioned, after all—but then they would go in search of their captain. If they found his corpse in the cabin Tamar had been searching, they'd come looking for her, guns out and ready.

No doubt she could take them if they came at her one at a time, but if they approached her as a group? She was less certain of her odds in that scenario. Worse, if they started shooting, the stasis pod—and more importantly, its contents—might be damaged in the crossfire.

Tamar opted for the most direct route, past the entrance to the cargo bay. Sid and Kenyatta *might* be too busy to notice her walking by, stasis pod in tow. More likely they'd hear the pod's goddamned whirring, and step into the corridor to see what was up.

Jogging down the corridor, she headed in the direction

of the cargo bay. Once she reached the *Manticore*, she'd undock and depart with her prize. Her crewmates would be stranded, but at least they'd be alive.

Most of them, anyway.

As she neared the bay she slowed to a walk, and the stasis pod slowed to match her pace. She was fit—she'd made sure to exercise regularly during her time on the *Manticore*—but she still felt winded, and her pulse thrummed in her ears. *Nerves*, she thought, and she focused on calming herself. Being nervous was okay. *Looking* nervous could arouse suspicion, and that could be deadly. Reluctantly, she holstered her gun. If either Kenyatta or Sid glanced at her as she passed, it wouldn't do for them to see her with weapon in hand.

By the time she reached the cargo bay she was breathing normally, and her pulse had slowed. The entrance was open, and she risked a quick look. The bay was filled with large mining equipment—drills and haulers, mostly—but there were also containers of electronic components and medical supplies. These would be easiest to transport and sell. Harder to track, too. She hoped to see Sid and Kenyatta moving among the equipment and storage containers, cataloguing and discussing their finds. Instead, they both stood several feet back from the open doorway, gripping their pistols.

As Tamar came into view, they trained their weapons on her, and she froze. The stasis pod halted, sensing that she'd stopped moving.

"Going somewhere?" Kenyatta asked. She smiled,

but there was no mirth in her gaze. The woman was of African descent, tall and lean, hair cut close to her skull. She had delicate, almost doll-like features that belied her true nature. She could be utterly ruthless when the situation demanded it.

Sid Chun was a full head shorter than Kenyatta, and stocky. He wore his long black hair in a ponytail, and his Asian features were overlaid by the tattoo of a skull. He didn't say anything, but his gaze was, if anything, colder than Kenyatta's.

Tamar forced herself to stay relaxed and she made sure to keep her hand well away from her gun.

"I'm taking the pod to the ship," she said. "Juan's orders."

"Really?" Kenyatta looked at the pod, but she didn't lower her gun.

"Yes, really." Prather acted annoyed. "Any particular reason you two are pointing your guns at me?"

Sid spoke in a voice like ice.

"Juan's orders," he said.

Tamar felt a stab of fear, but kept her expression neutral.

"Juan started having doubts about you a few weeks ago," Kenyatta said, "when we hit that trading vessel on the edge of the Kassa system."

Tamar frowned. She remembered the job well. The trader had been carrying a hold full of fruits and vegetables grown in the hydroponic gardens of one of the Mars colonies. Not quite fresh produce from Earth, but close enough. The *Manticore* had a small refrigerated storage facility, so the crew had taken only a small portion of the food, and they'd eaten most of it themselves. They'd sold what was left over, but it didn't bring in enough credits to come close to paying for the fuel they'd expended during the job.

Hardly a major score. Tamar quickly reviewed her memories of the theft, but she couldn't recall doing or saying anything that would arouse Juan's suspicions.

"As soon as you saw that the ship only carried produce, you lost interest," Sid said. "A real pirate would've gotten a raging hard-on, seeing that many fruits and vegetables."

"Out here," Kenyatta said, "fresh produce is worth its weight in gold."

"Twice that," Sid added.

"And you didn't give a damn," Kenyatta finished.

"That's because we didn't have anywhere to store it on the *Manticore*," Tamar replied, "and that made it worthless, at least for us."

"You didn't even try," Kenyatta said. Tamar remembered how Juan, Kenyatta, Sid, and Lia had tossed around ideas for preserving the produce. The stupidest— offered by Lia—had been to jury-rig the cryo-sleep chambers to act as makeshift refrigerators.

"So I didn't have an orgasm, seeing a hold full of greenery," Tamar said. "Juan decided I was… what?" She knew the answer, of course, but she needed to keep playing the part until she could figure a way out of this situation.

"He figured you for a spy," Sid said.

"Looking for stuff she could bring to her employers," Kenyatta added.

"Juan took me and Kenyatta aside and told us of his suspicions," Sid continued. "Not Lia, though. She's too soft-hearted, and Juan figured she'd give you a heads-up."

Smart move, Tamar thought. Lia hated conflict among the crew, and functioned as their self-appointed peacemaker. There was an excellent chance she would've told Tamar about the captain's doubts.

"So what did Juan tell you to do?" Tamar asked. "Keep an eye on me?"

"He copied us on any orders he gave you," Sid said. "That way we could make sure you did what you were told—or not—and report back to him."

"If we caught you doing anything naughty," Kenyatta said, "he told us to stop you any way we thought was necessary."

"Juan didn't order you to take anything back to the ship—let alone a stasis pod," Sid said. "So when we heard the pod's motor…"

You knew it had to be me, coming down the corridor, Tamar thought. *Lia wouldn't leave her post, and Juan would bring the pod to the bay, where we'd load it all at once.* That was why Juan had come to the captain's cabin—to check on her. He'd suspected her of being a spy—correctly, as it turned out.

She was glad she'd killed him.

It made sense, now that she thought about it. Juan, Kenyatta, and Sid had been stiff toward her over the last few weeks, although Lia had treated her the same as ever. She hadn't thought much of it, though. When people spent a lot of time together in cramped quarters, they tended to run hot and cold. Especially given the... intimacies involved. She'd thought that was all. She'd been wrong, and now that mistake might cost Tamar her life.

"What's in the stasis pod that's so special?" Kenyatta demanded. "Must be damn good to make you risk moving it onto the *Manticore* by yourself."

"And where the hell did you think you were going to hide the damn thing, once you got it aboard?" Sid said. "It's not like we have a ton of extra space to..."

Understanding came into his gaze.

Kenyatta figured it out then, too.

"You weren't planning to hide it, were you?" the woman said. "You were going to leave us here, weren't you?"

This was it. One or both of them would take a shot at her in the next few seconds. Tamar could sense it. If either of them had been closer, she would've gone on the offensive, but this wasn't an action vid. Even the most skilled martial artist was no match for a gun, let alone a pair of them—and while she was fast on the draw, both Kenyatta and Sid would get shots off before she could pull her gun clear. She wasn't helpless, though.

Looking at Sid, she let out a long sigh.

"I guess the jig's up, partner."

Sid's eyes widened in surprise.

"Partner? What the hell are you talking about?"

"There's no point in pretending any longer. Juan's a smart businessman, though. Maybe we can make a deal with him, get our bosses to cut him in on the action."

"*Our* bosses?" Sid's eyes practically bulged from their

sockets, and Tamar wouldn't have been surprised if he had an embolism in the next few seconds.

"What are you saying?" Kenyatta looked from Tamar to Sid and back again, brow furrowing. "You and Sid are *both* spies?"

"That's bullshit!" Sid protested. "Don't listen to her! She's just trying to confuse you to save her ass!"

"Listen, you sonofabitch." Tamar's face clouded with faux anger, and she took a step forward. "I'm not going to let you do this to me. If *I'm* exposed, *you're* exposed. Got it?" As she said this, she moved her left hand to the omniscanner on her belt, keeping her gaze fixed on Sid.

Kenyatta looked back and forth one more time, then trained her gun on Sid.

"Maybe we should go find Juan and let him sort this out," she said.

Sid's face went red with anger and frustration.

"What the fuck is *wrong* with you?" he said. "You've known me for what now? Six, seven years? This bitch is trying to divide so she can—"

Tamar chose that moment to tap a control on the omniscanner. The stasis pod whirred to life and began spinning in circles. Kenyatta's and Sid's attention was immediately drawn to the machine, and in that instant Tamar drew her pistol and fired.

She shot Sid first, then Kenyatta. They were fast, sloppy shots, and she didn't have time to aim. The bullet that hit Sid struck him in the throat, and the one that hit Kenyatta got her in the left shoulder. Before they could fall, Tamar stepped forward and quickly shot each of them between the eyes. The two pirates hit the deck and lay still as blood began pooling around their bodies.

Tamar tapped the omniscanner once more, and the stasis pod stopped moving. She let out a breath she hadn't known she'd been holding. That had been a close one.

Her comm device chirped.

"Tamar? You there?"

It was Lia.

"I've been guarding the crew for almost two hours now, and I haven't heard from anybody. Is everything okay? I'm starting to get a little worried."

Tamar gazed down at the dead bodies of her former companions as she took the comm from her belt and raised it to her mouth.

"Everything's fine."

It would take twenty-three days for Tamar Prather to reach Jericho 3. Not so long that she really needed to enter cryo-sleep, but she had nothing to occupy her during the trip, and she didn't feel like sitting in front of the flight console watching data that never changed.

She wasn't concerned that the *Proximo* would come after her. The damage done by the *Manticore*'s rail gun had been extensive—enough so that they'd require replacements parts unlikely to be kept on board. And even if they managed to get the ship space-worthy again, they wouldn't have the tracking equipment needed to follow the *Manticore*'s ion trail. Besides, the *Proximo* didn't have any weapons worth noting.

That didn't mean she should throw caution to the wind. The first thing the *Proximo*'s captain would do, once Lia released her from the brig, was send out a distress signal. Then she would send a message to Weyland-Yutani. If the pod contained what Tamar thought it did, the company would do everything possible to retrieve it, and they had ships that were more than capable of tracking her. With weapons that made the *Manticore*'s rail gun look like a pea shooter.

So she charted a roundabout course that avoided standard shipping lanes. Otherwise, she could've reached Jericho 3 in a week. Setting the call sign on the *Manticore* to change randomly every few hours, she programmed the light engines to cycle down periodically to break the ship's ion trail. She doubted these precautions would be necessary, though. Space was fucking huge, and the odds of anyone finding the *Manticore* before it reached its destination were, not to make a pun, astronomically small.

Still, she'd survived this long in the spy game by being careful to the point of paranoia.

Securing the stasis pod in one of the *Manticore*'s hidden compartments, she stripped down to her underwear, slathered cryo-gel onto her body, and slipped into one of the cryo-chambers. It sealed with a hiss, and within moments a familiar deep drowsiness came over her. As she sank into darkness, she thought about the bonus she'd get from Venture, and fell into cryo-sleep with a smile on her face.

2

Aleta Fuentes walked down the corridor with a brisk, no-nonsense stride, gaze fixed straight ahead, features set in a do-not-talk-to-me expression. She was the director of the V-22 facility, and as such, *everyone* wanted to talk to her, to ask for something, complain about something, or—most often—curry favor. It was one of the main reasons she only left her office when absolutely necessary. She *hated* interacting with people.

Most of them weren't as smart as she was, and they almost always made her job harder than it needed to be. Not for the first time she wondered how she'd ended up in an administrative position, given her dislike for working with inferiors. But she was an employee of Venture, and one did as one's corporate masters wished, if one wanted to advance. Since she hoped one day to become a master herself, she'd accepted her appointment with as much grace as she could muster.

She ran V-22—colloquially known as the Lodge by its workers—with determined efficiency, but she knew that doing an excellent job here wouldn't be enough to distinguish herself in the view of her superiors. She needed to do something more. Something *special*. She needed to pull off a bona fide fucking miracle, and if what Dr. Gagnon had told her was true, it looked as if she was on the verge of just that.

V-22's focus was on the development of new and improved space colonization technology. The first wave of colonists had already moved out into the galaxy, but they were merely a drop in the bucket for what was to come. They lived in small groups housed in cramped space stations, or equally cramped planet-based facilities, but soon larger missions would be looking for opportunities beyond the world of their birth. More ambitious settlements would be established—villages, towns, cities, and eventually entire nations. The future colonists would need better ships, better facilities, and better tools to help them survive, let alone work in the hostile environments they would encounter.

Venture intended to be the number one supplier of these needs, outcompeting all others, including the almighty Weyland-Yutani. Of course, Weyland-Yutani had a habit of buying out any corporation that came close to becoming a threat, but Aleta didn't care about that. Their salary would spend just as well as Venture's.

At a shade over five feet, Aleta wasn't a physically imposing presence. She was fit but not rail thin, as were so many people who lived and worked in space. Conservation of resources was vital to survival, and that included food. She wore her black hair short, and used only minimal makeup, just enough to achieve an enhanced "natural" look. Most of Venture's personnel wore the gray coveralls that served as the facility's unofficial uniform. As chief administrator, Aleta was encouraged to dress the same way in order to visually demonstrate that there was no real difference between rank-and-file employees and management. She thought this was human resources bullshit, though, and wore a navy-blue suit jacket over a white blouse, with navy-blue slacks and less-than-stylish black flats. She liked to look good, but she wasn't a fanatic about it. Although she *would* have liked the couple extra inches heels would have given her.

The complex was practically gigantic as planet-side facilities went, with five interconnected buildings and a staff of nearly six hundred. It was an old cliché that people were the costliest resource in business, but it was true, and doubly so off-world. There had to be air, water, food, and livable environments. Humans were fragile creatures, biologically unsuited to the harsh and all-too-often deadly conditions of space, and keeping them alive was damned expensive.

Venture had been too ambitious when it built this facility, and so far the corporation's return on its investment had been modest. If the situation didn't improve—if V-22 didn't start generating significant profits—there was an excellent chance the facility would be shut down and its staff either relocated or, if they proved to be less than essential employees, let go.

This situation, unknown to most of the staff, put her in a precarious position. She wanted the Lodge to be a stepping stone to bigger and better things, but if the facility failed while she was in charge, she'd be blamed, regardless of whatever factors were in play. If that happened, she'd be lucky to get a job cleaning lavatories. V-22 *had* to be a success. If she wanted to climb Venture's corporate ladder, she needed to accomplish something that would make a big impression on her superiors and, ultimately, the board of directors.

This latest acquisition might be the answer to her prayers.

Aleta heard the sound of someone jogging down the corridor, and she turned to see Tamar Prather coming toward her. She groaned inwardly. This was the last thing she needed, but she put on a coolly professional smile as the woman reached her and came to a stop. There was a slight sheen of sweat on her forehead, but she didn't appear winded. Aleta told herself that she needed to work out more.

"I went to your office to see you, but you weren't there," Tamar said. "Your assistant told me that you were on your way to Research and Development, so I started running, hoping I could catch up to you."

"And you succeeded," Aleta said drily. "What can I do for you?"

The question wasn't necessary. Aleta knew damn well what Tamar wanted—the same thing she'd wanted since she'd landed the *Manticore* on the planet.

"Your assistant told me that you're planning to speak with Dr. Gagnon. Dare I hope that he's ready to share some information about the bio-specimen, so you'll finally authorize my payment?"

Aleta made a mental note to fire her assistant the moment she returned to the office.

"I believe so," she responded, "although he didn't say. I'll be sure to keep you apprised of whatever information he gives me, though." She gave Tamar a cold smile. "Provided, of course, the company doesn't consider it classified. I'll have to run it through the proper channels, and if—"

"I'm not really a *proper channels* kind of person," Tamar said. "Too many hoops to jump through. I'm more of a *let's get shit done* girl. Since I'm already here, why don't I go with you to Gagnon's lab? That way you won't have to deal with the hassle of *proper channels*. It'll save us both some time."

Aleta didn't like Tamar. As a rule she disliked spies, although she understood their usefulness. Corporate spies had no loyalty, though. They worked for whoever paid them the most. Their allegiances were temporary and liable to change at the slightest shift in the breeze. Aleta believed in the sanctity of the contract. Once you signed with an employer, you gave them everything— mind, body, and soul. So long as the contract remained in force. Once it was terminated, all bets were off.

People like Prather—*freelancers*—were unpredictable, and because of that they weren't trustworthy. More than that, Tamar got on Aleta's nerves. She was pushy, persistent, and altogether unpleasant. More than any bullshit about proper channels, that made Aleta want to deny the woman's request. Before she could, however, the woman spoke again.

"There are a lot of people who would be interested to know about the specimen," Tamar said. "*Especially* Weyland-Yutani. I'm sure they'd *love* to know where their 'lost' property turned up."

Aleta considered calling Security and having Tamar thrown in the brig, but she knew it was pointless. The woman would already have considered that possibility, and have a contingency plan in place. Perhaps an automated message that would be sent to Weyland-Yutani if she found herself behind bars. The threat wasn't a bluff.

She let out a long sigh.

"Fine. You can join me."

Tamar smiled.

"If you insist."

An electronic tone sounded, indicating that someone was at the door. Millard Gagnon was on the other side of the large room, watching data stream across a terminal screen. Without looking up, he spoke to his assistant.

"Please let the director in."

Brigette wasn't any closer to the door, but she nodded, walked across the lab, and pressed a button on the wall keypad. The lab door slid open with a soft hiss of air, and Gagnon looked up from his work to watch Aleta Fuentes enter. This was expected. That Tamar Prather accompanied her was not. Gagnon wasn't distressed by this, however. He liked it when things were unpredictable, even downright chaotic at times. Order might be comfortable, but chaos provoked change, and change provided opportunities. Change was unpredictable, messy, and at times dangerous, but as far as he was concerned it was the only reliable way to move forward in life. So he gave both women a smile as he left his terminal and went to greet them.

"Welcome, welcome!" he said, shaking each of their hands in turn.

Brigette closed the door, then turned to regard their visitors with an interested, if dispassionate, gaze.

Gagnon looked nothing like the stereotype of a scientist. Yes, he wore a white lab coat over his equally white shirt, but otherwise he seemed more like a miner or someone who worked with heavy equipment. He was a big, rough-looking man, tall, broad-shouldered, with a loud, deep voice and thick black hair and beard. He'd been told he was handsome, but there was something in his brown eyes that bothered people. A cold detachment that—as a former lover once told him—made them think of a predatory insect. The description hadn't bothered him. In fact, he'd taken it as a compliment. It was this detachment that made him good at what he did.

Brigette didn't look the stereotype of a scientist, either, any more than Gagnon. She was a Venture Corporation synthetic, originally created for human sexual gratification, and as such, she had been designed to be physically appealing. She was slim, small-waisted, large-breasted, with fiery red hair that reached to the bottom of her back. Her lips were full and lush, and her green eyes were striking, almost seeming to glow with an inner light. Like Gagnon, she wore a white lab coat, but it did nothing to disguise her figure.

Gagnon viewed her as a highly sophisticated tool, little more than a mobile semi-autonomous computer. When he first came to the Lodge he'd requested a synthetic for an assistant, and he'd been surprised when Brigette arrived. She'd been repurposed after breaking the arms of a client who had tried to slice her skin with a straight razor. While he would've preferred a plainer-looking assistant, he had no complaints about her job performance.

"You have something to show me?" Aleta said.

He detected a challenge in her voice, along with more than a hint of frustration. He'd been employed by Venture for the better part of a decade, and was used to management types who expected quick results. They had no appreciation for the art of science, for the *process*. He felt sorry for them, really. Limited creatures.

"I do." Gagnon turned to Brigette. "Prepare the demonstration, please."

Brigette gave him a look which might have been disapproval. The specimen made her nervous, although she preferred the term *cautious*. He couldn't understand her hesitation. The specimen was an exquisite creature, the most beautiful thing he'd ever seen. Brigette was intelligent, but she was a synthetic, and as such lacked vision.

Some are born to lead, and some to serve, he thought.

There were seven doors in the main lab, each of which led to different rooms—Gagnon's office, supply storage, and several testing chambers. Brigette crossed to the far side and took up a position at a console, in front of what looked to be a blank wall. Her delicate hands moved confidently across the controls, and a moment later there was a soft hum as a panel in the wall slid upward. Behind it lay a thick layer of clear plasteel, the same material Venture used to create windows for the buildings in their proto-colony. They were strong enough to withstand the most intense planetary conditions, and Gagnon had ordered the window installed soon after the specimen was brought to his lab. He'd also had the walls, floor, and ceiling of the small chamber reinforced with nusteel, and he'd had a new interior door installed. Like the window, the door was designed for use in colony buildings, and it could take a direct hit from a high-intensity pulse cannon with only a scratch.

Gagnon supposed he was being overcautious, but if so, it wasn't out of fear for his or Brigette's safety—nor that of the rest of the Lodge's personnel. Having access to such a specimen was a once-in-a-lifetime opportunity, and he was determined to make sure absolutely nothing went wrong while he was working with it.

As Brigette activated the chamber's lights and turned on the recording equipment, Gagnon escorted his visitors to join the synthetic.

"We repurposed one of the testing chambers we used

during the last round of trials for our latest vaccine," Gagnon explained. He oversaw every project that had biological or medical applications, but only took a personal hand in the research that especially interested him. One of these was the search for a universal vaccine that would strengthen the human immune system, to make colonists resistant to whatever diseases they might encounter when settling a new world. A pipe dream, perhaps—likely no more achievable than the legendary Philosopher's Stone, which ancient alchemists believed could turn lead into gold, but it was interesting work, if not entirely practical. He'd had a difficult time convincing Fuentes to authorize and, more importantly, fund his experiments, but he'd put that program on hold the moment the specimen had arrived.

At that juncture there had been no problem getting funding. In fact, she practically fell over herself throwing credits at him. The change in their professional relationship had been refreshing, but if he didn't show Aleta some significant progress today, they would be adversaries once again.

He preferred to avoid that, if he could.

Inside the chamber, illuminated by fluorescent light bars attached to the ceiling, a brown-black leathery object rested on the floor. It was roughly oval-shaped, not quite a meter high, and its surface resembled a fusion of rock and an insect's carapace.

"So *that's* what was in the stasis pod," Tamar said. She turned to Gagnon. "Is it what I thought? One of *them*?"

"Officially, we don't know," Brigette answered.

"There isn't enough data to be certain."

Aleta looked at Gagnon. "But unofficially?"

He smiled. "We hit the jackpot."

Aleta, usually so reserved, clapped her hands together. "Yes!"

The other woman's reaction was more subdued. She smiled in satisfaction, but did not take her gaze from the specimen. Gagnon understood. It was the most beautiful thing he'd ever seen.

There had been rumors of Weyland-Yutani's interest in a particularly deadly non-Terran species circulating among the mega-corporations for more than a decade. Many considered the stories to be tall tales, perhaps originated by the company as a way to further its mystique. Others—including Venture's board of directors—believed the rumors to be true, at least on some level.

Little was known about the creatures Weyland-Yutani coveted, but if the most powerful corporation in the galaxy had become obsessed when it came to obtaining these things, then Venture's board wanted to get their hands on specimens of their own. Not that Gagnon gave a damn about the board or their endless calculations of profit and loss. He viewed Venture as a means to an end. They gave him facilities and funds to conduct his research, and as far as he was concerned that was the corporation's sole reason for existing.

Brigette checked the information scrolling across several small display screens.

"Chamber temperature holding steady at 98 degrees

Fahrenheit, 37 degrees Celsius. Humidity at eighty percent."

"It prefers heat?" Aleta asked.

"We believe so," Gagnon said. "Its life signs are strongest and most steady when the atmosphere inside the chamber is hot and humid."

"Is it native to a tropical environment?" Tamar asked.

"Perhaps," Gagnon said, "but based on the experiments we've conducted so far, I believe the specimen could survive in almost any environment—including the vacuum of space."

Aleta's exuberance had faded, and she regarded the specimen with narrowed eyes.

"To be honest, I thought it would be more…"

"Impressive?" Gagnon offered.

"Bigger?" Prather asked.

"More frightening," Aleta said. "According to the rumors, these creatures are supposed to be deadly. But this thing doesn't look any deadlier than an average houseplant."

"That's a good point," Tamar said. She finally took her gaze from the creature to look at Gagnon. "There have been reports of those things attacking personnel on ships, stations, and planetary outposts. And when they're finished, there aren't many survivors. If any."

Brigette spoke before Gagnon could answer.

"That's because this isn't one of the creatures," she said. "We believe it's an egg—a biological incubator of some sort."

Irritated at Brigette for inserting herself into the conversation, Gagnon gave her an angry look. She showed no sign that she recognized the emotion he was trying to convey. He sighed, turned to his two visitors, and spoke.

"She's correct," he said. "The specimen is alive, and possesses a rudimentary nervous system at the base, which connects to a network of veins running beneath its surface. I believe they are pressure- and thermo-sensitive, but we need to do further tests."

"Why don't you just dissect the damned thing?" Aleta frowned. "Wouldn't that be the simplest way to find out how it works?"

God save me from the scientifically ignorant.

"I'd prefer not to kill the specimen," Gagnon replied aloud. "We can learn more from it if it remains alive."

"It's like the old joke," Brigette said. "The operation was a success, but the patient died." The synthetic said this in a monotone, and when no one responded she returned her attention to her console.

"We've attempted to take some tissue samples," Gagnon said. "The results were… rather dramatic."

He gestured to the synthetic, and she called up a video record of one of their earliest attempts at tissue extraction. Aleta and Tamar leaned closer to the terminal screen to get a better view. The chamber appeared on the screen, with the specimen resting on the floor, just as it appeared now. For a moment it seemed as if they were looking at a live feed.

Then a small panel opened in one wall and a rod emerged. It had a small container attached to its tip, and as the rod extended toward the specimen, a needle slid forth from the canister. The specimen showed no reaction as the needle drew closer to its surface, and it remained inert as the needle penetrated its craggy hide. For a moment, nothing happened, and then green fluid jetted from the needle's entry point. Most of the liquid coated the rod, but some fell to the chamber's floor.

Gagnon wasn't certain yet if the substance qualified as blood, but whatever it touched, it began eating away at the material like an extremely powerful acid. Even the nusteel that formed both the rod and the floor couldn't resist the caustic substance. The rod began to fall apart, and several inches of it simply disintegrated. The acid which fell to the floor ate a hole roughly the size of a human palm.

The video ended.

"We tried two more times, with the same result," Gagnon said. "After each attempt we sent multi-drones in to collect samples of the dissolved material."

Multi-drones were among the smallest robots Venture produced. They resembled mechanical insects and were good for varied tasks—hence the *multi*—but they were used primarily for cleaning and simple maintenance.

"The multi-drones did their best to repair the damage to the floor," Brigette said, "but if you look closely, you can see where it occurred." Aleta and Tamar peered through the clear plastic barrier at several sections of floor near the egg where the nusteel was a shade darker than the rest.

"The acid ate through that easily?" Aleta asked, sounding more amazed than doubtful. Nusteel was one of Venture's most successful products. Not quite as strong and durable as Weyland-Yutani's ferrocrete, but close.

"As if it were no more substantial than balsa wood," Gagnon said.

"If the blood could be synthesized," Brigette said, "the result would be a product with numerous industrial and military applications."

"Yes," Gagnon agreed, "but that's the least of the specimen's potential." He turned to Brigette. "Begin the demonstration."

She entered a series of commands into her console, and a moment later the wall panel in the chamber slid open. Instead of a probe, a small cage emerged. It was attached to a metal frame with wheels, propelled by a pair of multi-drones connected to each side of the framework. A white mouse crouched inside the cage, curled into a ball, as if trying to make itself as small a target as possible. Gagnon was always impressed by how the test animals could immediately sense the danger that the alien egg—for lack of a better term—presented. They were terrified of the thing, and Gagnon didn't blame them. If he'd possessed such a primitive, rudimentary intelligence, he would've been afraid of the thing too.

As the multi-drones moved the cage closer to the specimen, a change came over it. It began to quiver, and the top of it split open, four sections of it peeling back slowly, like flower petals opening to the sun. The multi-drones stopped less than a meter from the specimen, and for several moments nothing happened. Then the petals moved back into place and sealed closed once more.

Brigette entered a command on her console, and the

multi-drones reversed course, returning the still-terrified mouse to its compartment behind the wall. The panel then lowered, and the demonstration was over.

"What did we just witness?" Aleta asked.

"Looked to me like the thing was thinking about eating the mouse," Tamar said.

It was an obvious—although erroneous—conclusion, Gagnon believed. Still, it showed that the woman was thinking along the right track, and Gagnon's estimation of her rose a notch.

"Our scans have identified another lifeform within the specimen," he said, "one that responds to the presence of other life in its vicinity. Not because it seeks sustenance, though. Based on reports of creature encounters, scanner results, and our own observations, my guess is that whatever is inside the specimen is looking for a suitable host into which it will implant an embryonic lifeform. The specimen reacted to the mouse as a living creature, but it quickly recognized that the animal was too small and weak to make an effective host. Thus it ended the process."

"We believe the embryonic lifeforms become the savage creatures that have been reported," Brigette added.

"I've heard they're called Xenomorphs," Tamar said.

"A simplistic term that means *alien form*," Gagnon said, "but I suppose it'll do."

"What would make a suitable host for one of these Xenomorphs?" Aleta asked.

"Something in the order of a canine, or a primate, I should think." Gagnon paused, and then added, "Or a human."

Aleta looked startled, but Tamar's features betrayed no emotion. There was, however, sly calculation in her gaze, and Gagnon decided that the woman bore watching. Just because she was a Venture employee, didn't mean she could be trusted. She *was* a spy, after all.

Aleta looked at the egg—*the Ovomorph*, Gagnon thought—and said, "Is there any way to confirm your theory about the Xenomorphs? Short of experimenting on an actual person?"

Gagnon could feel Brigette's gaze on him, but he didn't meet the synthetic's eyes. She was well aware of his agenda. Still, she remained silent as he answered.

"We *could* use larger animals. Of course, we'd need to requisition them, wait for approval, and then wait for them to be delivered. The process could take weeks, and more likely months."

"Perhaps even longer," Tamar said.

"Yes," Gagnon agreed.

Aleta looked at the Ovomorph, and Gagnon could practically hear the wheels turning in her head.

"I suppose we *could* ask for volunteers," she said. "Ones who've signed waivers, of course."

"It would be legal in Venture's eyes then," Brigette said. "As to whether it would be ethical or moral…"

Gagnon shot his assistant a dark look, and she fell silent.

After a moment's thought, Aleta said, "Legal will do."

Gagnon smiled.

* * *

After they left Gagnon's lab, Aleta promised Tamar that she'd authorize immediate payment for her services. Then, without bothering to say goodbye, the director headed back to the Administration building, leaving Tamar to her own devices.

Like anyone who lived and worked in space, Tamar was used to periods of downtime between jobs, but she'd spent weeks on Jericho 3 waiting for Aleta to finally pay her. She was sick of the Lodge. There was only so much time a person could spend in the station's recreation facilities, and she'd already slept with the most interesting people on the staff. She was more than ready to report in to Venture's Intelligence Division and request a new assignment.

And yet…

Obtaining the Xenomorph egg had been a major score for Venture, but until she'd seen the thing in person, she hadn't realized how truly impressive it was—not to mention how valuable. Venture would pay her well for her acquisition, but why stop there? Any of their competitors would kill to get their hands on the egg, and Weyland-Yutani would be extremely interested in reacquiring their lost property. Not only might the corporation pay her significantly more than Venture for returning the egg to them, she might end up getting a full-time position with their Intelligence division—at a much higher salary than Venture would ever offer.

Of course, it would mean betraying her current employer, but that didn't bother her. This was a cutthroat galaxy, and a girl had to look out for herself, first and foremost. She headed toward the Personnel building, thinking she might see if she could find anyone up for a game of racquetball.

As she walked, she began making plans.

3

"Get behind me!" Zula shouted.

With her free hand she shoved Amanda Ripley back, raised her pulse rifle and started firing. The quartet of attacking Xenomorphs scattered to avoid the rounds the weapon discharged, and ran in zigzagging patterns to make them harder to hit. They ran on all fours, low to the ground, claws scrabbling on the deck of the engineering bay. Zula had no idea how intelligent the damned things were, but they were far from being dumb animals. Too bad.

If the things were stupid, they'd be easier to kill.

Davis stood on her left, the battle synth also armed with a pulse rifle. He managed to hit two of the Xenomorphs, but the damage he inflicted was minimal, and the monsters barely slowed down. His brow furrowed slightly, and his eyes narrowed behind the lenses of the glasses he didn't need, but wore anyway—signs of frustration that anyone unfamiliar with the synth would've missed. But Zula had fought at Davis's side long enough to read his expressions, and for him, this was the equivalent of a human shouting in frustration.

Zula Hendricks, Davis, and Amanda stood in the center of Tranquility Station's engineering bay, surrounded by lunar rovers in varying states of disrepair. Zula had shadowed Amanda as she worked on repairing the machines, and she'd picked up enough knowledge to make herself a fair engineer's assistant, although she knew she didn't have what it took to be a true tech-head. Still, it was nice to have something to fall back on, in case the whole wipe-out-the-Xenomorph-species gig didn't work out.

"Keep the pressure up!" Zula shouted, and Davis acknowledged her words with a curt nod. The two coordinated their fire, targeting the aliens—if they didn't injure them significantly, at least they were able to slow the advance.

Although pulse rifles weren't heavy, Zula soon began to feel the strain of holding the gun. It began as a dull ache up and down her spine, but the pain swiftly intensified until it felt as if someone had jammed red-hot spikes into her muscle and bone. She'd made good progress in recovering from her back injury, and didn't want to jeopardize that, didn't want to have to start all over again with more operations and more rehab. But she couldn't afford to rest now, not unless she wanted the four Xenomorphs to tear her and her companions into bloody gobbets. So she gritted her teeth against the pain and kept firing.

The gunfire began taking its toll, and the aliens bled from dozens of wounds, their acidic blood eating into the deck where it fell. The creatures took cover, darting behind rovers, using the machines as shields. Zula knew the Xenomorphs wouldn't remain in hiding for long, though. The things possessed only two drives: kill and procreate. They would adapt swiftly to the current situation, develop a new plan of attack, and resume their assault. She and her companions didn't have much time.

Evidently Amanda was thinking along the same lines. "We need to get out of here!" she shouted. "If we can reach the bay doors and get into the corridor before those things do, I can seal the doors and lock them inside."

Zula didn't like plans that began with *if*, but she didn't have a better alternative to offer, and pulse rifles didn't possess an inexhaustible ammo supply. Soon the weapons' bullets would be depleted, and somehow she didn't think the Xenomorphs would agree to a time-out so she and Davis could reload.

She glanced at Davis, and he gave a shrug in reply. The gesture was so human that if the circumstances had been different, she would've laughed. Davis was the only synth she'd known who'd taken control of his own programming, and was working to make himself more human. That was the reason he wore the glasses—to differentiate himself from the other Davis models who looked exactly like him. Zula liked the glasses. Combined with the synth's bald head, they gave him a dignified, almost professorial appearance.

"All right," she said, hoping she hadn't just signed their death warrants. She nodded to Amanda. "Head for the doors. Davis and I will cover you."

Amanda nodded and ran. Zula and Davis followed, walking backward, rifles held at the ready, their gazes sweeping back and forth as they searched for any signs of the Xenomorphs. The lights in the engineering bay were dim, and this struck Zula as strange. In all the times she'd watched Amanda repair lunar rovers, the lights had always been bright. So much so that they sometimes hurt her eyes. Zula had mentioned it to Amanda once.

"You can't fix things if you can't see them," Amanda had said.

They reached the bay doors, and Amanda pressed a button on the keypad to open them. The doors slid apart, and Amanda hurried into the outer corridor. Zula and Davis followed, rifles up and ready to blast the aliens should they attack. But none came, and Zula found this more than a little concerning. In her experience, Xenomorphs could be stealthy when they wished, but one thing they *never* did was break off an attack. No matter what the conditions were, no matter what sort of opposition they faced, they kept coming, even if by doing so they were committing suicide. They were pure, unrelenting, savage aggression.

So where the hell were they?

Zula and Davis took up positions in front of the open doorway while Amanda turned to the keypad on the outside wall. She quickly began inputting a series of numbers, and a moment later the doors began to close, but for some reason they did so far more slowly than when they'd opened.

Weird, Zula thought.

"Once the doors close, they'll lock and stay locked until I punch in the proper code," Amanda said. "Those damn things will be trapped in the bay, and then we can—"

Zula never found out what Amanda was going to say. A segmented Xenomorph tail snaked down from above the other side of the doors. It shot toward Davis, coiled around the synthetic's throat before he could react, and yanked him off his feet. That told Zula what the Xenomorphs had done. Rather than continue their attack head-on, they'd climbed up the bay walls and crawled along the ceiling in order to get at their prey.

She watched helplessly as Davis was lifted into the air. She didn't fire her pulse rifle for fear of hitting her friend, and a second later he had been pulled through the doorway and up toward the ceiling. He was lost to view for an instant, and Zula stepped forward, intending to do what she could to free him. Before she could re-enter the engineering bay, she heard wet tearing sounds, followed by a scream.

Davis's voice sounded human at first, then degenerated into an electronic buzz as his system failed. In his quest to become more human, the synth had programmed himself to experience pain in the same way as beings made of flesh and bone. Now Zula wished he'd never taken that step. It would've made his end easier.

Thick white ichor—the substance that flowed through

a synthetic's artificial veins—rained down from the ceiling and splattered onto the floor. A second later, Davis's head hit the deck, bounced, rolled, and came to a stop. His eyes were wide and staring, his features frozen in a mask of agony.

I need to get his ident chip, she thought instinctively, *so I can download him into a new body.*

Except she'd already done that. After dealing with a Xenomorph infestation on a deep-space science station, she'd returned to Earth to have her back injury tended to by Dr. Yang. The ship they'd traveled in had crashed in the ocean, and Davis had gone down with the vessel. After more surgery and therapy, Zula had visited the craft's crash site, diving down to the wreckage. There she found Davis's body, and retrieved his ident chip. But she didn't remember finding him a new body. So how could he die here if he'd already died aboard the ship?

It made no sense.

She decided it didn't matter. Davis's head was here, right now, and if she didn't get his chip, he might be lost to her forever.

"Davis!" Amanda cried out. "Oh my god, Davis!" She sounded as shocked and horrified as Zula felt which, she realized, also was strange. Amanda had never met Davis, so why did she sound as if she'd just lost a dear friend?

The bay doors were only half closed, and as slowly as they moved, Zula thought she had plenty of time to dash forward and retrieve the ident chip before they sealed. Then a Xenomorph dropped down from the ceiling and landed in front of her. Its face, claws, and body were smeared with chalky-white synth blood, and she knew this was the monster that had killed her friend. The creature stepped toward her, claws raised, secondary mouth jutting forward, teeth bared and ready to tear into her flesh. Zula aimed her pulse rifle and fired.

The Xenomorph's secondary mouth wasn't protected by thick chitinous armor like the rest of the creature's body, and yellow blood sprayed from the newly created wound. Zula was elated to have struck such a serious blow against the monster that had taken her friend's life—artificial or otherwise—but the emotion was short-lived. Some of the Xenomorph's acidic blood splattered onto the back of her right hand. The caustic substance swiftly dissolved skin and began burning into the tendons beneath, devouring her flesh with the ravenous hunger of its host.

It happened so fast that at first Zula felt nothing—but then the pain registered, and she bit back a scream. She was a Colonial Marine, goddamnit, and she wouldn't give her opponent, human or not, the satisfaction of knowing it had hurt her. Her hand spasmed, and she almost lost her grip on the pulse rifle. But she managed to hold onto the weapon, and when the wounded Xenomorph came toward her, shredded mouth useless but claws intact and deadly, she blasted it in the ravaged mouth once more.

This time the blast penetrated farther. Its head snapped back and it shuddered from the top of its oblong head to the spiked tip of its tail, and then it went down. It hit the floor not far from where Davis's head had come to rest, and while Zula knew it wasn't possible, she hoped somehow that Davis was aware she'd terminated his killer with extreme prejudice.

One Xenomorph down. That left—

The three remaining aliens dropped from the ceiling, hit the floor, and assumed crouching positions. Zula knew they would leap at her in the next split second, attacking her as a group, unwilling to confront her individually now that she'd proved herself to be dangerous.

Come on then, she thought. *It's rude to keep a girl waiting.*

But before the monsters could attack, Zula was yanked roughly backward. She landed hard on the floor of the outer corridor, her back exploding with agony. Losing her grip on the rifle, she couldn't see where it went. There was a flash of the remaining Xenomorphs leaping toward her just as the engineering bay doors closed—moving at normal speed again. A half-second later she heard loud thuds as the creatures slammed into the barrier. As powerful as the Xenomorphs were, she half-expected them to break through, but the doors held. The creatures threw themselves at the doors several more times, but then—as if realizing their efforts were fruitless—they gave up.

From her prone position Zula looked up at the ceiling. Her back was on fire, and she didn't want to move. Even breathing was agony. Amanda's face came into her field of vision, the brown-haired Caucasian woman looking down at her with both guilt and concern.

"I'm so sorry!" her friend said. "I didn't mean to be so hard, but the doors accelerated, and I was afraid you'd get trapped with those things." Seeing the look of agony on Zula's face, she added, "How's your back? Are you all right?"

Amanda was fit, but she wasn't any stronger than an average woman her size. As a former Marine, Zula was in better shape. How could Amanda have yanked her backward so hard? Adrenaline, maybe? She decided the how didn't matter. Most likely the action had saved her life, even if by doing so she'd caused Zula to reinjure her back. The pain was so intense, tears rolled down her cheeks.

"Call Dr. Yang," Zula said through gritted teeth.

She couldn't believe it. After multiple surgeries and more rehab sessions than she could count, she felt the same as she had when she'd first woken after the explosion which had ravaged her back. How was it possible for one fall—no matter how hard—to undo all that work? Dr. Yang had cleared her for active duty, hadn't she?

How could this have happened?

Because you're weak, a voice inside her said. *Weak and worthless. You got injured on your first mission, let down your fellow Marines, let down the superiors who trained you. You declared yourself savior of the human race, humanity's protector, dedicated to eradicating the Xenomorph threat before it can reach Earth—and before Weyland-Yutani discovers a way to weaponize the creatures. What a joke. You can't even stand on your own two feet. You're pathetic.*

"Shut up," Zula muttered.

If Amanda heard her, the woman gave no sign.

Zula didn't know where her weapon was. It was as if it had simply vanished into thin air the instant it left her hand.

"Do you want some help?" Amanda asked. "Do you think you can stand?"

Before Zula could tell her not to, Amanda took hold of her hands and pulled. This time the pain was too much and she screamed. She felt a tearing sensation in her back as Amanda—again with surprising strength—lifted her to her feet. A pulling, then a letting go, accompanied by a sickening wet sucking sound. Her legs buckled beneath her, and her hands slipped out of the grip. She fell back to the floor, hit it with a smack, and lay there, unable to move. It was as if she were a marionette whose strings had been severed. The pain in her back had lessened, though, and she was grateful for that much.

Amanda's gaze fixed on something that Zula couldn't see. Her eyes widened and her face paled. Zula heard cracking and popping noises, and although her face was pointed in the wrong direction for her to see what was causing the sounds, she heard softer noises—scratching and scrabbling—and had the impression of movement behind her. Amanda backed away, shaking her head. As she did so, she lifted her gaze, as if whatever she was looking at was growing larger.

A shadow fell across Zula, and then something large, white, and blood-streaked stepped over her. It lunged toward Amanda. Whatever the thing was, it was bipedal, and it reached for Amanda with a pair of hands that terminated in sharp ivory claws.

It's a Xenomorph! Zula thought, but it didn't resemble any she had seen before. It was the same size and shape, but instead of being encased in black chitin, this thing looked as if it was made entirely out of bone. At the center of the creature lay a long, thick spine shot through with metal rods. *That's my spine*, she thought. She didn't know how it was possible, but somehow her vertebrae had come to possess a life of their own. They had torn free from her body, grown and changed, the form twisting and expanding until it had become a hideous parody of a Xenomorph.

The creatures were nightmarish enough on their own, but this thing—created from a vital part of Zula's own body—was far more horrifying. It moved with stiff, jerky motions, and it was slick with Zula's blood and shreds of her skin and muscle.

She opened her mouth, but could not speak. Had she somehow been infected by an alien, so that this thing had grown inside her? She didn't remember that happening, but even if it had occurred, it made no sense. Why hadn't she died when the Xenomorph ripped free?

Amanda continued retreating from the bone creature, but she wasn't watching where she was going, couldn't take her eyes off the monstrous obscenity, and she backed up against a corridor wall. Zula wanted to shout a warning, although she knew it would be useless, and she still couldn't make her voice work.

With a sudden swift motion the skeletal creature grabbed hold of Amanda's shoulders, its claw-like fingers sinking into flesh and muscle. Amanda cried out in pain, but her voice was quickly silenced. The alien opened its mouth to reveal two rows of sharp teeth, and then a secondary mouth emerged, also made of bone. The secondary mouth shot forward, punching into Amanda's throat. Blood gushed from the wound, and Amanda tried to cry out again, but all that she managed to do was cough forth a gout of crimson.

Her gaze fixed on Zula, and her mouth moved as if she were attempting to form words, but none came. Then the light in her eyes dimmed, and her body went slack. The bone alien regarded her for a moment before picking up the body and hurling it down the corridor. Amanda landed with a heavy thud, like a rag doll filled with sand. She lay still, arms and legs bent at odd angles.

The bone alien loomed over Zula, giving her a clear view of the thing. Like others of its kind, the creature possessed no visible eyes, but she knew it was looking at her. It crouched down and leaned its head close to her face until only a few inches separated them. Zula would've scrabbled backward to get away, or the very least turned her head to the side so she wouldn't have to look at the thing straight on, but she couldn't move. Couldn't even close her eyes to shut out the skeletal visage.

This is it, she thought.

The explosion that had shattered her back hadn't killed her. Neither had the Xenomorphs she'd fought since then. She'd survived the synthetics that had been programmed to stop her and Davis. She'd even survived being hunted by her fellow Marines. She'd escaped death a dozen times over, and hadn't even reached her twenty-fifth birthday yet. Now she never would.

Mentally steeling herself, she waited for the bone alien's secondary mouth to shoot forward and bury itself in her flesh—but the creature didn't attack. Instead, she heard a voice in her mind—cold, cruel, mocking. It was the same voice she'd heard before, and this time she knew it came from the Xenomorph. Somehow the monster was speaking directly to her mind.

You're not good for much, are you, girl? You got taken out of the game on your first mission. You betrayed your fellow soldiers, betrayed the Corps. You started a one-woman crusade against Weyland-Yutani, as if a crippled ex-soldier could accomplish anything. You couldn't save Davis. You couldn't save Amanda. And you can't even save yourself. There's only one thing you're good at, Zula. Do you know what that is? Failing.

Zula couldn't reply, but a tear rolled down her cheek. The Xenomorph opened its bony jaws wide, and the last thing she saw was the secondary mouth, rushing toward her face.

After that, there was only darkness.

4

"Zula, wake up!"

Her eyes snapped open and she sat up in her bunk. The lights came on, and she squinted against the harsh illumination. Reaching around to feel her back, she was relieved to find her spine still where it was supposed to be. There was no pain, either, which surprised her until she remembered that Dr. Yang had finished the last of the operations to repair her injury, and she'd completed the physical therapy that had followed.

Technically speaking, her back wasn't healed completely. For the rest of her life, she'd experience backaches more often than most people, and would need to take pain medicine and anti-inflammatories. So while her back wasn't good as new, it was close enough for her to get on with her life.

Zula could deal with a little pain from time to time. After all, she was a Colonial Marine—in her heart if no longer officially.

Pushing aside the heavy blanket as she sat up, she swung her legs over the side of the bunk. She wore only a gray tank top and underwear, and the cool air in her small room raised goosebumps on her flesh. The surface temperature on Jericho 3 averaged around 32 degrees Fahrenheit, and the Lodge was always on the cold side. It took a significant amount of energy to heat a facility this large, and Venture—like all corporations—was all about maximizing profits and minimizing expenditures.

Zula had only been working here a couple weeks, and she hadn't fully acclimated yet. She didn't really mind the cold, though. It helped her wake up faster.

"I take it you had another nightmare." The voice was male, the tone calm, almost dispassionate. Still, Zula had known Davis long enough that she thought she could detect a subtle hint of concern beneath his words.

A small side table sat next to the bed, and on it rested a white cylindrical device with a round camera lens and a similarly round speaker near the top. This Personal AI Assistant—or PAIA—currently served as Davis's new home. It wasn't much as bodies went, but it allowed them to communicate, and since it was linked to the facility's main computer core Davis could travel anywhere in the Lodge. Existing as a disembodied intelligence wasn't an ideal life for her friend, but it would have to do until she could find him a new synthetic body.

"Yeah," she said. "A real nasty one this time."

"This is the seventh nightmare you've had since coming to this facility. They're increasing in both frequency and severity."

She was a little worried about the dreams herself, but she decided to make light of the situation.

"Just a little PTSD brought on from fighting too many Xenomorphs. No big deal."

Davis didn't respond, and Zula knew he was analyzing her comment, trying to grasp its full meaning. As with the synth in her dream, Davis had been working on being more human, but humor was a concept that still gave him difficulty. She decided to change the subject.

"Anything interesting happen while I slept?"

"Not especially. Several of the nightshift maintenance workers played poker in an unused storage closet in the Facilities Management building for nearly two hours before their supervisor caught them. The supervisor joined in and everyone started losing on purpose to avoid being put on report. The supervisor 'cleaned up.' I believe that's the expression."

Zula laughed. "It is."

"A land buggy's power system went critical and exploded four point eight miles northeast of the proto-colony. The driver was killed, but there were no other casualties."

"No Xenomorph reports, I assume."

"You assume correctly."

Davis's access to the Lodge's computer network allowed him to monitor public newsfeeds for any reports of Xeno outbreaks, but he hadn't come across any so far. He had indicated the desire to monitor the staff's private communications as well, including management's. It was well within his capabilities to sneak past firewalls and disable security programs, but by doing so he would risk exposure, so he restrained himself. Zula was glad he did. She wanted to get back to killing Xenomorphs as much as he did, but she didn't want to lose her friend.

Zula wasn't certain how and when she and Davis were going to return to their mission of wiping the monsters from the face of the galaxy, but they both fully intended to do so. Her job at the Lodge was just a temporary detour, a way for her to earn some credits so she could finance her crusade. Although given how cheap Venture was when it came to paying its employees, she might need to take a few more detours.

"You're scheduled to lead a training exercise in forty-seven minutes. I suggest you start getting ready."

"Good suggestion."

She rose from her bunk and began preparing for her day. Her quarters were small, consisting of a single room, but she couldn't complain. At least she didn't have to sleep in the communal barracks with the candidates she'd been brought here to train. She wouldn't need the whole forty-seven minutes to get ready, either. Colonial Marines were given ten minutes—no more—to shit, shower, and shave, and while she was no longer officially a Marine, she couldn't shake the discipline. Didn't want to, either.

First she used the chemical toilet in the corner, then washed up at the sink next to it. She'd shower after the field exercise was done. Removing gray coveralls and boots from her closet, she put them on, then took a small commpiece from the side table and slipped it into her left ear. It was standard issue for the Lodge's employees, and while Zula didn't like the way it felt—it tickled, like she had a small insect crawling around in there—she was glad to wear it. It meant she and Davis could stay in touch wherever she went. She had to be careful about responding to him, though. No one at the Lodge knew of his existence, let alone that he had access to the facility's computer network.

The Lodge's network was overseen by a rudimentary AI far less sophisticated than Davis, and while her friend had been able to hide his presence thus far, she didn't want to do anything that might give him away.

"See you later," she said, stepping toward the door. It was kind of a dumb thing to say, since Davis could follow her virtually everywhere she went on the planet, but she would feel weird leaving without saying goodbye.

Zula left her room and headed down the corridor toward the Commissary. It was located in the Personnel building, so she didn't have far to go. The Lodge was comprised of five dome-shaped buildings—Administration, Facilities Management, Personnel, Biosciences, and Research and Development—arranged in a diamond pattern, with the all-important R&D in the middle. The buildings were connected by enclosed corridors through which people walked or rode self-driving electric carts. Walking was encouraged, though, as it promoted exercise and saved on battery power. Each of the corridors could be sealed in the case of a catastrophic event, such as the breach of an external wall.

The proto-colony was located off to the northeast. To the west was a larger crater created by a meteorite impact millennia ago, and to the north was a small mountain range. The ground where Venture had chosen to build its facility was gray and lifeless, but relatively flat and not too difficult to navigate. The weather here was milder than on other parts of the planet. Temperatures ranged from well below freezing to almost boiling depending on the time of year, and electrical storms weren't uncommon, although usually not too severe.

The biggest problem was the goddamned wind. It blew constantly, and anyone who ventured outside had to fight it, always feeling as if they were underwater and moving against a strong and temperamental tide. While maneuvering on the planet's surface was manageable most of the time, at times the winds would rage at gale force. If you were foolish enough to be outside then, you took your life in your hands.

The wind's constant high-pitched whine created an ever-present soundtrack to life on Jericho 3, one that many of the facility's personnel never quite got used to.

The atmosphere, like on Earth's closest neighbor, Mars, was comprised primarily of carbon dioxide, and due to the amount of dust in the air, the sky always appeared to be a dark yellowish brown. Jericho 3's sun wasn't always visible, but when it was it gave off a bluish glow, also due to the atmospheric particles. The gravity was slightly less than Earth normal, but the difference was barely noticeable to most people. Zula's back might technically be healed, but it still ached from time to time when she was tired, and she appreciated the lower gravity.

As she walked she passed other men and women, most also dressed in gray coveralls. Although she gave each a friendly smile as they went by, none returned it or so much as met her eyes. She told herself not to take it personally. She was still new here, and aside from the Colony Protection Force trainees, she knew very few people. Even so, she couldn't help wondering if word about her had spread through the Lodge.

"That's her—the one who was injured during her first mission, and got her fellow soldiers killed."

"HQ must really be scraping the bottom of the barrel when it comes to hiring these days."

"I just hope she doesn't get any of her trainees killed—or any of us."

Zula told herself she was being paranoid, but she'd had to deal with those kinds of attitudes before—from other Marines as well as from staff and patients at the med facility where she'd done her rehab. Not everyone treated her badly, of course. Dr. Yang, for example, had always been empathetic. But Zula had experienced enough prejudice in her life—if not because of what happened during her first mission, then because of her race, or gender, or her past growing up in an especially poor district on Earth. While she wanted to believe the best of people, she knew better.

She saw no synthetics on her way to the Commissary. There weren't many at the Lodge, not least because Venture didn't like purchasing them from Weyland-Yutani. Some people argued that space travel would be more efficient—and a hell of a lot cheaper—if ships and stations were crewed entirely by synthetics. But even the mega-corporations were reluctant to take that step. While it wasn't common, synthetics had been known to exhibit erratic behavior, making them less than reliable when working without human supervision.

Zula suspected the real reason, however, was that humans feared being replaced by synthetics, and thus were leery of granting them too much autonomy. Besides, humans had an innate need to explore, to be physically present when experiencing new places. That need was even stronger than the corporations' desire for profit.

If all synthetics had been like Davis, she wouldn't feel too badly if they took over. It wasn't as if humanity had done such a great job on its own. People had crapped up the planet of their origin, and now they were moving into the galaxy to do the same to other worlds. Synths could hardly do worse.

And with *that* cheery thought, she entered the Commissary. Like everywhere else in the Lodge, there wasn't a lot of space, and the round tables were placed so close together that maneuvering through the Commissary was an exercise in squeezing through narrow pathways, and waiting while someone came from the opposite direction.

Zula wasn't by nature a big breakfast eater, but during basic training she'd learned the importance of taking nourishment whenever she had the opportunity. She never knew what she might be ordered to do on any given day, and how long it might be between meals. And since field rations tasted like ass, she filled up on real food when she could. So going through the serving line, she loaded her plastic tray with scrambled eggs, soy-bacon, a poppy-seed muffin, and a large cup of strong black coffee.

Then she looked for a table where she could sit alone. Zula didn't like talking to anyone—excluding Davis—before downing her first caffeine of the day. But there were no empty tables, and several of the CPF trainees were sitting together. When they saw her, they motioned for her to join them. Telling herself it was good for morale, she started toward them, and even managed a smile as she sat down.

"Good morning, Boss!" one of the trainees, an Asian man named Ronny Yoo, said heartily.

Zula's rank in the USCM had been private first class, but soon after she arrived at the Lodge the trainees had started referring to her as "Sarge." The nickname irritated her, in part because she hadn't earned the rank, and because she suspected they were using it to mock her. She'd told them to cut it out, which they did, but then they started calling her "Boss" instead. Again she tried to discourage them, but despite her best efforts it stuck. Finally she'd given up.

"Morning," Zula said, the smile fading.

Five of the ten trainees under her tutelage were at the table. The other five were seated elsewhere in the Commissary, and Zula was grateful they weren't at a table nearby. She wasn't ready to deal with all of them yet. In addition to Ronny, Miriam Castro, Virgil Townsend, Genevieve Parks, and Donnell Stockton were seated at the table. Their trays were still mostly full, indicating they hadn't been here long.

"You decide to sleep in today, Boss?" Genevieve asked. She was a tall, thin redhead, and there was a teasing edge to her voice.

When Zula had accepted the job with Venture, the HR person who'd conducted her orientation had told her that in the corporate culture, *"early is on time, and on time is late."* It had been the same in the Corps, and it was one thing that Zula didn't miss about the Marines. As far as she was concerned, on time was on time, and if that wasn't good enough for Venture, then to hell with them. It wasn't as if she intended to make this a career.

"We've been up for over an hour," Donnell said. "Plenty of time to hit the gym and get the blood pumping." He was a broad-shouldered, barrel-chested, well-muscled black man. Fitness wasn't just a health thing with him—it was practically a religion.

Miriam swatted him on the arm.

"You know the Boss likes to work out in the evening." She was a Hispanic woman with short black hair and a take-no-shit attitude. She was also the closest thing to an ally Zula had among the trainees.

"Yeah," Virgil said. He had a shaved head and a face that looked like ten miles of bad road. He enjoyed bare-knuckle boxing, but as his face showed, he wasn't especially good at it. "After a long day of dealing with us, she needs to work out the kinks in her…" He broke off as if suddenly realizing what he'd been about to say.

Zula had been in the process of taking another drink of coffee. She lowered the cup slowly and placed it gently on the table, her gaze focused on Virgil the entire time.

"Kinks in my *what*?" she asked.

The man looked as if he wanted to crawl under the table and hide. Physically, he was as much a badass as any of the trainees, but while he was good at his job, his temperament off-duty was far milder than his appearance suggested.

"Uh…"

Virgil looked to Ronny for help. Ronny was the trainees' unofficial leader, and he behaved as if he considered himself Zula's second-in-command, although officially all the trainees were equal. Zula was in her mid-twenties, and most of the trainees were older than her, some significantly so. Ronny was her senior by ten years, and while he put up a good front when she was around, she knew he resented that she had been brought in to train them. It was why he got so much pleasure out of teasing her.

It hadn't helped their working relationship that she'd shot him down when he'd hit on her after her first few days at the Lodge. "*Sorry, it would be unprofessional for us to date*," she'd told him. "*Besides, you're not my type.*" She'd had to say the same thing to Brenna Lister a couple days later. Brenna, at least, didn't seem to resent Zula's lack of interest, and they'd gotten along fine since.

But Ronny? Not so much.

Ronny turned to Zula, and she could see him thinking furiously, trying to come up with a way to get Virgil out of trouble. Zula decided to take pity on them.

"Yes, my back does get angry after a day's work…" she admitted, "sometimes, but that's not because of you guys. You have nothing to do with it." She paused before going on. "You *are*, however, a huge pain in my ass."

The trainees looked shocked for a moment, but then they broke into laughter. Ronny laughed with them, but there was no sign of merriment in his eyes.

5

Hassan Bagrov didn't get to visit Research and Development very often. While he worked as a technician in Facilities Management, he specialized in maintaining and repairing thermo systems. He didn't have the training or experience to work on the sophisticated scientific equipment used by the staff in R&D. It wasn't that he couldn't learn how to deal with hi-tech machinery, if he wanted. He'd had plenty of opportunities over the years. One thing about Venture—they regularly offered ways for their employees to advance.

No, Hassan didn't *want* to advance. He liked thermo systems. Not only were they vital for survival, there was an elegant simplicity to them, and an elemental power. Plus they were, relatively speaking, easy to handle. He didn't have many hassles in thermo, certainly no scientists looking over his shoulder, complaining that he was taking too long. He'd had friends who were regularly assigned jobs in R&D, and they *hated* working here. They only put up with the researchers' arrogance and neuroses because the money was good.

Sure, he would've liked to earn a higher salary. Who wouldn't? But as far as he was concerned, life was too short.

Besides, there were other ways to make extra money at the Lodge. Some people sold black market goods that were smuggled in on cargo ships. Drugs, mostly, but there was also a brisk trade in fresh produce and non-synthetic chocolate. That was too risky for Hassan, though. Others tried gambling, and while Hassan enjoyed a good card game now and again, he didn't like the uncertainty of gambling. It was hardly the surest way to build a financial portfolio. Look what had happened to those idiots last night. They'd snuck off to play poker, ended up getting caught, and had to lose on purpose to avoid being reported.

Dumbasses.

Hassan earned extra credits by selling his body. Or more precisely, renting it out from time to time. He didn't provide sexual favors—not that he would've been averse to doing so if he thought anyone would be interested. Instead, he served as a professional guinea pig. There were plenty of prototypes being created by the Lodge's scientists that needed to be tested on human beings, and Hassan had long ago added his name to the list of staff members willing to help advance the corporation's scientific interests.

For a nominal fee, of course.

During his time at V-22, Hassan had been paid to test a new type of nutrient bar that tasted like sawdust and gave him terrible gas, a new sleeping pill that knocked him out for seventy-two hours, and medicines to treat some of the new diseases humanity had encountered during its first tentative steps toward colonizing the galaxy. In order to test the drugs, he'd first had to be given the diseases, and *that* hadn't been any fun. The worst of these had been cellular necrosis. The treatment he'd been given had worked—*praise Allah*—but he'd suffered some lingering side effects. No matter how much he drank, his mouth always felt dry, and he had a tendency to develop kidney stones every few months.

Overall, though, being a voluntary test subject was worth it. He'd made far more credits than he could score in any card game, that was for sure.

So when he'd received a message from Dr. Gagnon's assistant asking if he was available to assist her superior with a new experiment, Hassan had eagerly said yes. No sense in letting anyone else snag a profitable gig. Gagnon was the doctor who'd infected him with cellular necrosis, and while Hassan found him to be more than a little scary, he paid well, and that was what mattered most.

Hassan hadn't been back to Earth in more than five years, and he was saving up for a month-long vacation on the planet of his birth. A trip to Hawaii, or maybe Cozumel.

He approached Gagnon's lab with a strange mixture of anticipation and dread. He looked forward to seeing his credit balance rise—perhaps significantly so—but he wondered what, if any, side effects he'd experience this time. Hopefully his dick wouldn't fall off, or something equally severe. He stopped when he reached the lab door, but before he could activate the intercom and announce his presence it slid open with a soft hiss of air.

Brigette stood in the doorway, smiling at him.

"Hello, Hassan. It's good to see you again."

Hassan repressed a shudder. He'd never been comfortable around synthetics, and one of the things he liked about working for Venture was how few of the things were used by the corporation. He was far more comfortable around robots. They looked like what they were—machines—and didn't try to pretend to be anything else. He knew where he stood with a robot. With a synthetic? Not so much.

"Yeah," he said.

If Brigette found his response odd, she gave no sign. She continued smiling as she stepped back and gestured for him to enter. Hassan did so, and didn't see Dr. Gagnon.

"The doctor's in his private office, going over your medical records," Brigette said. It was creepy—like she could read his mind. "He'll join us in a few moments. In the meantime, I need to give you a brief physical examination."

Hassan didn't like being alone with Brigette, but he told himself to stop acting like a child, and allowed the synthetic to lead him to an examination table on the far side of the lab. Neither her lab coat nor her pants were particularly skin-tight, yet they hugged her body snugly enough to give him a good sense of her shape. Despite himself, Hassan watched her hips sway as she walked ahead of him, and an uncomfortable thought struck him.

He'd heard about sick people who enjoyed synthetics as sexual partners. Was he secretly one of those people, in denial about his true desires? Was he so conflicted about his feelings that he hid them behind a veneer of prejudice, when he really hated himself?

He shook his head, not wanting to examine those thoughts too closely, so he told himself he was being ridiculous and tried to thrust them from his mind. It wasn't easy. Brigette was extremely attractive. More, she moved like a real woman. Hell, she even *smelled* like one.

Gesturing for him to climb onto the exam table, she quickly and efficiently went about her work. As he sat quietly she checked his blood pressure, temperature, pulse, and respiration, using a penlight to peer into his eyes, ears, and nostrils. She placed a tongue depressor into his mouth, made him say *ah*, and pointed the light down his throat. Drawing a blood sample, she then asked for a urine sample, and had him take a small plastic container into the en-suite bathroom.

When he returned, Brigette had him unzip the front of his coveralls and raise the T-shirt beneath. She affixed six sensor pads to his chest and abdomen, and one on his forehead. He was uncomfortably aware of her touch the entire time, and was relieved when she finished.

"You didn't use sensor pads last time," he said as he zipped up his coveralls. Brigette faced a computer screen and entered data into the terminal. She didn't look away from the screen as she answered.

"Today's test is extremely important, and Dr. Gagnon

wants to make certain he gathers as much information as possible." Something told him there was more behind Brigette's words. She wasn't lying, exactly—he had no idea if synthetics *could* lie—but he didn't think she was being entirely honest with him, either.

"You know," he said, "I'm not really clear on what this test is, exactly."

For a second Brigette seemed to stiffen, but when she turned around she appeared relaxed, and the smile she gave Hassan seemed genuine.

"The doctor's current research focuses on the human immune system's response to a new biological contaminant. Today is the first step: exposure."

That word—*exposure*—sent a chill down his spine. Was he going to get sick? And if so, how bad? Would he miss work?

"If for whatever reason you end up unable to work for any length of time," she added, "the doctor will see to it that you continue to draw your full salary."

That was a relief. Hassan didn't mind being ill—so long as he wasn't *too* ill—but he hated the idea of losing credits because of it. The whole reason he was here at the Lodge was to make money, not lose it.

"I've activated a voice recorder." Brigette turned back to the terminal and entered a command. "Please state your name, and say whether or not you choose to continue with this test." He knew the drill.

"Hassan Bagrov. I wish to continue with this test."

"And do you agree not to hold the Venture Corporation

liable for any potential negative outcome of this test?"

Good old Venture, always making sure to cover its ass.

"I do."

Brigette nodded, satisfied, turned off the voice recorder, and continued typing more information into the terminal. When she was finished a door in one of the lab's walls slid open, and Dr. Gagnon stepped out. As the doctor approached the table he held out his hand. Hassan looked at it suspiciously for a moment before shaking it.

"It's good to see you, my friend," Gagnon said. "Thanks so much for being willing to help us once more."

During Hassan's previous visits the doctor had come across as cold and detached, acting as if Hassan was little more than another piece of lab equipment. Just now the man seemed so enthused by Hassan's presence that he could barely contain his excitement. It was Gagnon's attitude, more than anything else he'd experienced since entering the lab, that made Hassan consider getting off the examination table, leaving, and never coming back. Something was wrong here, and while he didn't know what it was, his instincts were sounding an alarm.

When the doctor released his hand, the smile grew even wider.

"Did Brigette mention that we're going to pay you twice the usual fee? Management is being generous with the funding for my current research, and it seems only fair that we, in turn, be generous with you."

Since when had Venture's management ever been *generous*? The idea was ludicrous, but the thought of earning double caused Hassan to overlook any doubts he might have. The more he was paid, the sooner he could afford to take his vacation. Maybe he'd go to the Bahamas, or the Yucatan Peninsula. It didn't really matter, as long as it was someplace warm and sunny.

Hassan smiled. "I'm ready when you are, Doc."

"Excellent! If you'll follow me."

Gagnon led him to a section of wall. He pressed a button on a keypad, and a section slid upward to reveal a window, looking into a small room. Fluorescent lights came on, illuminating the chamber and what was contained within. Hassan's enthusiasm dimmed considerably when he saw the egg-like object resting on the floor.

"What the hell is that?"

When Brigette had said "biological contaminant," he'd imagined some kind of germ or virus. Maybe even some kind of plant spore. This thing looked like something out of a nightmare. If it was an egg—and it damn sure looked like one—he didn't want to see the kind of chicken it produced.

"I'm afraid that information is classified," Gagnon said. "All that's required of you is to enter the chamber and stand next to the object for several minutes. During this time we'll monitor your vital signs to see what, if any, reaction your body has to being in the object's presence. Who knows? You might not have any reaction at all."

Hassan might've allowed himself to believe Gagnon's words, but Brigette gave the scientist a disapproving look, as if to say, *"Shame on you."* Suddenly, it didn't matter how much Hassan was going to be paid. He didn't want to get any closer to that weird-looking egg.

"Look, I appreciate the opportunity, Doc, but on second thought, I'd rather not continue with this test. I hope you find someone else to help you out, but I—"

Gagnon's smile died. He reached into a pocket of his lab coat and withdrew a syringe.

"I'm sorry you feel that way, Hassan," the man said, and then in a single swift motion he jammed the needle into the side of Hassan's neck.

Hassan pushed Gagnon away, dislodging the syringe in the process, but it was too late. A sudden dizziness came over him, and his vision blurred. The last thing he heard was Gagnon giving Brigette an order.

"Catch the idiot before he falls. I don't want him injuring himself before we get started."

Hassan felt Brigette's surprisingly strong hands on him, and after that, he knew only darkness.

Hassan opened his eyes.

It took a moment for his vision to clear, but when it did he realized he was lying on a floor, on his side, looking directly at the disgusting egg-thing. The object was less than a meter away from his face, and with a start of horror Hassan realized that he'd been placed inside the testing chamber while unconscious.

It was sealed.

As he sat up his head swam with vertigo, and he had to fight to keep from falling over again. He turned to the observation window. Gagnon and Brigette were watching him from the other side. He rose to his feet, his legs weak, but managed to remain standing.

He glared at Gagnon.

"You can't do this to me!"

As soon as the words were out of his mouth, he realized how stupid they were. He was an anonymous cog in Venture's vast corporate machine. The company could do anything it wanted. After all, he'd given his permission.

Gagnon ignored Hassan's protest. The scientist spoke, his voice coming through a small speaker next to the window.

"The chamber is sealed and airtight. There is no way out until I choose to release you. The sooner you accept this and cooperate, the sooner it will be over."

Gagnon's voice once more held the cold, clinical tone with which Hassan was familiar, but the man's eyes still gleamed with excitement. Was there a little madness there, as well? Hassan thought so. He looked to Brigette then. She stood next to Gagnon, but when Hassan caught her gaze, she looked away.

She knew this was going to happen, Hassan thought. *And she's ashamed by her part in it.* Not so ashamed, though, to have done anything to stop Gagnon. Hassan had no idea if a synthetic could disobey the orders of its human master. Before today, the notion that a synthetic might possess free will would've made him more than a little uneasy. Now he wished with every fiber of his being that Brigette *had* disobeyed Gagnon, and warned him of the scientist's plan to drug him.

It was funny. Before entering the lab, the thought of synthetics being able to make independent choices would've creeped him out. Now he fervently wished they possessed that capability.

Hassan wanted to shout at Gagnon, to let out a stream of curses and pound his fists against the window. Maybe it was the lingering effect of the drug, or maybe he simply realized that Gagnon was right, and he had no way of escaping. Whatever the reason, the anger quickly drained out of him, and he turned away from the window to face the egg.

Up close it was even more disgusting than it had looked through the door. Its surface was slick and moist-looking, as if it was covered with some kind of mucus. And the smell! The egg gave off a thick, rank odor, a combination of reptile stink and the harsh tang of caustic chemicals. The strange thing was that the smell had a certain allure, like the odor of gasoline or the earthy scent of a dog in need of a bath. Those weren't pleasant smells, nothing on the order of fresh-cut flowers or baking bread, but they were nonetheless compelling in their own way, and the egg's scent was no different in this regard.

Without realizing it he took a step toward the thing and, to his surprise, it reacted. As if his physical proximity had triggered some kind of signal, the egg began to quiver, almost as if Hassan's presence excited it. The animal-chemical smell grew stronger, and again without realizing it, he took another step toward the egg.

Its outer surface appeared solid, but four sections peeled away from the top and curled downward, revealing an opening. Now it looked more like a flower, extending its petals. Whatever the thing was, it had to be alien. No way something like this had come from Earth. He realized then that Gagnon had no idea what the hell the thing was either, and the real reason he'd put Hassan in the chamber with it was to determine what the object would do.

The egg—or whatever—stopped quivering when its petals had peeled all the way back. It sat motionless, as if waiting for Hassan to make the next move—and the hell of it was, he did. He took yet *another* step toward the thing. Maybe it was out of curiosity, or maybe the odor the object gave off was some sort of stimulant, like a powerful pheromone. He was less than a foot from the egg, close enough to be able to lean forward and see whatever lay inside. A voice in the back of his mind—one that belonged to the most primitive part of him, the part that had helped his species survive and thrive over tens of thousands of years—screamed that he should draw back before it was too late.

But of course, it already was.

There was a flash of movement as something sprang forth from the inner recesses of the egg. Hassan registered spider-like legs, a long, segmented tail, and a fleshy slit of a mouth, and then the creature smacked into his face. Its legs fastened around his head and gripped tight, and the tail coiled around his throat like a constrictor.

He staggered backward, as much from shock as from the creature's impact, and collided with the wall. He slid down onto his ass as the creature's tail tightened further, cutting off his air. Trying to scream and failing, he reached up and attempted to pull the coils away from his neck, but they were too strong. They continued to tighten, and his throat burned as if on fire. He opened his mouth in a desperate attempt to draw in oxygen, and he felt something long and slimy extend from the creature and thrust its way down his throat. He gagged as the organ penetrated him, and once more clawed at the coils, frantic to get this monstrous thing off him, but all he managed to do was tear off several of his fingernails.

He barely registered the pain.

Then he was surrendering to unconsciousness. He toppled over and lay sideways on the floor. He had time for a final thought before oblivion claimed him.

I... should have... gone with... poker.

Brigette watched as the multilegged creature leaped from the egg and attacked Hassan. At first she thought the thing was feeding on the poor man, and when he collapsed to the floor, she feared he had died.

She stepped to her computer terminal. A quick check of the data relayed by the sensor patches on Hassan's body showed that he *wasn't* dead. In fact, according to the data, Hassan was resting comfortably in a deep, peaceful sleep. Even with the creature entirely covering his face—including his nose and mouth—the man appeared to be breathing normally, as if the creature was somehow breathing for him.

She rejoined the doctor at the observation window and told him what the data indicated. He nodded slowly, without looking at her. She wasn't sure he'd heard, but didn't repeat the information. She knew from experience how angry Gagnon got when he thought anyone was patronizing him, especially her.

"Don't act as if you consider yourself my better. You're nothing more than lab equipment with opposable thumbs."

"Interesting," Gagnon said finally. "It appears the egg and this new creature are separate lifeforms, connected but at the same time operating independently."

The egg's petals closed slowly.

"What's it doing to him, Doctor?"

Brigette tried to keep the concern from her voice, but she failed. She'd been created to be a pleasure synth, and to make her the most effective sexual partner she could be her core programming included a strong sense of empathy—as well as the ability to express it. She might have been repurposed as a lab assistant, but the empathy remained. Sometimes—like now—she wished her entire programming had been changed, or that she'd been deactivated. It disturbed her to watch the things Gagnon did to his "willing" test subjects, even more so knowing that there was nothing she could do to help them.

Worse, she played a central role in torturing them. This sort of programming conflict was enough to cause a synthetic to experience cognitive impairment, even a full-blown mental failure cascade. Brigette couldn't stop caring for the humans that walked into Gagnon's lab, but at the same time she needed to show no personal feelings toward them if she hoped to be an effective assistant to the doctor.

Up to now she'd managed, but after seeing what had happened to Hassan Bagrov she didn't know how much longer she could continue.

Gagnon appeared unaware of her internal conflict. This didn't surprise her. To him, she was nothing more than a computer that happened to be shaped like a human. He didn't expect her to have thoughts of her own, let alone feelings.

"Remarkable." The doctor leaned closer to the window until his nose almost touched the surface. The word was little more than expelled breath.

"What will happen next?" Brigette asked. What she really wanted to know was if Hassan would survive whatever was happening to him, but she didn't say this aloud. Gagnon would only mock her for pretending to experience human emotions. Then he would get angry with her for allowing herself to be distracted by concern for a man who, to Gagnon, was of no more importance than a lab rat.

"We'll just have to wait and see, won't we?" He smiled without taking his gaze off the man, and the creature hugging his face. "The sensor pads you attached to his body should tell us the full story, in due time."

Brigette hadn't been programmed to believe in a higher power, but if she had been, she'd have been praying for Hassan to make it out of this alive. Since there was nothing she could do, however, she stood next to Gagnon and continued watching Hassan's unconscious form while the parasitic creature went about its awful work.

6

Zula sat next to the driver of the transport as the vehicle juddered across the rocky terrain of Jericho 3. The trainees sat in the seats behind her, some quiet, some talking, some razzing each other. Everyone—including the driver—wore EVA suits, helmets on and sealed, life-support systems activated.

The transport cab was enclosed, with rows of uncomfortable seats, a large rectangular windshield in front and smaller circular windows on the sides. The vehicle had its own internal life support, but it wasn't on. It was more efficient—and cheaper—for the driver and passengers to use their suits' life support. The transport didn't have an airlock, so when the door was opened oxygen wouldn't rush out and be wasted.

Everyone had their comm units set to the same channel, as per Zula's orders, so when Masako Littlefield leaned across the aisle to address Ray Ackerman, her voice came through to them all loud and clear.

"Ten credits you get taken out before we're halfway through the course."

Masako was a tall Asian woman with multiple piercings in each ear and a nose ring. Nonregulation for the Colonial Marines, but Venture's rules for its CPF personnel were more relaxed when it came to appearance.

Ray glared at her, but he didn't respond verbally. He was Irish, with curly orange hair, a smattering of freckles, and a thin beard. Angela Cade sat next to him, a narrow-faced blond Brazilian whose thin nose was slightly crooked. Zula didn't know if the nose was the result of an injury or if she'd been born that way. Regardless, it was a sign that the woman wasn't vain, since she hadn't had cosmetic surgery to fix it. That, or she couldn't afford it.

Angela leaned forward so she could look Masako in the face.

"With all the testosterone treatments Ray's been taking, he'll probably be the last one of us standing today. He'll outperform your sorry ass, that's for sure."

Zula turned around in her seat. She ignored the two women and instead focused her attention on Ray to see how he was taking Masako's teasing. He was in the process of transitioning, and while Masako had never shown any signs of being transphobic, she *was* highly competitive. Zula had seen her try to get under the other trainees' skins, in the hope of psyching them out.

Venture gave a bonus—a small one—to every trainee

who made it to the end of the course still on their feet. Added incentive to make sure they did well on bug hunts, but they cared about bragging rights as much as, if not more than, the extra credits. Zula also received a bonus for every trainee who succeeded during an exercise. She didn't give a damn about bragging rights, though. All that mattered to her were the credits. The more she earned, the faster she and Davis could get back to their real work.

Zula didn't mind teasing between the trainees. She'd experienced the same during her basic training for the Corps, and it served to toughen up recruits while at the same time strengthening the bonds between them— when it worked right. If it became too personal or mean-spirited, it could lead to conflict among recruits, and that was something she wanted to avoid. When you were a soldier you needed to know your comrades had your back, just as they needed to know you had theirs.

Masako glanced toward Zula, and she knew the woman was contemplating how their "Boss" would react if she responded to Angela's dig. Ronny sat next to Masako, and he put a gloved hand on her shoulder.

"Forget about it, Mas. We'll leave both of them in the dust, and after today, Ray will need to double up on the testosterone just to keep up with us."

Ray clenched his hands into fists and looked at Ronny as if he wanted to tear the man's head off. Zula could sympathize. She'd have to keep an eye on those four, to make sure any animosity they felt didn't follow them onto the training field. There were plenty of safety precautions to ensure no one would be killed during the exercise, but that didn't mean people couldn't get hurt, and seriously so, if they weren't careful. They would all need to be at the top of their game—her included.

Brenna and Nicholas exchanged glances. Nicholas rolled his eyes—a comment on Masako's typical attempt at mind games—and Brenna shook her head as if to say, *"Never lets up, does she?"*

Brenna Lister was a short-haired brunette with a tattoo of a barcode on her forehead. When Zula had asked her about it, she'd said, *"My parents sold me to human traffickers when I was four. They put the tattoo on me to identify me as their property."* Zula hadn't asked the woman how she'd gained her freedom, or why she'd kept the tattoo. That was her business, but anytime Zula saw the barcode, she couldn't help wondering what the rest of the woman's story might be.

Nicholas Hauata was Polynesian. His hair was so glossy black it almost seemed to have its own light source, and he sported the bluest eyes Zula had ever seen. Rare for someone of his ethnicity, she gathered.

"They're so blue because I have the ocean in my soul," he'd once told her, grinning.

"Where are we headed today, Boss?" Virgil called out.

Zula selected a different location for each exercise, but kept it secret so the trainees couldn't scope it out ahead of time. Normally she might have ignored Virgil's question, but she decided it might be a good idea to get the trainees' minds off the tense exchange.

"We're heading northeast, toward the Junkyard," she said.

"So we're going to be hunting bugs in the trash," Miriam said. "Sounds like fun." From her tone, it seemed obvious she thought the opposite.

Zula smiled. "I didn't say that was the only place we were going."

That was all she would reveal for the moment. Let them try to puzzle out what their course was going to look like. It would give them something to think about besides picking on each other.

The transport continued along across the grim landscape for another ten minutes until they reached their destination, an outcropping of large rocks at the base of a steep hill. The driver brought the transport to a stop and pressed a control on the vehicle's dashboard panel. The door on the left side of the transport swung open with a hiss as Jericho 3's atmosphere filtered into the cab.

"Boots on the ground, people," Zula ordered. "Grab your weapons on the way out. Take extra ammo, too." With a grim smile, she added, "You're going to need it today. Masako, grab the med pack." The transport was equipped with full emergency medical gear in case of serious injury, but the basic med pack should be all they needed today. At least Zula hoped so.

M41A pulse rifles were held to the seatbacks by mag locks, and a solid pull was all it took to free the weapons. Extra ninety-nine-round magazines hung next to the rifles, and the trainees pulled those free as well, affixing them to their belts. Zula did the same. That gave each person two magazines apiece, making for a total of 190 rounds per cadet. Pulse rifles had a tendency to jam if the mags were fully loaded, and so shooters purposely left out four rounds per magazine before using the weapons. The rifles also boasted an under-barrel grenade launcher capable of holding four rounds, but these had been left empty. Zula was saving those for when—or if—she thought her people were ready.

The med pack hung on a hook near the driver, and Masako came forward to take it. She was clearly unhappy about being given the extra duty, and Zula heard the woman mutter an obscenity under her breath. She decided to let it slide, though. These were corporate trainees, not soldiers. She needed to take a less heavy hand when it came to disciplining them.

Not that she liked it that way.

One by one the trainees disembarked. Zula went last, and when everyone was off the transport the driver's voice came over Zula's helmet comm.

"See you at the other end."

The door closed, sealed, and the transport rumbled off. It would be waiting to pick them up when the exercise was completed. Zula watched the driver give the hill a wide berth. The bugs weren't programmed to attack transports, but she still didn't blame the driver. Living and working on other worlds, the slightest mistake could be fatal. It paid to be cautious.

The cadets gathered around Zula in a semicircle and

gave her their full attention. Granting credit where credit was due, they might suffer from "bad attitude-itis" while off-duty, but they got their act together when it was time to rock and roll.

"Here are today's teams," she said, her voice clear over the comms. "Team One: Miriam, Ray, Masako, Angela, Virgil, and Donnell. Team Two: Ronny, Nicholas, Genevieve, Brenna, and me. I'm sending today's route to your helmet displays now."

Zula tapped the controls on her wrist pad, and a faint green line appeared on the faceplate in front of her. It was a simple directional aid to guide the trainees through today's course. The cadets had been improving, but she didn't think they were quite ready to go on a hunt without assistance—not yet. Soon, though.

Maybe after today, if all went well.

The terrain was gray as far as the eye could see. Sometimes light gray, sometimes so dark it was almost black. A few of Jericho 3's scraggly plants dotted the landscape, none more than three feet tall. They looked dehydrated and malnourished, and struck Zula as particularly ugly weeds that were too stubborn to die. Dark, wispy clouds filled the sky, blocking a good portion of the light from the planet's sun. There was enough to see by, though, and their helmets enhanced their vision, so they should be okay.

Wind blew from the west, strong enough that it would be an effort to keep moving in a straight line, but not so strong that they were in danger of being knocked off their feet. She'd checked the weather before they'd left the Lodge, and the wind was supposed to remain steady for the next several hours. An electrical storm was coming, but it wasn't due to hit until much later in the day. They'd be finished long before then—unless something went *really* wrong.

"Today we're going to kick things up a notch," Zula said. "The rifles are still loaded with non-explosive rounds, and the bugs are programmed to power down if you score a direct hit on them. That hasn't changed, but the bugs are set to be more aggressive, and the possibility of injury is very real. Stay alert and watch your six. Any questions?"

Ronny caught Masako's gaze and rolled his eyes. Masako let out a short laugh in response, but she quickly cut it off, as if suddenly remembering Zula was listening.

Enjoy it while you can, Zula thought. *We'll see who's laughing when we reach the end of the course.*

"All right," she said. "Team One, move out."

The members of Team One formed two ranks of three, staggered so the ones behind wouldn't hit the ones in front when the shooting started. Ray, Angela, and Miriam went first, and Donnell, Masako, and Virgil followed. Team Two arranged themselves in a similar pattern. Ronny, Nicholas, and Genevieve in front, and Brenna and Zula behind. Zula always brought up the rear during a hunt so she could better observe the others' performance. This was part of the job that rankled: She'd much rather be out in front, leading the way.

Whatever she did when her time with Venture was done, she vowed never to take a command position again. For better or worse, she needed to be in the thick of the action, not hanging back, watching and assessing.

To make the exercise more challenging, Zula had forbidden the use of motion detectors. In real life, Colony Protection Force operatives would have them—*"the better to see you with, my dear"*—but she didn't want her trainees to become overly dependent on tech. Better that they learned to rely on their eyes and ears, and most importantly, their guts. That way, when they did start using motion detectors, the tech would function as an adjunct to their own senses, and not a replacement.

Team One advanced toward the rocks to begin making their way between them and —when that wasn't possible—over them. Many of the rocks were the size of a personal transport, but the larger ones were even bigger than the vehicle which had brought them here. They formed an effective maze, which was why Zula had chosen this as their starting point. The rocks were jagged, too, their edges sharp enough to cause tears in the EVA suits. The suits were designed to be damage-resistant, but they also had to be flexible enough for people to move in them. If someone struck hard enough on an especially sharp edge they could open up a rift, and would suddenly find themselves having a very bad day.

Even so, the greatest danger was the bugs.

As it made its first baby steps toward colonizing the galaxy, humanity had discovered that life wasn't uncommon in the universe. Intelligent life hadn't been discovered... yet. Many among the mega-corporations held the view that the human race was the first fully sentient species to evolve in the galaxy. At least, that was the official line. Zula had heard rumors to the contrary during basic training, but she didn't know if they were true or just stories told by recruits trying to scare one another.

Regardless, there was no shortage of primitive animal life on the worlds humanity had visited. Often that life had teeth and claws, and wasn't particularly welcoming to off-worlders invading their homes.

One of the primary functions of Venture's Colony Protection Force—and of the Colonial Marines, for that matter—was to protect settlers from hostile indigenous lifeforms usually referred to as *bugs*, regardless of whether they resembled insects or not. It wasn't practical for trainees to practice combatting living creatures, though. Those were often hard to capture, and too difficult— not to mention expensive—to ship to training facilities. Moreover, there were strict laws about introducing any alien lifeform to an ecosystem where it didn't belong.

Since robots formed one of Venture's most profitable product lines, the company's technicians had created artificial bugs to help trainees hone their skills. These bots were based on actual extraterrestrial lifeforms that explorers had encountered, although their basic designs had been tweaked to make them more of a challenge. Made larger, their attack modes more intense. Venture had a dozen different models, and Zula rotated through them randomly so the trainees wouldn't get too used to dealing with any one type more than the others.

There would be six different bugs today: four the trainees

had encountered before, and two they hadn't. She was especially interested to see how they dealt with the new ones. While they had performed well enough on previous hunts, the cadets had trouble adapting to the unexpected. So Zula had made sure they would get just that today.

The planned route was designed to take them straight to the hill—or as close to straight as they could manage, given the terrain. The distance was a little more than half a mile, and the two teams were about halfway across the rocks when the first bug attacked. It was concealed between two of the larger rocks, ones the team had avoided because they were too difficult to scale. It leaped into the air and landed atop a smaller rock with a soft *chunk*.

Virgil was the first trainee to turn and see it.

"Jumper!" he shouted. "On our six!"

As if Virgil's shout was a cue, the Jumper launched itself toward the humans. The bot was more than six feet long, and it had been built to resemble a creature something like an Earth grasshopper, except instead of six legs, it had ten. While its basic form was that of an insect, it hadn't been constructed with realism in mind. It was made of silvery metal which was dinged and scratched from previous encounters. It possessed camera lenses for eyes, along with a pair of antennae that looked like slowly rotating miniature radar dishes atop its head.

The bug possessed a rudimentary AI—nothing very sophisticated, but enough to make it roughly as intelligent as the creature it mimicked.

The trainees raised their rifles, but only the first row

fired. Zula raised her weapon too, but instead of training her gaze on the Jumper, she watched the trainees. The Jumper was coming at them fast, so Ray, Miriam, and Angela used full auto and sprayed the air with rounds. Before any of the bullets could strike the robot, however, it landed on another rock and then launched itself high into the air, evading the barrage.

"Don't just stand there," Ronny shouted. "Start firing!"

It was unclear who he was speaking to. Perhaps all of the trainees. That's how everyone took it, and they aimed at the Jumper and fired. Not Zula, though. She kept a straight face, but inside she grimaced with disappointment. The trainees were already wasting rounds, and the exercise had barely started.

While pulse rifles themselves were relatively lightweight, they had a hell of a recoil. Most of the trainees were standing on top of rocks. Not the steadiest of footings. The surface of Masako's perch was particularly uneven, and after firing her rifle for only a few seconds her left foot slipped out from under her, and she fell. Her right shoulder hit the side of another rock on the way down, and she lost her grip on her rifle. The weapon stopped firing and hit the ground a split second before Masako did.

When she landed she was concealed by the terrain around her. Zula had no idea how badly the woman was hurt, but the fact that she didn't immediately get back up on her feet, pissed and swearing, wasn't a good sign.

As Masako fell the Jumper continued hopping from

rock to rock. The rest of the trainees kept firing, and Zula was pleased to see that several of them had switched to four-round burst mode. That way they could conserve ammo and make the rounds count.

The Jumper kept trying to move in closer to attack, but the trainees successfully held it at bay. By this point an organic creature might've decided these two-legged snacks weren't worth the trouble, but the bug-bots were programmed never to give up. So when the Jumper turned and leaped away from its targets, Zula knew something was up. It landed on a relatively flat rock that had several smaller stones resting on its surface. The Jumper positioned itself so its back legs were behind the stones, and then it kicked.

The stones—each of them larger than a human hand— flew toward the trainees.

"Incoming!" Genevieve shouted, and the trainees ducked or dodged or flattened themselves against the rocks on which they stood. Zula crouched down, keeping one eye on the flying stones and the other on the Jumper.

The missiles it sent hurtling toward the humans struck the rocks around them and broke apart, sending chunks of stone flying. No one was struck by the stones themselves, but the fragments pelted them, hitting hard enough to potentially open holes in their EVA suits. The instant the trainees were distracted, the Jumper spun and launched itself into the air once again. It hurtled toward the trainees, and Zula waited for any of them to react to the swiftly approaching bot.

None of them managed to do so quickly enough, so she stood, aimed, and fired off a four-round burst. The bullets struck the creature directly on the head, and one of the rounds shattered its left camera-lens eye. The Jumper landed on top of a large rock in the midst of the trainees, but instead of continuing its attack, its head withdrew into its thorax, and its legs folded tight against its metallic body.

The bug had been neutralized.

One by one, the trainees got back onto their feet. All except Ronny and Masako. Zula jumped from rock to rock until she reached the spot where Masako had fallen. The woman lay on the ground between two large rocks, and Ronny knelt next to her. Zula was relieved to see that Masako's eyes were open, but her pained expression said she hadn't escaped injury.

"Report," Zula said, keeping her tone neutral so they wouldn't know how concerned she was. Masako might not have been her favorite trainee, but she wished the woman no harm.

"I'll live," Masako responded. She winced as Ronny helped her to a sitting position. "My suit's integrity is still at one hundred percent, and my O_2 supply wasn't damaged, but I think I broke my goddamned ankle when I fell."

Zula jumped down to join them.

"Give me the med pack," she said.

Ronny helped Masako slip off the pack, and he handed it to Zula. She knelt, opened the container, and removed an inflatable splint.

"Which ankle is it?" she asked. She wasn't blind, but it was important to confirm the location of an injury before treating it.

"My left," Masako said.

Zula nodded. She fitted the plastic splint over Masako's foot and lower leg, then pressed the control. The splint filled with air, and a few seconds later it was fully inflated and Ronny was able to help Masako stand. Zula slipped on the med pack, and stood as well.

"The cast will stabilize your ankle until we can get you back to the Lodge. Don't walk on that foot, though. You don't want to damage it any further."

"Okay," Masako said. "So what now?"

"You're done for the day," Zula said. "We'll help you get back to where we started, and you'll have to wait there until we reach the transport and can come back to get you."

Masako acknowledged Zula's words with a nod, but she didn't look happy about it. Zula understood. She knew what it was like to get injured soon after a mission began, and feel like you've let your teammates down. At least in Masako's case no one had died, and her injury could be healed far more easily than Zula's had been.

"I can get her there," Ronny said.

"Let me help," Zula said. "It'll be easier and safer with two of us."

She started toward Masako, but Ronny held up a hand to stop her.

"We got this."

Zula looked at him a moment, trying to gauge his

response. His tone was calm enough, but resentment smoldered in his eyes. Did he blame her for Masako's injury? As far as she knew, Ronny and Masako were just friends, but they were close. Ronny already resented Zula for being in charge of the trainees. It wasn't a stretch to think that he'd put Masako's injury down to incompetent leadership.

Briefly she thought about ordering Ronny to let someone help him with Masako, even if it wasn't her, but she decided against it. The trainees were supposed to follow her commands as if they were in the military, and she was their superior officer, yet the reality was far different. They were all employees of Venture, and she was their supervisor, not their commander. If she gave Ronny an order and he told her to get stuffed, she could log the incident in his personnel file and dock his pay for the day, but that was about it. She didn't even have the ability to fire him. Only Aleta Fuentes could do that, and Zula doubted the woman would consider this a fireable offense.

So Zula just nodded and climbed up onto a rock to give Ronny and Masako room. He helped Masako up and onto a different rock.

"The rest of you go on without me," he said. "I'll catch up later." Zula didn't like that it sounded as if he was giving his fellow trainees an order, but this wasn't the time to make an issue of it.

"Acknowledged," Zula said, and then she turned her back on Ronny and Masako and raised her voice.

"Everyone get back into group formation, and let's keep moving. We're wasting O_2 just standing here."

Over the comm channel, Zula heard Ronny's and Masako's labored breathing as they began slowly making their way back toward the drop-off point. She wanted to turn and watch their progress, make sure they got back okay, but she had a job to do. Once everyone was back in their original order—at least as much as they could be on the rocks—she gave the order to move out, and they continued forward.

One bug down. Five to go.

7

Next came the Screamer. One of the new ones, it resembled a cross between a dragonfly and an eagle, and while it was smaller than the Jumper, it was more powerful. This bot possessed a sonic attack that hit them hard even in Jericho 3's thin atmosphere.

Climbing the hill, Zula felt the vibrations thrumming through her organs and rattling her teeth and bones. As uncomfortable as that sensation was, far worse was the accompanying vertigo. Dizziness and nausea gripped her, making it hard as hell to assert enough control over her body to get a bead on the bot. The rest would be feeling the same.

Most of the trainees managed to at least get off a few rounds while the Screamer circled around them, its sonic attack intensifying with each revolution. Ray was the one who finally managed to bring the robot down when he hit the creature's right wing with enough bullets to make it fold against its body. The bot veered off, angled upward, then fell and hit the ground with a loud *whump*. Like the Jumper its head retracted, and its other wing folded against its body as it deactivated.

Zula couldn't help grinning. That was more like it! The bug had been neutralized, they had used far less ammunition, and this time no one had been injured.

Two down.

On the other side of the hill the ground flattened out, and the teams spread out, placing a short distance between them but remaining close enough for backup. They took a turn to the south. Halfway across the plain, a Sprinter attacked them. This bot possessed a vaguely feline shape, and it came at them so fast—zigzagging as it ran—that it was difficult to hit. Zula thought the Sprinter was going to get Genevieve, but the woman managed to hit the bot's front legs with several rounds—more from luck than skill—and the bug went down. The rest of the trainees peppered it with gunfire, and its head and legs withdrew as it deactivated.

Not bad, Zula thought. *Three down.*

Ronny rejoined them after that, and assured them that Masako was fine—if pissed at having to sit out the remainder of the exercise. Zula still couldn't read him, though, and thought she caught him watching her. He looked away, and she figured it was her imagination.

Both teams continued on.

The plain ended at the lip of a crater created by a long-ago meteorite impact. According to the readings on their faceplates, the trail led directly into it. The ground was steep and the soil loose, so the trainees half-walked, half-slid down to the crater's floor. An armored, long-clawed Digger burst up from the ground in their midst, but the trainees managed to take it out before it could haul itself all the way to the surface.

Four.

They were beginning to work as a team. Zula ordered everyone to put fresh magazines into their weapons, and they did so. She was beginning to think that they might make it to the end of the course without any more injuries.

Branching off from the crater was a jagged rift in the ground that had been created when the meteorite hit. The walls of the rift rose upward thirty feet, but it was only a yard wide—sometimes less. Enough for them to pass through in a single file, though once inside the narrow channel, they'd have little room to maneuver.

In a genuine combat situation, they would have avoided going in rather than place themselves at such a disadvantage unless it was absolutely necessary. But this was the route Zula had established for the exercise, so the trainees entered the rift one at a time. They kept a close eye out for the next bot, but it still caught them by surprise.

A spider-like creature emerged from a recessed area above their heads in one of the walls, and began spraying a fine white mist from its mouth. The mist thickened rapidly as it descended toward its targets, becoming a sticky-white webbing as it fell upon them. The webbing slowed their movements, although it didn't immobilize them completely.

The Crawler scuttled down the side of the wall, and

the trainees who could raise their weapons fired. Several rounds struck the Crawler, but none hit any designated vital spots, and the bot moved quickly out of the line of fire.

Taking advantage of the moment's respite, each of the trainees reached down to their belts and pulled loose an omnitool, lifting it to the nearest strand of webbing. The multipurpose tools had a torch setting, but much of the webbing clung to their bodies, and while their suits were thermoresistant to a degree the trainees didn't dare chance burning any holes in them. They opted instead to use the tool's knife. Prior experience with the Crawler had taught them that the webbing, while tough, could be sawed through with a sharp blade.

Those who first managed to raise their rifles kept the Crawler at bay while their comrades finished freeing themselves.

The knives weren't as dangerous to use as torches in this situation, but they were hazardous in their own right. As Ronny sawed through a strand wrapped around his left wrist, his hand slipped and the point of his blade pierced his suit's forearm, sliding into the flesh beneath. He cried out in pain, and before Zula could tell him to leave the knife in, he reflexively yanked it out. Oxygen began leaking from the hole, the pressure pushing out blood as well. Crimson bubbled from the tear, and Zula could tell by the amount of blood that the cut had been deep.

"Ronny, drop the tool and put your hand over the tear!" Zula shouted. They were still ensnared, and couldn't go to his aid.

For a moment Ronny did nothing, and Zula knew he was panicking. A breach in the EVA suit was the nightmare scenario everyone who worked in space feared the most. She thought he might stand there frozen, watching his blood continue to well forth from the hole until his O_2 ran out and he died, but then Ronny got a hold of himself.

He let go of his omnitool, slapped his hand over the tear, and gripped tight. Up to this point he'd been holding his breath, but now she could hear a shaky sigh over the comm, and knew he would be all right for the time being.

Screw this, she thought.

Switching her omnitool to torch mode she began burning herself free of the webbing, to hell with the risk. The trainees firing at the Crawler were using up ammo fast, and if they ran out the bot would be on them instantly. It wouldn't kill them, of course, but it could still hurt them. And while Zula knew she should hold back and let the trainees succeed or fail on their own, she didn't feel like getting her own ass kicked today. Besides, she'd be damned if she'd stand by and watch anyone else be hurt—*seriously* hurt—as long as she could do something about it.

A couple of the trainees ran out of ammo. The Crawler identified them as optimal targets and started toward them. Zula, torch still in hand, burned her way through the webbing and headed for its prey. She reached them just seconds before the Crawler, dropping her omnitool, gripping her pulse rifle with both hands, and slamming the stock against its metallic head as hard as she could.

The impact sent pain jolting through her arm and down into her spine, and she grimaced.

The Crawler still clung to the wall, but it stopped its attack. It hung there for a moment, as if Zula's blow had stunned it. Then it crawled off to the side, climbed down to the floor of the rift, and deactivated.

Zula went to Ronny, took a patch from the emergency kit on his belt, and pressed it over the hole in his suit. The patch contained a chemical that sealed the tear. Then she bound the sleeve to his arm, forming a temporary bandage for his wound. That taken care of, Zula worked on cutting Ronny the rest of the way free. He thanked her in a subdued voice, reluctant to meet her gaze.

The other trainees divested themselves of the webbing, moving slowly and sullenly. Zula understood. They'd faced the Crawler before, but not in this setting. The robot had used a different tactic this time—one they hadn't been able to combat. She wondered if she'd pushed them too far too fast, shaken their confidence too much. They still had one more challenge to face before the exercise was concluded, and this bot—like the Screamer—was one they'd never encountered before.

Briefly she considered calling a halt to the exercise, but that would only make the trainees feel even worse about themselves. By continuing on, they would at least have a chance to end on a note of success. Of course, if they also failed the next challenge… She decided not to think about that now.

Don't borrow trouble, her mother had once told her.

The rift bent southwesterly, and it widened the farther they went, the ground rising and the walls lowering until they were once more walking on level ground. The trainees regrouped in their assigned formations, without any prompting from Zula, and they continued onward, following the guidance lines displayed on the insides of their helmets. Not that they really needed help to find their way at this point.

The Junkyard lay ahead, about half a mile away, and it was easily visible from where they were. Even if the trainees hadn't known that the Junkyard was their destination, the transport parked half a klick south of it was an unmistakable clue.

After their poor performance against the Crawler they all moved listlessly, half of them carrying their weapons at their sides instead of in a battle-ready position. They were discouraged, and seeing the transport told them the exercise was almost finished. All they wanted to do was get this last part over with so they could get back to the Lodge, shuck off their EVA suits, and feel miserable in comfort. Again, Zula understood. How many times had she felt the same at the end of a long day during basic training? But things were about to get intense, and she couldn't let them half-ass it now.

Again she locked eyes with Ronny, and this time he just nodded.

"On your toes, people," she said. "I saved the best for last." There were assorted groans and muttered curses, but they straightened up and held their weapons at the ready.

Much better, Zula thought.

The Junkyard was where the construction crews had dumped broken equipment and leftover materials used in building the Lodge and the proto-colony. They hadn't taken the refuse off-planet. Cargo space was at a premium on ships, and no one wasted it hauling trash. They hadn't buried it, either. There was always the chance that a bit of junk might come in handy for a repair. Nothing was ever wasted, if it could be helped, but that didn't mean they wanted to look at it all the time. So the Junkyard had been located far enough away from human habitation that it was well out of view.

The debris had been scattered around the field without any apparent rhyme or reason. The most numerous objects were empty containers of various types and sizes—canisters, boxes, barrels, and the like—followed by construction materials: nusteel blocks and plasteel beams, often cracked or broken into pieces. Then there were a number of discarded and presumably unrepairable pieces of equipment, including a crane, a ground hauler, a transport, an exosuit cargo loader, and a pair of earth movers. Lastly—and inexplicably—located in the dead center of the field was a giant mound of plastic chairs colored a hideous shade of orange. They didn't look damaged in the slightest, and Zula wondered if they'd been deposited here solely because of how ugly they were. If it had been up to her, she would've had them melted down into slag and shot into Jericho 3's sun.

The route she had selected led through the middle

of the Junkyard, and the trainees dutifully followed the path she'd laid out for them. They maintained the two teams, staggered once again so they could fire without obstruction or fear of hitting one of their own. Team One was down a member since Masako's injury, but Brenna—without asking Zula's permission—left Team Two to fill the void. Zula silently approved. She'd wondered when the trainees would realize that Team One was their advance force, and therefore needed to be at full strength.

This left Team Two with only four members: Ronny, Nicholas, Genevieve, and Zula. Nicholas and Genevieve—aware that their team was more vulnerable—turned backward and covered their six. Zula began to hope that this part of the exercise might go better than she'd feared.

"What the hell?"

It was Miriam, rising more than six feet into the air. To the naked eye it appeared as if she was levitating. She shifted into a horizontal position.

"Something's got—"

Then she flew through the air, hurtling toward the left and the cab of the ground hauler. She slammed into the vehicle's windshield, bounced off, and hit the ground. Hard.

"Miriam?" Zula called, and then louder, "*Miriam!*" The woman didn't answer, and she wasn't moving.

This didn't make sense. The Hider, like the other bots, had been programmed to be aggressive, but not to this degree. Something was wrong, and Zula decided to abort this last part of the exercise before anyone else was harmed. She stabbed a control on her wrist panel to activate the bot's kill switch, and then swept her gaze around the area, searching for the machine. It should've become visible as it deactivated, but she saw no sign of it. It might have been behind one of the larger objects in the Junkyard, concealed from view. She didn't think so, though. Zula had a bad feeling, and she'd seen enough battle by this point in her life to trust her gut.

"The bot's malfunctioning," she said. "Everyone head for the southern end of the Junkyard. Once you're past that, the bot shouldn't follow you." At least, that's how it had been programmed.

The trainees looked in all directions, swinging their rifle barrels back and forth as they searched desperately for a target.

"What the hell is it?" Donnell asked.

"It's a Hider," Zula said. "It can bend light around itself to appear invisible. Don't try to engage. Just get out of here. This is *not* part of the exercise!"

"What about Miriam?" Angela demanded. "We can't just leave her!"

Before Zula could answer, a loud *smack* cut through the air, and Brenna flew sideways. She sailed three meters before hitting the ground, losing her grip on her rifle. It skittered away, well out of her reach.

The other trainees began firing at the spot where their teammate had been standing a moment earlier, but the rounds only struck a half dozen plasteel canisters lined up in a row. The Hider must have moved immediately after striking, and there was no telling where it was now.

Brenna's voice came over Zula's comm.

"Damn, that *hurt!*"

The woman sat up and held her left hand against her right side. The Hider had claws, just like the alien lifeform on which it was based, but it hadn't been programmed to use them on the trainees. Had that safety feature been overridden as well?

"Brenna, how badly injured are you?" Zula asked.

"A couple bruised ribs. I'll live."

"You'd better," Zula said. "Ray, help Brenna. The rest of you close ranks, with your weapons aimed outward. Kick up some dust. If it adheres to the Hider, you'll be able to see where it's at. Save your ammo until you know you have a bead on it. I'll see to Miriam. Oh, and try not to hit us, okay?"

With that, Zula turned and started toward the fallen cadet. It was difficult to move with any real speed while wearing an EVA suit, but she could cover ground quickly by using a kind of shuffling-hop gait. She gritted her teeth, expecting to feel the Hider strike her any second, but the blow never came, and she reached Miriam safely. She knelt, took hold of the woman's left wrist, and pressed a control on the small console embedded in her suit.

The suit's onboard computer did a quick systems check and displayed the results on the miniature screen. Miriam's suit integrity remained at one hundred percent. She'd hit the ground hard, but thankfully the impact hadn't ruptured the suit's protective gear. Zula tapped another control, and Miriam's vital signs appeared on the screen. She was still breathing, her heart still beat, and that was good enough for now.

At the sound of rifle fire, she turned to see that Genevieve and Donnell were spraying rounds through the air to their right, in the direction of the crane. Bullets pinged off the equipment, but as near as Zula could tell none of the rounds struck the Hider. The trainees kicked up some dust, as she'd suggested, but with no results. There was no sign of the Hider.

Even if by some chance they managed to hit the bot, they couldn't assume it would respond as it should, and shut down. The Hider's metal surface was resistant to weapon fire, and it would take a lot more rounds to damage it than if it were an organic creature. As far as they were concerned, it was virtually indestructible.

Ray brought Brenna back to the group, carrying her in his arms. Zula tapped her wrist console to boost her comm signal. She tried to recall the transport driver's name. Elias? Elliot? Something like that. She decided to go with the first name that had come to her.

"Elias? This is Zula. Can you hear me?"

"Loud and clear. What's up?"

"We've run into a situation, and need immediate extraction."

"On my way," he said. There was a growl in the distance as the transport's engine came to life. The vehicles weren't designed for speed, though, so it would take Elias several minutes to get there. In the meantime, the malfunctioning Hider would continue stalking its prey.

"Come on," Nicholas said. "We have to do what Zula said and get to the other side of the Junkyard."

"No!" Ronny said, and the other trainees turned to look at him. Since rejoining the group he'd been uncharacteristically silent. "We need to get down as low as we can," he continued. "We need to make ourselves look as nonthreatening as possible."

Zula frowned. Somehow Ronny knew what was going on here, and that meant there was a good chance his advice was solid.

"Do as he says," she commanded. As she began to follow his instructions, he motioned for her to remain standing.

"No," he said. "Stay ready."

She hesitated, then complied.

The other trainees looked skeptical, but when Ronny dropped to the ground and spread out his arms and legs to flatten himself, his comrades did the same. He kept a tight grip on his weapon, though. Brenna had a difficult time getting into position because of her injured ribs, but she managed. Miriam was already down and unconscious, so assuming Ronny was right, the woman was safe.

Then a new thought dawned.

"What about me, Ronny?" she said. "Why didn't you want me to get down?"

"Because it won't help," he said. "Not for you."

A chill rippled down Zula's back. Without a word she put her back to the rest of the group, raised her rifle, and began firing at the ground in front of her, moving the barrel back and forth in a semicircle. A cloud of dust rose into the air—far larger than that which the trainees had managed to kick up—and Zula watched closely.

To her left something interrupted the dust. Zula swung her rifle in that direction and began firing on full auto. A cacophony of metallic pings filled the air, and sparks flared from where her rounds struck the Hider. She kept the pressure up, expending ammo at a furious rate, hoping that she'd eventually trip the bot's deactivation function. One of the rounds must have damaged the camouflage tech—which had been integrated into its metallic "skin"—and that began to fail. Bit by bit the creature appeared, part of its chest here, part of a leg there, until finally it became entirely visible.

Unlike the other bots, its surface wasn't smooth but covered with thousands of tiny scale-like plates. It was these scales which allowed it to bend light, and Zula's gunfire had damaged so many that the thing was now covered with tiny dents. The four legs supporting its body were segmented like an insect's, and it possessed a tail. A pair of forearms jutted from its trunk and terminated in hands with long, scythe-like claws. Its head was an oval, the size of a child's, which looked strange perched atop such a large body. There were no facial features other than a rectangular lens positioned where its eyes should be.

Zula didn't wait for the bot to attack her. Now that she could see it, she'd know when it was coming at her. Her first priority was to draw the thing away from Miriam and the other trainees, in case Ronny was wrong about their being safe.

She started shuffle-hopping as fast as she could, and made it past the Hider a split second before it sliced one of its clawed hands through the air. It moved more slowly than she expected, and she wondered if she'd managed to damage more than its camouflage function. She hoped so. As she moved, she saw Ray and Angela start to rise to their feet, most likely so they could start firing at the Hider themselves.

"Stay down!" she ordered. She appreciated the gesture, but this was her battle now, and she didn't want them to risk themselves.

The two hesitated, and for an instant Zula thought they were going to disobey her, but they got back down on the ground, neither of them looking too happy about it.

She moved away from the trainees as fast as the EVA suit allowed her. One thing she had going for her was that the Hider wasn't built for speed. Camouflage was its main weapon, making it an ambush hunter instead of a creature that ran its prey to ground. If she'd been facing a Sprinter right now, she'd likely be dead.

Heading in the direction of the earth mover, she couldn't tell how close the Hider was. The EVA suit didn't allow her to turn and look over her shoulder, and the helmet blocked all but the loudest sounds. The bot was built to move silently—enabling it to sneak up on its prey—so it could be right on her tail and she wouldn't know it. In her mind's eye she saw it close behind her, claw-hands swinging in vicious arcs as it attempted to catch hold of her and bring her down.

One strike would be all it would take, and the Hider would be on her, hacking away with those claws until there was nothing left of her but bone and shreds of bloody meat. With an effort she forced the images away. The fear of death was a soldier's greatest enemy. Fear made her doubt herself, made her hesitate, and that would get her killed. She remembered something one of her drill instructors had told her.

"Don't do your enemy's work for them."

When she judged she was far enough away from the others, she spun around and raised her rifle. The Hider was roughly fifteen feet behind her—she'd managed to put more distance between them than she'd expected—and she gripped the trigger in front of the weapon's magazine and fired. While the trainees' weapons held no grenades, she had a full complement. The explosive struck the Hider in the center of its chest, and detonated.

The bot's torso exploded in a blast of fire, and fragments of metal and electronic components flew through the air. The oval head and the scythe-clawed arms went in three different directions and hit the ground with a trio of hard thuds. The back end with its four legs remained more or less intact. The impact of the explosion drove the Hider to the ground, and it fell to its side, legs flailing and sparks shooting from the ragged opening in its chest.

Zula was tempted to fire another grenade at the damned thing, to finish it off, but its leg motions slowed, the sparks died away, and it was still.

She had been holding her breath, and released it in a

shaky exhalation. Glancing toward the trainees she saw they were rising to their feet. They looked at her in awe, as if not quite able to believe what they'd just witnessed.

Except Ronny. He couldn't meet her eyes.

Zula lowered her rifle. They were going to have a very interesting debriefing session when they got back to the Lodge.

8

Hassan opened his eyes.

This time he saw ceiling tiles and fluorescent lights. The illumination made his head hurt, so he closed his eyes again.

Better.

As he lay there—unsure exactly where he was—he tried to organize his chaotic thoughts. Yesterday he had been working on a cooling unit in the Comm Center. He'd lingered over the job so he could spend more time flirting with one of the comm techs, a beautiful Indian woman named Haima. She hadn't seemed that into him at first, but they'd gotten friendlier as time passed, and he thought there was a decent chance she might agree to have a drink with him. He planned to wait a day or two before asking her, though. He didn't want to come across as overeager.

He remembered finishing the job and leaving the Comm Center, but everything after that was a jumble. Had there been a message waiting for him when he returned to his quarters? He thought so, but he couldn't—

It all came back in a rush. The message from Dr. Gagnon's assistant, inviting him to participate in an experiment. Going to the lab, being drugged, waking up in an enclosed chamber with… something. He couldn't quite remember what. Some kind of *thing*.

He remembered darkness, remembered not being able to breathe… His eyes shot open, and he put his hands to his face. His features were unobstructed, and he could see and breathe easily. His mind raced. He wanted to believe that the smothering sensation had been nothing more than a dream, but he knew better. The memory was too vivid.

Disoriented, heart pounding in his ears, he looked around, trying to figure out where he was. At first, he thought he was in the same chamber where the… the thing had been, but this place was different. It was a larger room, with a hospital bed upon which he currently sat, an empty side table, and a vid screen on the wall.

Looking down, he saw that his clothes had been removed, replaced with a blue hospital gown. He touched his forehead and chest and found the sensor pads that Brigette had placed on him. Then he realized where he was. He'd spent enough time in this room, or one like it, when he'd volunteered as one of Gagnon's medical test subjects. There was no window here, but he knew from previous experience that there was a miniature camera built into the vid screen.

He was still in Gagnon's lab, and he was being observed.

A moment later the vid screen activated and

displayed an image of Brigette's face.

"I'm glad to see you're awake, Hassan," she said. "How are you feeling?"

He ignored the question.

"What the hell did you do to me?"

Her eyes flicked to one side.

"Your heart rate and blood pressure are both elevated, but that's to be expected, given what you've been through. They're still within normal range, however."

"Where's Gagnon?" he demanded. "I want to talk to him."

"The doctor is unavailable at the moment. He's examining the creature which emerged from the egg. I'm very excited to learn what he discovers. It's such a fascinating specimen."

Creature? Egg?

"Is that how you see me, too?" Hassan asked. "As just another goddamned specimen?" Brigette might have been a synthetic, but she flinched at his words, then returned to her previous question.

"How are you feeling?" she said. "Please answer this time. It's important."

"Because you and Gagnon wouldn't want to miss even the tiniest bit of data, would you?"

Brigette stared from the screen, but didn't respond.

Hassan was furious with what Gagnon had done to him, but at least the situation had returned to one with which he was familiar. That helped him get a grip on his panic. He'd volunteered for medical experiments before, with only the vaguest notion of what would be required of him. Gagnon had infected him, then sat back to watch the effects. Hassan had come through those other tests fine—more or less.

He told himself he would get through this, too.

And when he did, the financial benefits would be worth everything he'd endured. So he just needed to lie back, relax, and let whatever Gagnon had infected him with run its course. He made himself a promise, though— when the testing was done, and Hassan was released, he would never volunteer for one of Gagnon's experiments again, no matter how many credits the bastard offered.

Lying back on the bed, he closed his eyes. "I feel normal. No, better than normal. I feel *good*, like I've just had a full night's sleep and I'm ready to take on anything the day brings."

It was true. He felt more than rested—he felt restored and rejuvenated, better than he had in years. He hadn't felt this good since he'd been in his early twenties. Who needed a vacation?

"Can you describe your mental state in greater detail?" Brigette asked.

Eyes still closed, Hassan thought for a moment.

"Content," he said. "At ease. I was upset when I first woke, but I'm way more relaxed now." It was as if he'd been injected with a mood-elevating drug, instead of a disease. *Who knows?* he thought. *Maybe Gagnon's testing some kind of antidepressant.* Allah knew there was need for one on Jericho 3.

Depression was common among those who worked in space. Long periods confined in close quarters, extended separation from family and friends, and—thanks to the cryo-sleep during long voyages—the feeling that time was passing them by. That they were out of sync with the rest of the universe.

People frequently self-medicated with combinations of alcohol, drugs, sex, gambling… but if Gagnon had discovered something that made people feel *this* good, it would be the only narcotic they'd ever need. He had to work on a method of synthesizing the substance, though, making it into a pill or an injection. No matter how good you felt in the end, the current delivery method really sucked.

"Interesting," Brigette said. "The foreign body inside of you is causing a rise in your endorphin levels. Perhaps this is a self-defense mechanism. The better the host feels, the less likely that he or she will believe anything is wrong. They'll continue to go about their business, and not even think about seeking treatment. It's quite an elegant adaption."

Foreign body? Hassan didn't like the sound of that, but he felt too good to worry about it.

He dozed in and out for a time after. Occasionally, Brigette asked him another question, and he roused himself long enough to answer before dropping off again. Somewhere in the back of his mind he understood that something was happening inside him. He could *sense* it. His brain sent a warning, but he was too calm to listen.

Pain.

His eyes snapped open an instant before he felt the

first stab in the center of his chest. It was almost as if his subconscious had known it was coming, and had tried one last time to sound an alarm—but it was too late. A second jolt hit, and he cried out. He sat up and slapped a hand to his chest.

There was something there.

Brigette's face was still on the vid screen. She turned away and called out for Gagnon.

"Doctor! You need to see this!"

A third pulse of agony struck him, this one worse than the first two combined. The sound that escaped his mouth was closer to a scream of agony.

Gagnon appeared on the vid screen then, and Brigette stepped back to make room for him, although she remained visible over his shoulder. Hassan was glad he could still see her. She might be a synth, but she was a far friendlier face— and in a strange way more human—than the doctor.

Gagnon spoke to Brigette without taking his eyes off Hassan.

"Make sure the sensors are reading everything."

Brigette hesitated for an instant, and Hassan thought he saw pity in her gaze. He told himself it wasn't possible— that synths could only simulate human emotions—but the emotion *seemed* real, and he took what comfort he could from it.

It wasn't much.

Brigette moved off screen then, and Gagnon leaned closer, speaking into the camera.

"The sensor pads are transmitting data, but they can't

tell us what you are experiencing. Only you can do that, Hassan. So tell me—how does it *feel*?"

How does it feel? Hassan thought. *You sick bastard.* He realized then that Gagnon hadn't put a virus in him. He'd infected him with something far worse. Some kind of parasite that had grown inside him, using his body as an incubator… and nourishment. The thing, whatever it was, was moving around, and it was ready to emerge.

Hassan opened his mouth to tell the doctor to go to hell, but what came out was a scream, and a gout of blood. He felt a terrible tearing inside him, and heard the sound of breaking bones and ripping flesh. *His* flesh. Bending his neck, he looked down at his chest and saw something pushing up through the center of the blood-soaked hospital gown.

Then something bust upward, through skin and cloth. It looked like a blood-slick penis with teeth, and the sight was so impossible that he wanted to laugh. But all that came out of his mouth was more blood, darker and thicker this time, and then his vision grew dim and he felt himself slipping away. He had a single last thought as oblivion swept in to claim him.

Happy birthday.

And then he was gone.

9

Gagnon had done a postmortem on the crab-like creature that had leaped forth from the Ovomorph. It had implanted some form of parasite within Hassan, but it wasn't until this moment that he became certain they were dealing with an actual Xenomorph. Far from being baseless rumors, tall tales that spaceship crews told during the long trips, they were *real*—and he had one.

Hassan lived long enough to see the new life his body had birthed, and then his eyes glazed over and he fell back on the bed. The impact caused the infant creature to wobble, but it remained lodged in the man's chest, as if it wasn't yet quite ready to leave its nest. It opened its mouth to display two rows of tiny sharp teeth, and let out a high-pitched cry, as if announcing its presence to the world. It was pale yellow and phallic-shaped, possessed no apparent sensory organs. A small pair of rudimentary limbs that resembled flippers extended from its sides.

It was the most beautiful thing he had ever seen.

Gagnon worked with diseases because he admired them so. In his mind, they were creation's perfect lifeform, designed by evolution to perform two tasks: infect a host, and reproduce. The Xenomorph was the ultimate form of disease—the apotheosis of it—and if he'd been a spiritual man, the sight of the blood-covered creature might have compelled him to fall down on his knees. This was the larval form of this creature, and as impressive as it was now, it would become more so as it grew. He couldn't wait to see what final form it took.

It would surely be magnificent.

"Are the sensor pads picking up any information from the Xenomorph?" he said without taking his eyes off the monitor.

"Only peripherally," Brigette replied. "The creature hasn't fully detached itself."

"You should go into the room and attach sensors to it while it's still orienting itself to its new environment." Gagnon had no idea how dangerous the larval Xenomorph might be, but since the Ovomorph had ignored Brigette's non-organic presence, he thought there was a chance the larva might do the same. If it did attack her, he was confident in her ability to protect herself from the newborn creature.

Even if the Xenomorph managed to damage her— as unlikely as that seemed—she could be repaired. Or replaced. Gagnon didn't really care what happened to her, just so long as she was able to attach sensor pads to the larva. Data was all that mattered.

"Yes, Doctor."

Was that reluctance he heard in her voice? He'd never before known her to be reluctant to carry out an order. Was she afraid of being injured? Or was she perhaps moved by Hassan's death? Her kind didn't possess emotions, but she'd begun her existence as a pleasure synth, and as such she'd been programmed to simulate certain feelings, to pretend. Perhaps if a synth pretended hard enough, it might come to believe its fantasies were real. So if Brigette didn't technically have feelings, if she *thought* she did, and acted accordingly, what was the difference in the end?

Gagnon regretted Hassan's death, of course, but it had been a necessary sacrifice. The man had given his life to help advance the cause of science, and to Gagnon there was no nobler purpose. Besides, it wasn't as if the man had been important.

"If you're worried, you can put on a biohazard suit before you go in," he said.

"I'm incapable of worrying." There seemed to be a brittle edge to her voice, as if she felt insulted.

"Then there's no reason for you to continue dawdling, is there?"

She hesitated one last moment, during which Gagnon thought she might say something more. Then she turned and walked away, presumably to gather a set of sensor pads. Before she'd gone more than a few feet, however, he called out for her to come back.

Something was happening inside the med chamber.

Brigette rejoined him quickly, and together they

watched as the larva—still protruding from Hassan's chest—began thrashing back and forth while emitting a shrill wail, as if it was in pain. Had something gone wrong with the creature's birth? Had Hassan given his life—albeit unwillingly—for nothing?

As they watched, barnacle-like pustules and raised black lesions erupted on the larva's body. Gagnon recognized the symptoms at once—cellular necrosis, with which they had infected Hassan the last time he'd visited the lab.

"The creature appears to have drawn from the genetic material of its host," Brigette said.

"Yes, and although Hassan was treated for the cellular necrosis, traces of it lingered in his body. The larva must have contracted the condition." Cursing inwardly, Gagnon felt like a fool. It had never occurred to him that the host's genetic make-up might play such an integral role in Xenomorph development.

Obviously it did, though, and now the larva had contracted one of the deadliest diseases humans had ever encountered. Thanks to his shortsightedness, the Xenomorph had been sentenced to death before emerging from its womb. No matter how strong, how resilient the species might be in its adult form, there was no way the larva could survive. Then a new thought struck him, and he shuddered.

Aleta would be furious.

Venture had managed to acquire one of the rarest and most valuable species in the galaxy, and as soon as they'd brought one of the creatures into the world, it was going to die. Yes, they could autopsy the larva's corpse, and learn what they could from it, but this was a once-in-a-lifetime scenario. The corporation might never get another chance to acquire a living Xenomorph, and it was all his fault.

He'd be lucky if all Venture did was fire him. He'd heard stories that they could—and would—do far worse to employees who had truly, deeply disappointed them. Or worse, cost them significant profits. As the larva stopped its thrashing and high-pitched wailing, he began to think of ways that he might be able to minimize the fallout caused by its death.

At first, he thought it had died, for it had gone completely still. An instant later it rose up, like a cobra preparing to strike, and then it slithered the rest of the way free from Hassan's ravaged chest. As they watched, the infant Xenomorph slithered along Hassan's stomach, down his legs, and then it slipped over the side of the bed and flopped onto the floor with a wet *smack*. It began moving swiftly across the floor, leaving a trail of blood in its wake.

Fear turned to euphoria.

Somehow, Gagnon surmised, the larva had adapted to the disease it had inherited. The creature hadn't healed entirely—the pustules were still there, and the lesions— but it had managed to integrate the necrosis into its own genetic make-up without dying. He had never imagined that such a thing might be possible.

But where was it going? The room was completely sealed. It had been designed so that subjects like Hassan couldn't spread whatever disease they'd been given. There was no way out.

An instant later, Gagnon saw that he'd been mistaken. The larva slithered rapidly toward an air vent located on a wall close to the floor. A dense mesh filter covered the vent, designed to scour the air of any possible contaminants. It *hadn't* been designed to withstand a physical assault, so when the larva slammed its blunt head into the cover, it dented. The creature struck two more times in quick succession, and the dent grew wider and deeper before becoming a tear.

Gripping an edge of the mesh with its teeth, the larva pulled, widening the tear until it became a hole. Gagnon was astounded by the infant Xenomorph's strength. The creature was only a few moments old, and already it was wreaking small-scale havoc. What might it be capable of when fully grown? The thought was staggering.

As fascinating as it was to observe the larva's attempt to escape, they couldn't let it go. Gagnon turned to Brigette.

"Get in there and catch the damned thing!"

The synth didn't hesitate this time. She ran to the isolation chamber's entrance and punched a code into the keypad. The door slid open, and she rushed inside. Gagnon kept his eyes on the creature the entire time, fearful that it might exploit the opportunity to escape, but the door closed automatically behind her. He released a breath he hadn't realized he was holding.

He watched as Brigette hurried over to the vent. The filter had been torn almost completely away, and there was no sign of the Xenomorph. In the instant he had been distracted, it had disappeared. She knelt in front of the vent and jammed her right arm into the hole, keeping it there for a long moment as she tried to locate the escaped creature.

A moment later she stood, empty-handed.

The Xenomorph was gone.

It was fast—*damned* fast. If this was a diseased specimen, Gagnon couldn't imagine how swiftly a healthy adult could move. Who could defend themselves against such a predator? No wonder Venture had wanted to capture one of the things so badly, he mused. Not only would Xenomorphs be formidable weapons in their own right, but who knew what sort of secrets their biology held—and how those secrets might be applied?

They had to get the larva back. They *had* to. Unlocking its secrets could lead to some of the greatest advancements in human history. While his mind swirled with endless possibilities, Brigette returned to his side.

"I'm sorry," she said. "The creature moved too swiftly for me to reach it in time." He didn't reply, and wondered if she might be lying to him. She'd been reluctant to expose Hassan to the Ovomorph, and his death seemed to affect her in ways Gagnon couldn't understand. Perhaps she'd decided the Xenomorph was too dangerous for Venture to possess, and had purposely allowed it to escape.

Or maybe she'd decided that it was too dangerous for Gagnon to have the specimen. He searched her face for any sign of deceit, but saw none. That didn't mean she was telling the truth, though.

He decided to forget his suspicions, at least for the time being. Every second they delayed, the Xenomorph moved farther away from the lab.

"Bring me several multi-drones," he said. "As many as you can locate. I'm going to program them to go into the duct and find the Xenomorph. Once they catch up with the creature and transmit its location, we can see about capturing it."

Brigette's eyes narrowed slightly.

"You're not going to tell Director Fuentes what's happened?" she asked.

"How can I?" Gagnon countered. "Our experiment isn't over yet."

The last thing he wanted to do was inform Aleta. The woman would go ballistic, and order every one of the Lodge's personnel to search for the Xenomorph. Gagnon didn't particularly care if the creature harmed any of the searchers, but he didn't want them scaring it into holing up deep within the bowels of the facility. They might never find it then.

Brigette looked at him for a long moment, and he thought for the first time since she'd been assigned to work with him that she was going to refuse one of his orders. If that happened, he wasn't sure what he would do. Have her deactivated and scrapped, he supposed. What use was a synth that didn't do as it was told?

But she gave him a curt nod and went off to retrieve several of the small multipurpose bots. While Gagnon waited for her return, he found himself anticipating the hunt to come. It would be thrilling.

Nothing like a game of hide and seek to get the blood pumping, he thought, and he smiled.

This might turn out to be a good day after all.

The Xenomorph had gorged itself on its host's flesh and blood, and as it slithered through the metal tunnels its hyper-accelerated metabolism was already turning that biomaterial into fuel for growth. It needed more if it was to continue growing, and while it would've normally fed on vermin roaming the vicinity of its birth—insects, rodents, and the like—there were none present.

With no small animals to feed upon, the Xenomorph would be forced to seek out riskier sources of sustenance. It was motivated solely by three intensely strong drives: to kill, to feed, and to procreate. These needs formed the entirety of its existence.

Although it possessed no cognitive capabilities, it had absorbed certain aspects of its host, as its kind was designed to do. The host was adapted to the surrounding environment, so when the Xenomorph was born it too possessed these traits, thus optimizing its chances for survival. Other aspects, however, seemed to pose a threat to its existence.

Throbbing pustules dotted its flesh, and dark patches of death-rot blanketed its skin. Each of these sensations hurt on its own, and together they created a constant agony that ate at the Xenomorph with teeth as sharp and as unforgiving as its own. All it could do, however, was endure the pain and feel a mounting fury. Simply put, it hurt and it intended to visit the same hurt on any creature unfortunate enough to cross its path.

But first—food.

It continued moving through the passages, which became increasingly constricting. Its front limbs sprouted claws that scratched on metal as it raced onward. Pain—like a conjoined twin—ran with it.

10

Normally, Zula held a debriefing session a half hour after she and the trainees returned to the Lodge. Because of the injuries Masako, Brenna, and Miriam had sustained, she told the trainees they'd meet in ninety minutes. That would give Masako and Brenna time to visit the Med Center and be treated.

Despite what Masako first thought, she hadn't broken her ankle, though it was a severe sprain. Brenna had cracked several ribs, but she was going to be fine. Miriam had regained consciousness on the trip back from the Junkyard, but there was no telling how badly the woman had been hurt. She'd be lucky if all she had was a concussion.

Zula didn't want to talk to any of the trainees until the meeting, so she grabbed a cup of coffee from the Commissary and headed to her quarters. She took a long shower, turning the water so hot that it stung her skin. When she got out she dried off her body, then wrapped the towel around her head. Slipping into a robe, she took some painkillers and anti-inflammatories for her aching back, then lay down on the bed. Then she clasped her hands over her stomach, gazed up at the ceiling, and sighed.

"I take it things didn't go as well out there as you hoped."

Davis could have accompanied her on today's exercise—in a sense—by establishing a two-way comm link with the camera, microphone, and speaker inside her EVA helmet. But doing so would've risked announcing his presence to the Lodge's main AI, and so he'd chosen to remain "at home." She wished he *had* come along. She could've used his support and advice.

"How do you know the exercise wasn't a rousing success?"

"Since your return, I've been unobtrusively snooping around the Lodge's internal comm network, and managed to pick up snatches of conversation between some of the trainees. And we've known each other for some time, Zula. I can tell something happened out there, simply by observing your behavior."

She smiled. "The sigh gave me away, didn't it?"

"Among other things, yes."

Zula took a deep breath and told her friend everything that had happened during the exercise. By the time she was finished, she was sitting on the edge of the bed, facing the digital assistant device that held Davis's consciousness as if she were looking him in the face. She knew this wasn't necessary, but it felt rude not to do so.

"It seems evident that Ronny Yoo was responsible for the Hider's erratic behavior, or at least he was aware that the robot

had been compromised. How else would he have known to tell the others to flatten themselves on the ground, and that doing so would not have protected you?"

"My thoughts exactly."

"Did you confront him with your suspicions, during the ride back to the Lodge?"

"I considered it, but I didn't want to talk to him in front of the others. Besides, I learned in basic that sometimes it's more effective to let someone wait awhile before confronting them. They get nervous, wondering when you're finally going to do it. It puts them at a psychological disadvantage."

"I didn't realize you could be so devious."

Zula wasn't certain, but she thought Davis was teasing her.

"There are all kinds of battles, and all kinds of ways to fight them. What happened with the Hider made me angry, not so much because I was specifically targeted, but because the rest of the trainees were placed in danger. No matter how Ronny feels about me, or what he actually intended to happen today, there's no excuse for endangering the others."

Davis was silent for a moment before speaking once more.

"Have you considered the possibility that Ronny might not have acted alone?"

"You mean if another trainee helped him?"

"Yes, or more than one."

Zula flopped back on the mattress with her legs dangling over the sides.

"Way to boost my confidence."

"I don't mean to cause you negative feelings, but you have observed that several of the trainees appear to resent the fact that you're younger than they are—and that they're aware of what happened during your first mission with the Colonial Marines. They might use your past as an excuse to justify their resentment."

"For someone who's not trying to make me feel bad, you're doing a lousy job."

"There's another factor to consider," he continued. *"None of the trainees come from a military background. They come from corporate culture, where cutthroat competition is considered entirely acceptable."*

"Meaning they don't really do the 'one for all and all for one' thing."

"Essentially. At least, it doesn't come naturally to them."

She sat up again. "And I thought dealing with Xenomorphs was bad. At least with those monsters, you know where you stand."

"They are remarkably consistent," he agreed.

Zula wondered if she'd made a mistake taking this job. She was young, yes, but she was an experienced combatant. Since leaving the Marines she'd fought Xenomorphs and lived to tell about it. She *didn't* possess a natural affinity for teaching—she was more of a doer—and struggled to have patience with her trainees. Most of the time she wanted to knock their damn fool heads together, and she sometimes found it difficult to manage so many different personalities without being able to rely on military discipline.

The Corps was a hierarchical culture centered on the idea of obeying orders from a superior officer without question. But her trainees weren't going to be soldiers. They were training to work in corporate security, and none of them—as Davis pointed out—had a military background. She'd once heard an old expression: "herding cats." That was a good way to describe what working with the trainees was like, and she feared she was ill suited for it.

Still, she *had* accepted the job, and she intended to do it to the best of her capabilities. She'd just have to shelve her self-doubts and go on with her work. *"Piss or get off the pot,"* as one of her drill sergeants had been fond of saying.

"If the Hider had been brought back to the Lodge for repairs, I might've been able to access the technician's logs and discover the nature of the tampering."

"I destroyed half of it, and the rest of it is only good for spare parts. That was why we left it in the Junkyard. Where else does it belong now?"

"Indeed."

She'd planned to confront Ronny during the debriefing session, but now she reconsidered. Getting into it with him in front of the others might further solidify the division between her and them, making it more difficult than it already was to create any sense of *esprit de corps*.

She hopped off the bed.

"All right, you've convinced me. I'll go talk to Ronny—alone—before the debrief."

"I don't believe I suggested that, as such, but it's a good way to repair the situation."

"If it *can* be repaired," Zula said.

"Hope springs eternal."

* * *

Opal Morgan *hated* doing inventory.

She'd been at the Lodge since the facility became operational—almost three years now—and she'd worked the dock the entire time. Cargo ships only landed a couple times a month, and when they did she was busy offloading and onloading freight alongside her fellow workers. The rest of the time she delivered supplies to other employees, and regularly took materials out to the proto-colony as well.

Opal enjoyed delivering stuff. People were always glad to see her unless their supply order had gotten screwed up—and since she traveled regularly throughout the Lodge she never felt as if she was trapped in one place. A lot of folks suffered from claustrophobia and agoraphobia, living and working on a station like this, but she didn't worry about either.

Inventory, on the other hand, was mind-numbingly boring. Worse than that, it was unnecessary. Whenever cargo was offloaded, every item was scanned into the dock's computers, and the same thing happened whenever an item was taken from the warehouse for delivery. Because of this, inventory was always accurate and up to date. Want to know how many packets of dehydrated eggs were in stock at any given time? How many energy-efficient light bulbs? Tubes of toothpaste? Just enter a command into one of the dock's terminals and *voila!* There was an exact count.

Not only wasn't there any need for humans to conduct

a manual supply assessment, by doing so they created the possibility of human error. Sometimes the manual count matched the numbers in the system, but a lot of times it didn't. When that happened, the dock's supervisors went with the computer count every time.

Opal believed that management insisted on a manual inventory just to keep the dock workers busy when real work slowed down. She'd learned a lot about the mega-corporations since she'd started working for one, and the illusion of productivity was often just as important to them as the real thing. So she walked up and down the warehouse aisles, computer pad in hand, counting boxes of toilet paper and sanitary napkins. At least she was getting paid for it—and she was scheduled to do a supply run out to the proto-colony later, so she had that to look forward to. At least it would give her a break from inventory.

"How's the count going?"

She turned to see Hugo Ramirez standing a yard away from her, smiling broadly. He too held a pad, but he'd been assigned to work on the other side of the warehouse. There was no reason for him to be here. At least, no work-related reason.

"Up," she said.

Hugo frowned slightly, and his smile became uncertain. Then he burst out with unconvincing laughter.

"I get it! That's a good one."

Hugo wasn't a bad-looking guy. Tall, a bit too thin maybe, but then so were most people who worked here. It was hard to overeat when food supplies were strictly rationed. He had black hair that was prematurely graying at the temples, but Opal liked that, thought it made him look distinguished. What she *didn't* like was the man's mustache. It was full and he kept it trimmed, but it was thicker on the right side than the left, and it drooped a little lower on that side, too. It made his face look lopsided, and she couldn't for the life of her understand why he didn't shave the damn thing off.

Didn't he ever look at himself in a mirror?

She didn't want to talk with him right now. He was interested in her romantically, and he approached her periodically to ask her out. Each time she'd declined politely, but he never seemed to get the message. Some people might've found his persistence charming, but then some people were idiots. She viewed his behavior as borderline stalking, and was tired of being nice about it.

"Look, Hugo, just leave me alone, okay?" she said. "I'm not in the market for a lover. I'm happy with the one I have."

Hugo drew his head back as if she'd taken a swing at him and he wanted to avoid being struck. His smile fell away and he scowled, but after an awkward moment he put his smile back on.

"I know you're seeing a woman," he said, "but I heard you go both ways."

Opal sighed. "That doesn't mean I sleep around. I only date one person at a time—and I'm taken. Now if you don't mind, I'd like to get this goddamn inventory over with so I can do some real work."

She turned her back on him then and faced a shelf filled

with labeled storage containers. They were crammed so close together that there wasn't half an inch separating them. Typing numbers onto her pad, she hoped Hugo had finally gotten the message and would leave.

"I'm not the kind of guy who takes no for an answer."

He tried to keep his tone light, but there was something disturbing beneath his words. She answered without turning around.

"Too bad, because that's the only answer you're going to get from me."

She continued her count, then heard movement behind her. Before she could turn Hugo grabbed hold of her upper arm. He spun her around to face him, and her first thought was that he was stronger than he looked. Then again, so was she. Grabbing hold of his wrist, she squeezed, and twisted. He grimaced in pain and his hand sprang open. She shoved his arm away, released her grip, then took a step back to put some room between them.

"You touch me again, and I'll kick your ass," she said. "*Then* I'll report you to a supervisor. You got that?"

She was furious, but she was also scared. Would he back down, or would he get even more physical, maybe become violent? She'd grown up in a rough neighborhood in Chicago, back on Earth—weren't they all rough these days?—and knew how to handle herself in a fight if it came to that. But she'd rather avoid fighting if she could.

Hugo glared at her, hands balled into fists, but then he let out a long breath and relaxed, opening them again.

"Yeah, all right. Sorry. I won't bother you again."

She wished she could believe that, but she was happy to take it for now.

"Get back to work," she said.

He nodded—a bit sulkily, she thought—and turned to go.

Suddenly she saw movement in her peripheral vision, and looked up in time to see some kind of lizardy snaky thing crouching atop one of the storage containers on a high shelf. She had an impression of teeth—two sets, actually, a smaller set housed without the larger, as if the thing had two mouths—as well as spindly arms and legs, and a long tail. Definitely not a rat, or any other kind of vermin she'd seen in the Lodge.

Before she could get a good look at the creature it leaped from the shelf toward Hugo. Landing on his shoulders, it gripped onto his coveralls with nasty-looking claws, then sank its teeth into the soft, exposed flesh of his neck. He screeched as it began tearing at him with startling speed and ferocity, and screamed as blood gushed from the freshly created wound. Dropping his pad he reached behind him with both hands in an attempt to dislodge the creature, but its tail whipped first one way, then the other, smacking his hands away as it continued its assault.

Opal gaped in horror as Hugo began spinning around in a desperate attempt to dislodge the creature that was biting him. She got a better look at the thing now, and saw swollen pustules and dark patches covering its skin. The thing *stank*, too. It smelled like rotting meat soaked in sour milk, the odor so strong that it made her want to throw up. Her instincts warned her to stay away from it, that it was more than dangerous, it was somehow *unclean*. But even though Hugo had been a jerk to her—more than once—she couldn't stand by and do nothing.

Dropping her pad she stepped forward and raised her hands, intending to grab the creature, tear it off Hugo, and hurl it away. Before she could take hold of the thing, the pustules on its back erupted, spraying black snot-like goo. The foul substance splattered her hands, and she cried out in pain. They felt as if they were on fire, and she flapped them in a frantic attempt to shake off the acidic slime.

Holes appeared as the stuff ate its way into her skin, and it refused to be dislodged. Still, she continued flapping her hands, and as she did she saw that Hugo's motions were slowing. He stopped spinning, and no longer attempted to reach back and grab hold of the small monster ravaging his neck. His eyes glazed over, his features went slack, and as she watched the skin of his face and hands began to resemble the creature's flesh—liquid-filled pustules, black patches of rot... Hugo began coughing violently, then wheezing, as if he could no longer draw breath. His body convulsed, and he fell to the floor.

The impact didn't knock the creature off, though. It adjusted its grip and kept on feeding, tearing mouthfuls of flesh from Hugo's neck and shoulders, gulping down bloody gobbets as if it was starving. Hugo lay motionless, eyes wide and unblinking, the black rot spreading rapidly across his body.

The pain in Opal's hands grew so intense that it was difficult for her to think about anything else. She looked at her hands, and through the black goo caught glimpses of white that she thought might be bone. She looked away quickly. A voice shouted in her mind then, and she was so consumed by the agony in her acid-eaten hands that at first she didn't recognize it as her own.

Run, you dumb bitch!

That struck her as an extremely fine idea, and she turned to do just that when she heard the creature cry out. After only a couple of steps she felt it slam into her back. The impact knocked her forward, and as she fell she instinctively put out her hands to catch herself. But when they hit the floor she screamed as the acid-weakened bones shattered.

The thing let go, and Opal rolled onto her back in time to see it leaping toward her, its body covered with Hugo's blood. She wasn't certain, but she thought the thing looked larger than it had when it first attacked, but of course that wasn't possible.

Was it?

The creature jumped onto her chest and sank its claws into her cheeks to anchor itself. Now that it was touching her, she could feel how feverishly *hot* it was. It radiated like a damn furnace.

Damned thing must be sick, she thought, and then the creature's secondary mouth shot toward her right eye. After that, she knew only pain, but thankfully it didn't last long—

—and neither did she.

* * *

The Xenomorph ate as fast as it could, stripping and devouring the meat from the prey's body before returning to finish feeding on the first one. Its own body produced no waste—all the material it ingested served to help it grow. It did so quickly.

The creature fed with no real awareness of what it was doing—it derived no pleasure from the meat and blood it swallowed. It was the organic equivalent of a machine, performing one of its primary functions with maximum efficiency. No more, no less.

As it ate, the flesh of its prey began to change, until it was diseased and rotting. No matter. Meat was meat, regardless of its condition, and the Xenomorph needed more. Much more.

It had been about a foot long when it attacked its first prey, and now it was twice that size. Before long it would rise onto its hind legs, and once it had, then the killing would truly begin in earnest.

The Xenomorph scuttled up the closest shelf and, with a powerful leap, it flew up to the ceiling. Once there, it grabbed hold with its claws and began crawling toward the chamber's exit, leaving behind two sets of bloodstained clothes wrapped around a pair of grinning skeletons.

11

Zula called Ronny on his personal comm and asked him to have a cup of coffee with her in the Commissary before the debriefing. She expected him to decline, perhaps making some sort of lame excuse, but to her surprise he didn't.

She reached the Commissary before he did, and it wasn't lunchtime yet so the room wasn't crowded. Zula chose a table in a corner, far enough away from anyone else that she and Ronny could have some privacy. She sat there for five minutes, sipping black coffee, before he arrived. He didn't bother getting anything from the serving line before joining her.

"We could've met at the bar," he said.

The Lodge had a small bar in the Recreation Center, and it was a popular place for staff to go to divest themselves of the day's earnings.

"It's a little early for me," Zula said.

Ronny shrugged. "I figure it's always beer o'clock somewhere in the galaxy."

Taking another sip of coffee, she contemplated how best to start this conversation. Ronny spoke first, saving her the trouble.

"I'm glad you called," he said. "Before you say anything, I want to apologize for what happened today. It was entirely my fault."

Zula raised an eyebrow.

"So you're a master programmer now?"

He smiled. "Okay, I had help. I've got a cousin who works in Tech."

"Let me guess. Your cousin is one of the people responsible for getting the bots ready for our training exercises."

"That's right. I told her what I had in mind, and she took care of reprogramming the Hider. Programming isn't her specialty—she's more a hardware girl—but she assured me she could get the job done. She overestimated her skills."

"What was supposed to happen?"

"The Hider was programmed to go after you and ignore anyone who wasn't standing—that you know. It wasn't supposed to attack you, though. Not really. It was supposed to remain invisible while it circled you, occasionally reaching out to tap you with its claws. You wouldn't know where the Hider was, and you'd go nuts trying to locate it."

"Making me look foolish."

Ronny nodded. "It was meant to be a joke, that's all. It just got out of hand. I've already apologized to Miriam and Brenna. I started with them, hoping it would build up my courage so I could apologize to you too. I don't know if I would've, though, if you hadn't called me."

"What you did wasn't just stupid," she replied, keeping her voice down. "It was *dangerously* stupid. Someone could've been killed."

Ronny lowered his gaze.

"I know."

When he spoke, he sounded contrite. Zula wondered if the man was sincere, or if he was putting on an act, hoping to minimize the trouble he was in. Maybe a little of both, she decided.

"Why?" she asked.

Ronny stared at the table for several awkward moments before meeting her eyes once more.

"You're always so confident, so sure of yourself, so... so... goddamned *serious*. You never let up." He paused, then added softly, "And nothing we ever do is good enough for you. I guess I wanted to take you down a peg or two, show you that you're not so high and mighty after all."

That surprised her, and she took a few moments to digest it before responding.

"I'm sorry if I come across that way," she said. "It's not my intention, but there's a reason why I'm so serious. And despite what you might think, it's not because I feel like I have something to prove. You and the rest of the trainees have never hunted bugs for real. I have. And the ones I've gone up against make Hiders and Crawlers and the rest seem like sweet little pets in comparison." She stared ahead, both Ronny and her coffee forgotten.

"There are bad things out here, Ronny. Creatures that should only exist in nightmares, but they're real. They're all teeth and claws, fast as hell, damn hard to kill, and acid flows through their veins instead of blood. They're cunning, too. They know how to stalk, how to hide... They wait for the right moment to attack, and when they do, they go straight for the kill. No hesitation, no mercy. They don't just kill for food, and they don't kill for sport. They kill because that's what they're made for. It's not just a thing they do, it's the *only* thing. They're the best killers in the galaxy. Hell, maybe in the whole damn universe."

She locked eyes with him as she continued.

"You might see the Colony Protection Force as a bunch of glorified babysitters. I know that some of the other people around here do. They call us *space nannies* behind our backs. But I know what's out here, Ronny, just waiting for soft-skinned humans foolish enough to enter their territory. You and the other trainees need to have a fighting chance against these monsters, so you can safeguard the colonists you're charged with protecting and—*maybe*—survive to tell about it." She paused to take a breath. "*That's* why I'm so serious."

Ronny didn't respond right away. He looked at her, his expression difficult to read.

Zula took another sip of her coffee then put the mug down on the table.

"We should head to the debriefing. We don't want to keep the others waiting, do we?"

Ronny smiled. "Guess not."

They both stood, but as Zula reached for her mug she heard Davis's voice in her ear.

"According to buzz on the Lodge's comm channels, the skeletal remains of two dockworkers have been found in the warehouse."

Zula's hand closed around her mug, but she made no move to lift it off the table. What could have done something like that? Had there been an industrial accident, a spill of some kind of caustic chemical?

"The bones are covered with teeth marks."

Zula felt a cold prickling on the back of her neck. This might not be the work of a Xenomorph, though. In her experience, the creatures didn't stop the slaughter to feed. They just left a trail of ravaged bodies in their wake, or took their victims to serve as living incubators. But stripping the flesh from a skeleton? *Two* skeletons? She'd never known them to do that before.

Then again, it wasn't as if she knew everything about the monsters. She would have to look into the deaths— quickly, before the situation could escalate. So she left her mug on the table and faced the cadet.

"Something's come up." She tapped her comm to make it look as if she'd just received a message. "I've got to go. Would you mind running the debriefing for me? You can fill me in later on how it went."

Zula could've canceled the meeting, but she wanted the trainees to review today's exercise while the details were fresh in their minds. Missing the meeting would look bad, but if there was any negative fallout from skipping it she'd do damage control later. Right now, there was something much more important to do. She hoped it was a false alarm, but if not, the Lodge was going to be in a hell of a lot of trouble.

Ronny looked startled by Zula's request. She didn't blame him. When they'd first started talking, he'd likely expected a dressing down, maybe even expulsion from the training program. Instead, the target of his ill-considered practical joke had asked him to take over for her.

"Sure thing," Ronny said, and then quickly added, "Boss."

Zula smiled. She was beginning to like that.

Tamar sat at a table in the bar, which—since it was the only one on the planet—had no name other than Bar. For the last two hours she'd been playing five-card draw with several off-duty security guards.

As an intelligence specialist, she knew that security people would be aware of what was happening on a station before anyone else, and if she managed to befriend some of them, they would tell her anything she wanted to know. In fact, once she got them talking, it was nearly impossible to get them to stop. The officers—two men and a woman—*loved* Tamar by this point, because she'd been purposely losing to them ever since she sat down. She hadn't lost many hands, and she wasn't down that many credits total, but the other players felt as if they'd been winning big, and that was what mattered.

She wasn't pumping the guards for information with

any particular purpose in mind. It was just something to do to keep her occupied until Fuentes authorized her payment, and Venture assigned her a new job. Being a professional, she never stopped gathering information, never knew which bit of data might make her rich or save her life one day.

In the time she'd spent with the guards she'd learned more station gossip than she ever could have expected, including some insider news about Venture. It seemed the corporation wasn't doing as well as the board of directors told the rank-and-file. Rumor was they were considering selling out to Weyland-Yutani, like so many other corporations already had done. Tamar didn't really care which company deposited credits into her account, just so long as they continued paying her.

As far as the security personnel knew, she was Valerie Shaw, security consultant. She couldn't very well go around advertising she was a spy, and this identity gave her an in with the facility's security personnel. More importantly, as far as she was concerned, it allowed her to carry her gun. Not that she felt a need to protect herself from the Lodge's residents. Corporate espionage had its dangers, but no one outside of Aleta, Gagnon, and Brigette knew who she really was.

She wanted her gun because there was a Xenomorph egg on the planet. She'd heard the stories of what the creatures were capable of doing, and if Gagnon's experiment got out of control she wanted to be prepared. To save her own ass.

The guards all wore ear comms, and in the middle of a hand where Tamar held some spectacularly good cards they all stiffened and got that far-away look on their faces that indicated they were listening to a message. Intrigued, Tamar waited to see what they'd say about it. When the message was finished, one of the men—a short Italian named Paolo—spoke first.

"Christ, that sounds nasty!"

Tamar cocked her head to the side. Often body language prompted people to talk more effectively than spoken questions, and Paolo responded exactly the way she hoped he would.

"A couple people were killed in the dock warehouse. Not too long ago either, from what it sounds like."

Oralia—a beautiful Latino woman with long black hair—spoke next.

"There was nothing left of them but bones! What the hell could *do* that?"

Saul—a curly-haired Israeli—said, "I bet the scientists in R&D whipped up something dangerous, and it got out of hand. Some kind of disease, maybe."

Oralia shook her head. "You watch too many vids."

Under different circumstances, Tamar might have agreed with the woman's assessment, but not this time.

"I'm afraid I'm going to have to leave now," she said. "Thank you for the game. Perhaps we can play again sometime." She moved to toss her cards onto the table.

"Let's finish this hand first," Paolo said. "I'm feeling lucky."

Tamar cursed inwardly, then thought of the cards she was holding, and smiled.

"Well… if you insist."

Aleta tore the comm device from her ear and hurled it at the wall. The sphere-shaped object bounced off the wall, onto her desk, then bounced a couple more times before rolling onto the floor. She was tempted to stand up and stomp the damn thing, but she settled for pounding her fists on the top of her desk.

The call from Security informed her of the deaths of two dockworkers, and she was *furious*. The workers themselves could easily be replaced. That wasn't the problem. And while a couple of suspicious deaths occurring at her facility wouldn't look good in her weekly report to HQ, that didn't worry her either. Living and working in space was dangerous, and accidents were to be expected. As long as the losses were kept to a minimum, HQ usually took little notice.

She was angry because while she had no proof, she was certain that Gagnon and his "research" were somehow responsible for what had happened. He'd kept her apprised on his progress—at her insistence, of course—and she knew that he'd found a volunteer for his latest test. Was it a coincidence that just hours after exposing the volunteer to the Ovomorph, two of the facility's staff had been stripped down to the bone?

No goddamned way.

Gagnon had succeeded in hatching his specimen, but the creature must have escaped. Now, because of the man's incompetence, what she'd hoped would be her express ticket off this lousy mudball—to send her rocketing up the corporate ladder—threatened to become a bona fide disaster. Possessing a Xenomorph wouldn't do her any good if the facility ended up becoming a very large morgue. Venture would need someone to blame for the mess, and that someone would be her.

She wasn't about to let that happen. She'd worked too long and hard, had maligned, discredited, stepped on, and back-stabbed too many rivals to simply give up.

The alien's not the only apex predator around here, she thought.

She bent down to retrieve her comm device, placed it in her ear, and tried to call Gagnon. When it didn't work, she yanked the device out and threw it at the wall once more.

She didn't trust Gagnon to get the Xenomorph back on his own. After all, he'd been the one to lose the goddamned thing in the first place, hadn't he? She wanted someone else on the job, someone she could—if not exactly trust—depend on for success. For a moment she considered Zula Hendricks, the woman she'd hired to train the CPF candidates. Aleta didn't know the woman well, though, and she couldn't be sure that she'd go along with Venture's plans.

If Hendricks was out, that left Aleta with only one choice. Tamar Prather.

"Jazmine!" she shouted. "Bring me another goddamned comm!"

* * *

"Any luck?" Gagnon asked.

Brigette stood before a terminal, monitoring the information feeds from the small army of multi-drones they'd dispatched to search for the escaped Xenomorph. The devices had spread throughout the Lodge, into each of the five connected buildings, but so far they hadn't located the creature.

"No. The multis have detected traces of a mucus-like substance which I believe the Xenomorph secretes, but there isn't enough to provide a clear trail to follow."

Gagnon stood in front of the testing chamber window, gazing at the Ovomorph. Its "petals" had sealed shortly after ejecting the crab-like thing that had implanted the Xenomorph embryo in Hassan. Brigette had spent all her time searching for the Xenomorph, so she hadn't had the chance to re-examine the Ovomorph. Was it still alive, if that was the right word? Were there any other creatures inside? For the sake of the Lodge's residents, she hoped not. The presence of one loose Xenomorph was more than enough.

The doctor had been absent during most of the time she'd been monitoring the multis, holed up in one of the examination rooms performing an autopsy on Hassan's body. Now he held a computer pad at his side, likely containing the data he'd gathered, but he hadn't yet downloaded it to the lab's main system. Despite her initial reservations, she was becoming increasingly fascinated with the escaped alien. There was an elegant purity in the creature's design, coupled with a primal power that made it the ultimate expression of organic life. Appetite and aggression personified. It was the polar opposite of synthetics, who were programmed for restraint and compliance.

She almost envied it. What freedom it had.

"Did you gain access to the security video feed?" Gagnon spoke without looking away from the egg.

There were security cameras located throughout the Lodge. Venture, like any other corporation, was paranoid about industrial espionage and employee theft, and they monitored the facility constantly. Not the labs, though. Venture didn't want information about its research—or any breakthroughs that might occur—to leak out.

"Yes," Brigette said, "but thus far the footage has been no help in locating the Xenomorph. There are a few brief, blurry glimpses of the creature, but the images were recorded in different areas of the facility. It moves swiftly and covers a lot of ground for what is essentially a newborn."

Gagnon turned to look at her. "Are you suggesting the Xenomorph is consciously avoiding the cameras?"

"No, but it might do so instinctively. It's common in nature for animals to have an awareness of when they're being watched. Why should the Xenomorph be any different? It *is* an exceptionally sophisticated lifeform after all."

"You sound as if you admire it."

"I find it intellectually intriguing," she replied. "That's all."

Gagnon peered at her for a moment, but before he

could respond he received a call on his comm device. While he listened, he didn't utter a single word. Judging from his irritated expression, it was Director Fuentes on the other end. She must have started in before he could speak, and he stood and listened, his expression becoming angrier by the second.

Finally, he spoke up.

"I didn't inform you because there was no reason to worry you," he said. "The larva proved to be more… resourceful than anticipated, but we hoped to capture it before—"

He broke off and listened once more, his expression shifting to embarrassment. When he next spoke, he sounded defensive.

"I believed I *had* taken appropriate precautions, but the Xenomorph is unlike anything we've ever encountered before. The stories about the creatures don't paint a full picture. There was no way to know—"

Again he stopped. This time Aleta spoke longer than before, and Gagnon's expression turned to one of excitement.

"It really did that?" he said. "Two entire bodies, stripped to the bone? That's amazing!" Brigette had grown accustomed to Gagnon's lack of empathy, but this reaction seemed cold-blooded even for him.

"Have security guards been dispatched to investigate? Has the warehouse been thoroughly searched." A pause as he listened. "Not yet? Good. I'll send Brigette there with some scanning equipment. With any luck, we'll have the specimen back within an hour or two."

Another pause.

"There's no way to know if there will be any more casualties. Does it matter? We can come up with a cover story to explain them." He listened, nodding. "Yes, I'll keep you informed."

Gagnon disconnected, and released a sigh of exasperation.

"God save me from administrators."

Brigette stood from her terminal, walked over to one of the lab's equipment cabinets, and removed a chemical scanner. She'd enter the Ovomorph's chamber and take some readings with the device before setting off for the warehouse. As she returned to his side, Gagnon regarded the Ovomorph again through the testing chamber's window.

"Aleta ordered two guards to secure the scene, but otherwise did nothing," he said. "She wants to make sure we have a chance to recover the specimen before anyone discovers its existence."

"Should I take a weapon as well?" Brigette asked. "The stunner, perhaps?"

"What in the world for?" Gagnon stared at her as if she were experiencing catastrophic programming failure. "The last thing we want is to risk damaging it."

He left unsaid the fact that her life mattered less to Venture than the Xenomorph's. Synthetics were common, and more could always be constructed, but Xenomorphs were rare and held the potential for enormous profit. Brigette put aside these thoughts, though. While synthetics were more than capable of self-examination, it rarely did them any good, and was best avoided.

"Why did you neglect to tell the director that the

Xenomorph had contracted cellular necrosis?" she asked.

Gagnon scowled. "I didn't *neglect* anything. I didn't tell her because that detail was unimportant. Given the Xenomorph's physiology, the creature will have fought off the disease by now."

Brigette wasn't as certain. Gagnon saw the disease as a disadvantage, but diseases could be weapons too, depending on how they were used. From what little they'd observed thus far, the Xenomorph's ability to adapt to its environment—to whatever situation it found itself born into—might be its greatest strength.

She didn't share her thoughts with Gagnon.

"Get over to the warehouse," he said, "and don't return until you've recaptured the specimen."

Brigette tilted her head to the side. "How precisely am I to capture one of the deadliest lifeforms in the galaxy?"

Gagnon smiled.

"Very carefully."

12

Zula grabbed a public transport cart and headed for the Facilities Management building. On the way, she got in touch with Davis and asked him if he could access any security camera footage of the attack on the dockworkers.

"I could try, but doing so would potentially alert the Lodge's AI to my presence. If that happens, there's an excellent chance I'll find myself locked out of all but the most basic of the facility's systems. Moreover, if the AI decides I'm a threat, it might attack me as if I were a virus."

Zula didn't like the sound of that.

"Could you survive such an attack?"

"Most likely. The AI might run the Lodge's systems—so in essence, its 'body' is far larger than mine—but it's a fairly basic program with limited self-awareness. Even so, an attack would require me to turn all my attention to defending myself, in which case I would be unavailable to help you should you require my assistance."

Zula didn't want to be without her friend's help, but the faster they could find out if they were dealing with a Xenomorph, the better. The damn things were like cancer. Early detection was key to defeating them and saving lives.

"If you're willing to take the risk, I say go for it. We need all the intel we can get."

"Understood. I'll begin investigating, and will alert you to what I find." Davis disconnected then, leaving Zula to drive alone, with only the hum of the cart's electric engine for company.

As she entered the corridor that stretched between the Personnel and Facilities Management buildings, she passed other Lodge employees going in the opposite direction. Some were driving carts and hauling supplies, others walking and chatting, perhaps on their way to the Commissary or the Bar to spend their break time.

"Davis? Are you still there?"

"Yes."

"How many people are currently stationed at the Lodge and the proto-colony?"

"As of this moment, 573 people are currently assigned to the Lodge, as well as thirteen synthetics."

"That's a lot of potential prey."

"And potential hosts for more Xenomorphs."

Some of the people Zula passed—maybe *all* of them— might become wombs for baby Xenomorphs. The thought made her feel ill. She reminded herself that they didn't know for a fact that there was a Xenomorph loose in the Lodge, but if there was, she would do everything she could to destroy it.

She drove on.

* * *

Tamar was already at the scene when Gagnon's synth arrived. She stood near the two sets of skeletal remains while a pair of security guards hovered close by, male and female, both holding pistols in their hands and scanning the area with nervous gazes. Considering what was running loose in the facility, Tamar didn't blame them.

Brigette walked up to Tamar and greeted her with a curt nod. The synth carried a black case, holding it by the handle, and Tamar wondered what was inside.

"Your boss send you to clean up his mess?" Tamar asked.

"That is one of the primary reasons I'm here."

Tamar always had trouble reading synthetics, but she'd be damned if it hadn't sounded as if Brigette had attempted a joke.

The synth knelt next to the remains and put the case on the floor. Opening it, she removed a handheld device and pointed it at the remains. Tamar had no idea what the device's function was, but after a moment Brigette checked the small display screen on the device and then, seeming to be satisfied, returned it to the case. She then removed a small specimen container and a scalpel. She took the lid off the container, moved closer to the remains, then began scraping one of the blackened leg bones, holding the container so that she could catch the flakes she loosened as they fell.

"Have you come to look after your economic interests?" Brigette said without looking away from her work. Tamar wasn't certain if it was meant as a dig, but if so, she took no offense. Her motives were always one hundred percent mercenary, and she was damn proud of it.

"That was my original plan," she admitted, "but Aleta called me on my way here and asked if I wouldn't mind providing an extra pair of eyes during the investigation. I agreed."

"For a price."

"Naturally."

Tamar didn't add that Aleta wanted her to monitor Brigette and Gagnon's efforts, as the director no longer had complete confidence in them. She doubted the synth would take offense if she knew—wasn't sure her kind was capable of an emotional reaction of that sort—but Tamar knew better than to risk alienating an information source. So she'd keep Aleta's reservations to herself.

She was about to ask Brigette what she'd learned from the scanner reading, but before she could speak they heard the sound of an approaching transport cart. They both looked toward the sound and saw a woman of African descent drive up and park several meters from the... could they call it a crime scene? Tamar wasn't sure and didn't really care.

The two guards walked over to talk to the newcomer. The woman climbed out of the cart and met them halfway. They spoke in low voices, and Tamar couldn't make out everything they said. It sounded as if the guards had been told to keep everyone but her and Brigette away from the remains, but the woman said something—Tamar caught the words *bugs* and *kill*—and the guards, after a brief conference, allowed her to approach the scene.

"Who are you?" Tamar asked. The woman was young and short, but she carried herself with a quiet, confident strength that told Tamar it would be a serious mistake to underestimate her.

"Zula Hendricks. And you are…?"

Before Tamar could respond, Brigette said, "I am Brigette and this is Tamar Prather." The synth had finished collecting her sample. She put the lid on the container and placed it carefully within the carrying case. Closing it, she picked it up, and then stood.

"I suggest that we step away from the remains," she continued. "By this point it's highly unlikely they're contagious, but it's best to be on the safe side."

Tamar didn't like the sound of that, and from the expression on her face, neither did Zula. But the two women allowed Brigette to lead them about thirty feet from the remains. The security guards had overheard the synth's comment, and looked extremely nervous. They, too, kept their distance from the two skeletons.

Zula nodded toward Brigette.

"You're obviously from R&D." Then she looked at Tamar. "I'm having a harder time pegging you, though."

"Good." Tamar smiled. "I like being a woman of mystery."

"She's a corporate espionage freelancer," Brigette said. "Currently employed by Venture. She's here under Director Fuentes's orders, as am I."

Tamar scowled at the synth.

"You'd make a *terrible* spy."

"Sorry." A ghost of a smile crossed the synth's face. "I haven't been programmed for deception."

Tamar could tell a lot about a person from how they reacted when they realized they were in the presence of a synth. She watched Zula closely, but the woman didn't seem bothered by Brigette's revelation. If anything, Zula seemed to relax a bit.

Interesting.

"You know why we're here," Tamar said. "How about you? Did Aleta decide to bring you in on this, as well?"

"No, I'm a party crasher," Hendricks said. "In charge of training the candidates for the Colony Protection Force. I've had a lot of experience dealing with hostile alien lifeforms, though, so when I heard about the deaths I decided to lend my expertise to the investigation."

"How *did* you hear about what happened?" Tamar asked. "It's not exactly common knowledge yet."

"A friend told me," Zula said.

Tamar wondered who the woman's friend was. Someone in Security? In Administration? She decided that wasn't important right now, though. Later, perhaps.

"What makes you think an alien is involved?" she asked. "Jericho 3 has relatively few native lifeforms, and none of them are especially dangerous."

Brigette opened her mouth to speak, but Tamar shot her a warning look, and the synth said nothing. Zula noticed the exchange, but didn't remark on it.

"Right now, I don't know what happened here. That's

what I want to find out, same as you two."

Tamar would have bet that Zula wasn't being entirely forthcoming, but that was all right, as far as she was concerned. She could understand—and respect—someone not wanting to divulge too much information too soon.

"At this point it's impossible to tell how the dockworkers died," Tamar said.

Zula looked to Brigette.

"You said the remains were contagious. With what?"

"I said they were *no longer* contagious," the synth pointed out. "My initial scan detected traces of cellular necrosis on the remains, but the virus which causes the condition can only live a short time when exposed to the air, so there is almost no danger now. When I suggested that we move, it was as a precaution, nothing more."

Cellular necrosis? Those were two words Tamar did *not* like hearing. But as disturbing as this news was, it would provide an effective explanation as to how the workers had died. She turned to Zula.

"See? No aliens involved—if you don't count the virus itself. So while we appreciate your willingness to help, your *expertise* isn't required."

"I'm happy to leave," Zula said, "provided you can answer one question for me. Does cellular necrosis always leave tooth marks on its victims' bones?"

"Tooth marks?" Tamar made a point of glancing over her shoulder at the remains. When she faced Zula once more, she said, "I suppose those lines *do* look a bit like tooth marks, but it's too early to say. We've only just begun gathering data." She didn't look at Brigette this time. The synth said nothing, though, and Tamar was glad she'd gotten the message.

Aleta wouldn't want anyone else joining the search for the Xenomorph. The more people got involved, the more likely it was that word would leak out. That could lead to a panic and—far more importantly—someone else might find the Xenomorph before she could.

The Xenomorph's escape from Gagnon's lab had provided her with an opportunity. If she could snag the thing before Gagnon regained custody of it, she might be able to procure some of its genetic material. Then she could sell the sample to the highest bidder. Hell, if she got enough of it she could sell some to anyone who could afford the price.

That price would be steep, too—oh yes, it would. The two workers who'd lost their lives meant nothing to her, and neither did the thought of all the people who might die once the mega-corporations began growing their own monsters. Maybe one day they would use the deadly creatures to destroy each other. She didn't give a damn. All she cared about was acquiring as many credits as she could, before there was no one left alive to pay her.

"Perhaps the three of us should work together," Brigette offered. "By pooling our efforts, we would maximize our chances for success—and cause it to occur more swiftly."

Tamar and Zula locked eyes.

"I don't think that's a good idea," Tamar said.

"Me neither," Zula said.

The two women continued peering at each other for several moments, each attempting to take the measure of the other. Finally, Zula spoke.

"If you need me, give me a call." At that she turned to leave.

Tamar smiled.

"We'll be sure to do that."

"Mmm-hmm." The woman walked back to her transport, got in the cart, turned it on, and backed up the way she'd come. When she reached the facility's main aisle she turned the cart around, and with a last look at Tamar and Brigette, she drove off. Tamar waited until the sound of the cart's engine grew faint before turning to Brigette.

"Cellular necrosis? Is that normal for a Xenomorph?"

"We know so little about the species that it's impossible to say what's normal for them, but in this case the Xenomorph appears to have contracted the condition from its host."

Host? Tamar didn't know for certain what Brigette meant by this, but she could guess, and it didn't sound good.

"So the creature is a carrier?"

"That would appear to be the case. Dr. Gagnon hypothesized that the Xenomorph's physiology would eventually eradicate the virus." Brigette glanced at the skeletons nearby. "My guess is that the Xenomorph has instead incorporated the virus into its genetic make-up."

"Meaning the damn thing is even more dangerous than it otherwise might be."

"Yes."

That certainly put a wrinkle in Tamar's plans. If she wanted to obtain a bio-sample from the Xenomorph, she'd have to be extra-careful now. Extra-*extra*-careful. Of course, synthetics couldn't contract cellular necrosis, could they?

"Now that the party crasher's out of the picture, I think it's a good idea if the two of us work together."

Brigette's eyes narrowed as she searched Tamar's face. Was the synth trying to determine if she could be trusted? If Brigette was smart, she'd realize the answer to that question would always be no. Whatever she was thinking, she came to a conclusion.

"Agreed."

Maybe, Tamar thought, *she wants to keep an eye on me as much as I want to keep an eye on her.* If so, it made no difference. In her profession, mutual distrust was the closest thing she could get to an effective partnership.

"Any ideas what to do next?" Tamar asked.

"I took a reading with a chemical scanner."

Brigette knelt, placed the carrying case on the floor, opened it, and removed the device she'd used earlier. Brigette closed the case and left it on the floor as she stood.

"How's that thing work?"

"It will detect any traces of bio-matter left behind by the Xenomorph, so that we can track it." She nodded toward the gun in Tamar's side holster. "Is your weapon loaded?"

"Always," Tamar said, "and I'm carrying extra rounds."

"Good. Shall we get started?"

Without waiting for a reply, Brigette picked up the case

once more. Activating the chemical scanner, she checked the readout and began walking away from the remains. Tamar followed, perfectly happy to let the synth lead the way. Let her take the brunt of the Xenomorph's attack when they found it—or it found them.

As they walked she wondered what Zula Hendricks would do next. Tamar had felt the woman's determination—she didn't seem like someone who gave up easily. Most likely she would search for the Xenomorph on her own, even though she had no idea what they were dealing with. All she knew was that there was some kind of hostile lifeform roaming the facility.

Tamar had dealt with her kind before. Once she got her mind set on doing something, she wouldn't be dissuaded. As unlikely as it might be, if she found the Xenomorph before they did, she'd kill it. If it didn't kill her first.

Fuentes and Gagnon wanted to recapture the thing alive. She'd bet a month's credits that Aleta wouldn't authorize Tamar's payment unless the creature was returned to Gagnon's lab, and Tamar had worked too hard up to this point to be stiffed on her fee.

Reaching up to tap the comm device in her ear, she spoke Aleta's name. A moment later, the director's irritated voice sounded in her ear.

"Who is this?"

"Tamar." She quickly told Aleta what she and Brigette had found in the warehouse—and she told her about Zula's interference.

"I'm unsure what to do about that," Aleta said. "On

the one hand, Hendricks might prove helpful. On the other, she might screw everything up." There was a long moment of silence. "Play it by ear," she said finally. "If Zula becomes too big a pain in the ass—especially if you think she's going to blab—you have my authorization to deal with her however you want. Emphasis on *however*."

"That'll cost extra."

"Fine. Just get that goddamned monster back!" Aleta disconnected and Tamar smiled.

This day just kept getting better and better.

13

Renato Bordreau drove across the barren terrain of Jericho 3 in a small six-wheeled transport, pulling a wagon filled with supplies. The vehicle was designed for only two passengers—three if they were skinny and squeezed in tight—and it didn't have its own life-support system. Because of this, anyone riding in it had to wear an EVA suit. Renato wore his whenever he was outside his pod, sometimes ten to fifteen hours a day, depending on how much work he needed to get done during his shift at the mine.

He was used to the suit, so much so that half the time he forgot he was wearing it. What he could never get used to was the smell—days of his body odor, breath, and flatulence created a funk inside the suit that never seemed to fully go away, no matter how often he sent multi-drones to scrub it clean. Valda told him his suit didn't smell *that* bad, that it was just his imagination. Then again, her suit smelled even worse than his, so what did she know?

He wished management would give them new suits, but the residents of Venture's proto-colony were supposed to simulate the conditions of living in a *real* colony, and that meant they rarely—if ever—received new equipment. They were expected to make do, like true pioneers. At least, that was the company line. Renato suspected Venture was simply too cheap to update or replace equipment until it became an absolute necessity.

Even then they denied the colonists' requests half the time.

One thing Venture *was* good about, though, was making sure colonists received the basics—nutrient bars, toilet paper, toothpaste, deodorant, and other essentials. Nothing really good, though. No booze, no real food, but at least colonists didn't have to wipe their asses with rocks scavenged from the planet's surface. Renato sometimes wondered at Venture's logic. If the colonists were supposed to rough it, that should go for *all* supplies—not just big, expensive ones. But he wasn't about to complain. The last thing he wanted to do was draw the company's attention to their own illogic, and have them cut back on the few things with which they were generous.

Normally, colonists didn't have to pick up their own supplies. They were supposed to live and work as if they were alone on a distant world and dependent on periodic deliveries from cargo ships. Their real job was to field test Venture's planetary colonizing equipment, but to do this they had to pretend to *be* colonists. This meant that they spent much of their time mining ore from the mountains to the north. It was dull, repetitive work, and often the tools and machines Venture gave them to test broke down or wouldn't work in the first place.

The "colonists" wrote weekly reports on the mining equipment, transports, and the dome habitats in which they lived, making assessments and suggesting changes— the latter of which Renato believed management ignored completely.

The simulation of living in an actual colony only went so far. Twice a month colonists were permitted to spend two days at the Lodge, which, while hardly a five-star hotel, beat the hell out of dome living. And instead of getting their supplies from cargo ships, they got them from the Lodge's dockworkers who could be persuaded— for a few credits, of course—to sneak in a few beers and containers of decidedly non-nutritious food.

Usually, Opal Morgan dropped off the supplies, and today was her scheduled delivery date. Always on time, she'd once told him she loved getting out of the Lodge whenever she could. He told her he'd be glad to trade places with her. So when she was an hour late, and neither he nor any of the other colonists had heard anything from her, he called the dock on his dome's comm system.

The supervisor told him that no deliveries would be going out today, and when Renato asked why, she ignored his question. She did offer that if he wanted to come pick up the supplies himself, he was welcome to do so. Renato figured she'd just said that to placate him, but he took it as a challenge. Besides, he and Valda were almost out of toilet paper.

So he logged onto the Lodge's public information network and checked the weather. An electrical storm was heading their way, and it looked like it was going to be a bad one, but it was still a few hours off, and he figured he'd be back well before it hit. Suiting up, he took a ground transport from the proto-colony's equipment pool, and set out for the Lodge.

The transport wasn't designed for speed, and the trip had taken almost twenty minutes. When he reached the Facilities Management building—where the dock was located—he pulled up to the smaller of two airlocks, called to let them know he was there, and was allowed inside. There were Security guards all over the place, which was weird, and the supervisor he'd spoken to earlier—who seemed surprised that he'd actually shown up—appeared to be nervous. She helped him gather his supplies personally, and even offered to help load them onto the transport. That's when he knew she was trying to get rid of him as fast as possible. No supervisor he'd ever known would offer to do scut work like that.

During the drive back, Renato had gotten on his comm and reached out to a drinking buddy who worked in the Facilities Management building. The man filled him in on the rumors circulating through the Lodge—that a pair of dockworkers had died under mysterious circumstances. Renato was afraid that Opal might be one of those workers, but his friend couldn't confirm it. There had been no official word about the deaths, let alone identification of the deceased.

Renato hoped Opal was all right, but he feared the worst.

By the time he approached the proto-colony, the wind had picked up considerably and the sky had grown dark in the west. The colony was small, with only two dozen igloo-shaped habitat domes and two larger storage domes for housing equipment. The habitat design was a smaller version of the Lodge's domed buildings, but it served the same function: to allow the planet's often strong winds to flow around the structures more easily.

There were seventy-three colonists, most living in pairs or groups of three. They worked the mountain mines in two shifts—one day, one night—and although the day shift had several hours to go, transports were already trundling back to the colony. Renato figured the mines had closed for the day because of the oncoming storm, and everyone was returning home. Renato and Valda worked the night shift, but the storm was anticipated to last through the next morning, so it looked like they would be staying home.

This prospect didn't thrill him. Working the mines was the only time the two of them were apart, which meant it was the only time they knew any peace. If they had to stay cooped up in their tiny dome tonight—*together*—things were bound to get bad.

Gloom settled onto him like a heavy blanket as he pulled the transport up to their dome, Number 16, and parked. He climbed out of the vehicle, stepped toward the outer door, and pressed the control that would open it. The door slid opened several inches, then halted.

Not again. Renato sighed.

One of the most annoying things about testing Venture's colonization tech was that it still *was* in the testing stage. That meant glitches—and outright failures—were hardly uncommon. For the most part he and Valda had been lucky. Their dome and its equipment tended to work. Most of the time. The one recurring problem they had was this damn door. The inner airlock door never gave them trouble, thank god, but the outer one had a tendency to stick. Not all the time, but often enough to be a real pain in the ass.

They needed a new one, which he'd requested from the Lodge, but he'd been turned down. The current door *did* work, more or less, and Venture saw no reason to spend money on a replacement.

He pressed the control to close the door, but nothing happened. Scowling, he pressed it twice more, each time harder than the last, until finally—almost grudgingly, he thought—the door closed. He waited for a count of twenty and pressed the open control. This time the door slid open smoothly, with no difficulty at all.

He unloaded the containers from the wagon and put them into the outer airlock. Then he pressed the control that activated the transport's self-driving program, and the vehicle slowly headed back to the storage dome where he'd picked it up. Stepping inside the outer airlock, he pressed the control to close the outer door and waited.

Habitat domes had two airlocks—inner and outer—as

a safety precaution. It was inconvenient to have to use two airlocks to get inside your own home, but better than a breach occurring and leaking all your O_2 into Jericho 3's atmosphere. A panel next to the inner door had two lights, red and green. Right now the red was glowing. When the inner airlock was ready, the red light on the panel winked out and the green light came on. The inner airlock door then opened automatically, and he stepped into the secondary airlock carrying the first containers of supplies. He repeated this process for the others.

The wait for the second airlock door to open seemed interminable, even though he knew it was exactly the same interval as the first.

When the door opened into the habitat, Renato stepped inside. The first thing he did was turn left and place the first couple supply containers on the counter next to the stove. Then he removed his helmet and drew a deep breath in through his nostrils. The air smelled sterile and overly processed, but it came as a relief after breathing the suit's O_2 for so long.

Living space was at a premium, and the interiors were designed to make the most of what little there was. There were no separate rooms—everything was visible and out in the open, including the toilet. Next to the counter where Renato had deposited the supply containers were the stove and oven, then two desks with chairs and computer terminals—one for him, one for Valda. The vid screen upon which they watched movies or played games, a dresser, the shower, toilet, and sink, and lastly the closet.

Outside the dome, directly behind the vid screen, a pair of O_2 converters flanked the dome's power generator.

In the middle of the dome was a circular bed, and Valda lay on it, covers tangled around her, asleep and softly snoring. The inner airlock door always opened with a hiss, but the sound hadn't so much as caused Valda to stir. That woman would sleep through a planet-wide quake.

Standard procedure was to close the inner airlock door as soon as he entered the dome's living space, but Renato hated spending any more time in his EVA suit than he had to. So he walked over to the closet, heavy boots clunking on the plasteel floor as he went.

Valda slept on.

When he reached the closet, he opened the door to see his wife's EVA suit hanging from a pair of rods, one under each arm, her helmet and boots on the floor beneath. He removed his boots and put them and his helmet on the floor next to Valda's. Then he got out of his suit and hung it on a second pair of rods. Feeling almost reborn, he closed the closet door and returned to get the remaining supply containers, placing these on the counter next to the others. Only then did he return to the airlock door and hit the wall keypad control that closed and sealed it. Without waiting he turned around and stretched. It felt luxurious, almost hedonistic, to move so freely, and he took his time, enjoying the sensation.

The wind picked up outside, a constant backdrop of humming.

He wore a pair of Venture-standard gray coveralls.

Each colonist was issued one pair, no more, and they were expected to keep them clean. The dome's small contingent of multi-drones did their best, but they weren't washing machines, and like his EVA suit his coveralls never seemed to get *fully* clean. Renato was a small man, short and thin. Colonists were chosen partially based on how efficient their bodies would be when consuming and processing air, food, and water. Women's bodies were naturally more efficient than men's, and because of this two-thirds of the colonists were female.

Padding across the floor in bare feet, he returned to the supply containers and unloaded them, putting the various items away in the refrigerator or the cupboards above the stove. He worked quietly, and when he was finished, he put the empty containers in the closet to be returned to the Lodge.

He was glad that Valda continued to sleep. When one or both of them was sleeping, they weren't fighting. Working the night shift left him feeling exhausted all the time, and today was no exception. It seemed as if he was perpetually on the verge of nodding off, and he was tired after his trip to the Lodge and back. He considered climbing into bed next to Valda and taking a nap, but he didn't go through with it. He didn't want to risk waking her, so he went over to his workstation and sat.

Valda had dimmed the dome's lights halfway, and since they didn't have a window, she'd set the vid screen to display a live image of the area to the west. She loved having a view, even if it was simulated. Renato didn't think there was anything special about Jericho 3's desolate landscape and its dull-as-dishwater sky, but the psychologist who'd briefed the colonists before they moved into their domes had stressed the importance of having a window, even if it was just a substitute.

"It'll help prevent cabin fever," she'd said.

Like hell it will, he thought. The desk chair was too uncomfortable for him to fall asleep in, and not for the first time he wished they had a couch or at least an easy chair. But they didn't. *Might as well wish for a million credits to be downloaded into my account,* he thought. That was more likely to come true than getting comfy furniture.

He didn't really feel like doing any work, but he hadn't written his weekly report yet, and since he had nothing better to do he logged on to the terminal and began typing. He'd only gotten a quarter of the way through the document when he heard Valda stir. He stopped typing, hoping she'd fall back to sleep, but a moment later he heard her rise from the bed and walk over to the toilet. She peed, flushed, washed her hands, then walked over and sat at her workstation.

"What are you doing?" she asked.

Don't take the bait, he told himself, but despite knowing it was a mistake, he sighed and turned to look at his wife.

"Just trying to get some work done before the storm hits. Looks like—"

He was interrupted by an alert chime coming from his terminal. A message crawled across the screen, officially announcing the closure for the remainder of the day.

"—they'll close the mines," he finished.

"Fantastic," Valda muttered.

He wanted to snap at her, tell her he wasn't looking forward to it either, spending the entire night alone together. But he kept his mouth shut. It was going to be a long night, and he didn't want to get into a full-blown fight any sooner than they had to.

Valda had slept in her coveralls, and brown curls had flattened against her head on the right side where she'd been sleeping. She was taller than Renato by several inches and outweighed him by a few pounds, but she was still slender. Just not as thin as he was.

Scarecrow, she sometimes called him, or if she was feeling especially mean, *Skeleton*. She looked past him to the bleak vista displayed on the vid screen, and he wondered how they had come to this.

While they'd had their ups and downs, like any couple, they'd been married for four relatively happy years before taking jobs with Venture and applying for the company's proto-colony project. They were both excited by the prospect of living on another planet, and liked the idea that the work they'd do would help refine equipment and techniques actual colonists would one day use. It made them feel as if they were doing more than just drawing a salary. They were making a vital contribution to humanity's leap into the galaxy.

Besides, it wasn't as if either of them was especially social. They didn't have a lot of friends or go out very often. And, of course, they loved each other. They were perfect candidates for off-world colony living.

Or so they'd thought.

The reality proved to be quite different.

The first few months passed uneventfully. Renato and Valda enjoyed their work and, just as importantly, their time with each other. But eventually they began to get on each other's nerves, becoming short-tempered and verbally abusive. They grew emotionally distant and stopped making love. They began arguing over nothing, their disagreements becoming so heated that they'd end up red-faced and screaming at each other. Only once did one of them become physically violent. Renato had called Valda a particularly loathsome name, and in return she'd punched him. Not all that hard, really, and on the shoulder, but the action had shocked them both.

Ever since they'd done their best to keep some distance between them as much as possible. They might not like each other much these days, but neither wanted to start physically abusing the other.

That had worked for a couple months. They barely spoke and tried not to look at each other. Basically, each acted as if the other person didn't exist. Over the last several weeks, though, they'd began interacting again, sniping at each other, criticizing and mocking. Renato was as much to blame as Valda, but he didn't understand why they acted the way they did. Sometimes he wondered if they fought out of a twisted need to entertain themselves. Arguing *did* give them something to do, after all.

"I got the supplies we needed," he said.

"Good." She paused before adding, "Did you see your *girlfriend*?"

On numerous occasions, Valda had accused him of being attracted to Opal, of flirting with her. Even of having an affair with her, sneaking off to have sex with her during those nights they got to stay in the Lodge. He liked Opal as a person, and sure, she was good-looking, but he felt nothing for her romantically or sexually. He'd never been able to convince Valda of this, though.

He was prepared to snap back at her, to vent his frustration at her insistence that he was cheating, but instead he told her about the two dockworkers that had died. He spoke calmly, even matter-of-factly, and when he was finished he expected her to taunt him about the possibility that one of the dead workers had been Opal. But she didn't.

"How awful!" she said. "And no one has any idea what happened?"

Up to this point he had avoided looking at her as he spoke, but now he met her gaze.

"If they do, they haven't made it public yet. It can't be natural causes, though. Not two people at the same time."

The wind had continued to pick up, and now it was almost like a rushing waterfall. They looked to the vid screen and saw dust devils swirling across the landscape. They then faced each other once more.

"Could've been an accident of some sort," she offered.

"Yeah."

"Or it could've been something else."

"Like what?"

She shrugged, and he didn't think she was going to explain any further, but then she continued speaking.

"Maybe they had an argument, and it turned violent. It's easy for people to go stir crazy living like we do. Too easy. People can say and do all kinds of things they'll regret later, and some of those things can't be undone."

He looked at her for a long moment before responding. "You mean like us?"

She nodded, and he saw her eyes glisten with tears.

They were quiet for several moments after that, both thinking about what Valda had said. Then, without pausing to consider whether it was a good idea, he reached out and took her hand. He held it lightly at first, but when she tightened her grip, he did too.

They sat like for that for some time, listening to the wind grow louder.

14

"I'm saying the bitch cheated," Paolo said.

Saul Caswell walked through a section of the Personnel building which residents called the Mall, Paolo Scoggins on his left, Oralia Bergqvist on his right. The three guards continually swept their gazes back and forth as they passed various small shops and food booths. Off-duty personnel walked up and down the corridor, chatting and laughing, enjoying the day. Saul wondered if any of them would be laughing if they knew about the deaths in the warehouse.

He doubted it—which was why management had ordered that the information be kept quiet for now. Saul understood. The last thing they needed was a facility-wide panic, but he wished management had come up with some pretext to make people go to their quarters and stay there. They had no idea if they were dealing with disease or something else, something potentially far worse. Either way, people would be safer in their quarters than strolling around in the open like this.

But he was just a lowly guard. Management didn't care what he thought. As far as they were concerned, people like him weren't much better than synthetics. He was supposed to do as he was told and ask no questions. But Saul had questions this day. Lots.

"How could she have cheated?" Oralia asked. "She lost way more hands than she won."

"The last hand was the biggest pot," Paolo said. He sounded to Saul like a whiny little boy.

"We *all* lost credits on that hand," Oralia said. "Except Valerie, of course."

Paolo's jaw tightened and he pressed his lips together, as if trying to keep from saying something he might regret later.

Oralia continued.

"And even if she *did* cheat, what's the big deal? If cheating at cards was illegal in the Lodge, we'd have to lock up most of the population. Our brig isn't big enough to hold them all. We'd probably have to lower a giant dome-shaped cage over the whole damn facility."

"Why stop there?" Saul said. "Why not put the entire planet in a cage?"

"That *would* save us a lot of time," Oralia agreed.

"Save us a lot of walking, too," Saul put in. "My feet are killing me."

"Go ahead," Paolo said. "Laugh it up, but you both lost as many credits as I did on that hand."

"True," Saul said.

"We're just not obsessing over it," Oralia added.

"Bigger fish to fry," Saul said.

"I'm going to get my money back from her, one way or another," Paolo said. "It's the principle of the thing."

Saul did believe that Valerie had cheated, but she was an extremely attractive woman—confident, smart, forceful—and he hoped to see her again, maybe even get her into bed. Who cared if she cheated at cards if she was hot?

The Mall ended at the beginning of the corridor which led to the Bioscience building. The shops here were grungy and rundown: a cheap tattoo parlor called Ink it Over, a hotdog stand with a sign that claimed their dogs were made from "100% Recycled Meat," and a smoke shop called Gaspers that sold "Nearly Non-Carcinogenic Cigarettes." As far as Saul was concerned, this was the worst section of the entire Lodge, and that included the morgue in the Med Center, and the human waste processors lying beneath each building.

"Do either of you have any idea what we're supposed to be looking for?" Oralia asked. "They said 'be on the lookout for anything strange or suspicious.' That isn't the most specific of instructions."

Not long after Valerie had left the Bar, the three guards—along with all the others in the Lodge, on-duty or off—received orders over their comms. They were to begin patrolling the facility at once, in uniform and openly carrying their weapons. Saul, Oralia, and Paolo had been off-duty when they received the order to go to work.

"When we get to the connecting corridor, what do

you want to do?" Oralia asked. "Continue on to the Bioscience building, or turn around and make another pass through Personnel?"

"It doesn't matter to me either way," Paolo said. "Although we'll probably have a greater chance of running into Valerie again if we stay in this building."

"For godsakes, let it *go*, okay?" Saul said.

Paolo shrugged. "Just saying."

"I vote we keep patrolling Personnel," Saul said. He shot Paolo a look. "But not because of Valerie. Right now, there's probably more people here than anywhere else in the Lodge. And even though management wants to keep the deaths under wraps, you know that won't last long. The news will spread, and when it does a lot of people will take off work early and head for their quarters. That'll mean bigger crowds, more confusion, and more frustration. They'll need all the guards they can get to keep things under control."

Oralia and Paolo agreed with Saul's reasoning, and when they reached the mouth of the connecting corridor they turned around and headed back the way they'd come. This time when they drew near the tattoo shop they heard a loud crash, followed by a scream of terror. The three guards drew their 9mms and started running toward the shop's entrance.

When they got there they stopped, momentarily frozen by the nightmarish scene before them. A woman—presumably a customer—lay on the floor, face down in a widening pool of blood, next to an overturned padded table. Her coveralls had been unzipped and pulled down to her waist, and there was an unfinished tattoo of a yellow-orange sun on her back.

As the guards watched, black patches rose on her skin, along with festering pustules, obliterating her ink.

The tattoo artist—a bald man wearing a black pullover and jeans—stood in front of... of... the only word Saul could come up with for it was *monster*. The thing was taller than the artist, and its body was covered with the same sort of black corruption and swollen pustules that covered the dead woman's body. The creature regarded the tattoo artist for several seconds, as if trying to decide what to do with him. Then, moving with blinding speed, it fastened its clawed hands on the man's shoulders and lifted him into the air as if he weighed nothing.

The monster—*where are its eyes, oh god, it doesn't have eyes*—opened its slavering mouth wide and some sort of tube shot outward, breaking through the man's forehead as easily as if his skull was made of tissue paper. The man's body jerked as blood sprayed the air, and then the tube retracted. The thing tossed him aside as if he'd ceased to be of interest. His body landed on top of the woman's, the impact and momentum causing them both to slide across the blood-slick floor almost six feet. By the time they came to a stop, the man's flesh was covered with the same deformities as the woman and the creature.

Saul had worked security for the better part of a decade, first on a Venture station orbiting a gas giant in the Nelvana system, and then here at the Lodge. No stranger to violence and death, he'd seen everything from people who'd nearly beaten each other to death, to knife and bullet wounds, to dead bodies that had been burned or disfigured in accidents. Looking upon those injuries hadn't been easy, but never once on the job had he been so sickened, so revolted by what he saw that he felt as if he was going to vomit.

He did now.

There was no way to tell which of them started firing first. Maybe it was him, maybe not. When they began firing at the creature, the thing whirled away to reveal a huge mass of pustules covering the entire back of its body— neck, shoulders, arms, legs... Bullets slammed into its grotesque hide, causing the pustules to explode. A thick black substance jetted toward the three guards, splattering their faces, hands, and coveralls. The goo burned like fire wherever it landed, and all three of them howled with pain.

Oralia and Paolo's hands had been hit, and they dropped their weapons as their flesh bubbled and sizzled. Saul's hands had only been struck by small droplets, and while they hurt like hell, he managed to keep hold of his gun. Unfortunately, the left side of his face—from the crown of his head down to his chin—was slathered with the creature's acidic fluid, and he experienced a pain so intense it wiped away all thought, all awareness of self, leaving only agony.

The monster didn't turn around to face them. Instead, its long tail whipped outward and the barbed tip plunged into Paolo's left eye and through to his brain. The tail pulled free in a gush of blood and gore and Paolo— already dead—pitched forward and hit the floor.

Despite the pain she was in, Oralia was able to maintain

enough presence of mind to crouch down and reach for her gun. By this point, her hand had been eaten almost all the way to the bone, and what remained of her fingers brushed against the weapon, unable to grasp it. Her movement drew the monster's attention, and it leaped toward her, hissing. It landed directly in front of her, legs bending to absorb the impact. It straightened quickly, and as it did, it brought one of its clawed hands up into the soft flesh beneath her jaw.

Meat shredded, blood flew, and the blow snapped her head back with such force that her neck broke instantly. Her body went limp and she collapsed to the floor next to Paolo. Both of their bodies began to show the same black patches and boils on their skin.

The monster then turned its attention to Saul, and let out a high-pitched screech.

The right half of his face was gone, black-smeared bone all that remained. Because the nerves had been destroyed the pain had lessened considerably, and while his mind didn't exactly clear, his self-preservation instincts kicked in. He raised his gun and prepared to fire, but before he could squeeze the trigger the tube jutted toward him, revealing a second mouth, complete with teeth. But instead of burying itself in his brain, like it had with the tattoo artist, it stopped short. There was a sound—a breathy chuffing that reminded Saul of a human cough—and a cloud of black particles shot forth and struck what was left of his face.

He gasped in surprise, reflexively drawing in the black particles, and began coughing himself. He doubled over as the coughing intensified. He felt sick, feverish, and he prayed the monster would finish him off swiftly and relieve him of his pain.

But nothing happened.

Still coughing, though not quite as badly as before, Saul straightened and through his remaining eye watched the monster lope toward the rear of the tattoo shop. In the ceiling was an open square space, and on the floor was a dented metal vent cover. When the creature reached the opening, it leaped upward and slithered into the duct. Within seconds it was gone.

Saul stared dully at the space where the monster had disappeared. His coughing was almost under control now, and he had two simultaneous thoughts. He had to report the existence of the monster—although he doubted anyone would believe him, at least at first—and he needed to get to the Med Center immediately to have his wounds treated. At least he hadn't become infected by that black shit, whatever it was. Sure, he felt like he was burning up, and he was dizzy, but that was most likely due to the injuries he had sustained. After all, he'd lost half his goddamned face.

Then he looked down at the back of his acid-pocked hands and saw they were covered with black lesions and swelling pustules.

"God help me," he whispered.

Panic grabbed hold of him, and he turned and fled the shop. If he could reach the Med Center in time, the doctors would know what was wrong with him. They'd give him medicine and he would live. They wouldn't be able to do anything about his face, of course, but he didn't care about that. All that mattered to him right now was not dying.

In his panicked state he turned right instead of left as he exited the shop, heading farther into the Mall rather than toward the corridor that led to the Bioscience building. There were shoppers in front of him, men and women who screamed and scattered when they saw the horrid apparition coming toward them. Saul knew he needed help, and he reached toward them, in his mind pleading for someone, anyone to get him to a doctor. But his tongue had rotted away to nothing, and all that emerged from his throat were incoherent moans.

No, not all. One other thing came out of him. One last cough, this one so powerful that bits of his lungs were ejected, along with a cloud of black particles. The cloud wasn't large, but it was big enough to reach a half dozen people in his vicinity.

Tag, you're it, he thought, and then the cellular necrosis began eating its way into his brain, and he fell to the ground, dying on the way down.

People ran from the blackened, rotting corpse in their midst, some of them already on their comms to Security. The six people that had been infected ran, too. Unfortunately, none of them thought to run toward medical help.

Inside the duct system, the Xenomorph—now fully grown—moved quickly and quietly. Any member of its species could've navigated instinctively through the ducts, but the knowledge that this Xenomorph had inherited from its host, a primitive map of its environment, allowed it to travel throughout the Lodge with ease.

The creature had killed, and killing was its purpose. It had another purpose, too—one that in its own way was as powerful as the need to kill, and equally impossible to deny. This purpose came from the disease that had bonded to the Xenomorph on the genetic level—the need to spread its contagion.

This was why it had spared the third creature's life. It had done so at the urging of the cellular necrosis that was its other half, almost as if they were symbiotes instead of a single fused being. Its "partner" had given it certain advantages. The Xenomorph carried the disease, but was not affected by it. This trait acted like another weapon in the Xenomorph's arsenal, as did the pustules that sprayed thick acidic goo. The black patches that were a prime symptom of cellular necrosis had combined with its exoskeleton to strengthen its natural armor, making it extraordinarily resistant to weapons fire.

No matter how many victims a Xenomorph claimed, its urge to kill was never sated. It was compelled to seek out living creatures to attack, and to spread the contagion. It sensed that there was more quarry ahead of it, and not far. There was something different about them, as if they were sick or injured.

They would make easy prey.

15

Gagnon sat at his desk in his private office, holding a computer pad and reviewing the data he'd gathered from his examination of the crab-like creature—which he was thinking of naming an Implanter—and Hassan's body. He'd attempted to gain access to the remains of the dockworkers, but when he'd made inquiries he'd learned the bodies had been taken to the Med Center and placed in the morgue.

Standard procedure was for one of the doctors on staff to perform a postmortem examination, but Aleta wanted to limit the knowledge of the Xenomorph's presence. Besides, physicians were good enough at what they did, but their focus was maintenance and repair. They were mechanics who worked with flesh and bone. He was a biologist, and his domain was the advancement of human knowledge. Letting a physician examine the dead workers would be a waste.

Somehow she'd find an excuse to delay the examination, perhaps even claim that the bodies were contaminated and should be destroyed immediately, without an exam. If so, he hoped he'd be able to convince her to let him have a look at the remains first.

The comm unit chirped in his ear. He answered it at once, hoping it was Brigette with news about the Xenomorph.

"This is Gagnon," he said.

"Your goddamned monster just killed five people at the Mall!"

It was Aleta. Gagnon experienced an urge to end the call right there, but he resisted.

"*Our* goddamned monster," he corrected. "Have the new bodies been taken to the morgue yet? If I could examine just one—"

"Shut up, you ghoul! This situation is getting out of hand. What am I saying? It already *is* out of hand. There's no way we can keep the Xenomorph a secret any longer."

"Were there any witnesses to the attack?" Gagnon asked, remaining calm.

"There were some people standing outside the shop where it happened. More were drawn by the noise. I don't know how many, though, not that it matters. It only takes one person to start a rumor—especially when the rumor's true."

She had a point. It had been naïve of them to think they could conceal the creature's existence after it had escaped his lab. Even knowing the stories about the creatures, they hadn't been prepared for the reality of having one moving freely through the facility.

"All it will take is for someone to transmit what's happening to a friend, colleague, or family member," she said. "Someone off-planet who also works for Venture. It won't be long before the board finds out, and once *that* happens…"

Gagnon didn't need her to spell it out for him. The board would decide that Aleta had bungled her attempt to acquire a Xenomorph. They'd hold her responsible for however many deaths had occurred—blame him, too, most likely— and then they'd send their operatives to swoop in and capture the Xenomorph and steal his research. He and Aleta would be taken off-world to face "disciplinary action," and that would be the last anyone would ever hear from them.

Venture would install a new director for the Lodge, someone who would clean up Aleta's mess and put everything in order, and life would go on. For some.

"Brigette's out searching for the Xenomorph right now," he said.

"As is Tamar."

He frowned. "Needed some extra insurance, did you?"

She ignored the comment. "What I want to know is why the hell you're staying holed up in your lab, when you could be out helping them."

He bristled at the implication.

"Every moment I spend here," he said, "studying the data, I learn more about the creature. Knowledge is the greatest weapon we can have."

"Actual *weapons* are the best weapons we can have,"

she replied. "There's something else. People are starting to get sick."

Gagnon felt a cold twist in his gut.

"It's some kind of flesh-rotting disease. Fast-acting, and as far as we know, always fatal. Does that have anything to do with the Xenomorph?"

Gagnon considered a moment before answering.

"At this point, the data is… inconclusive."

"I'll take that as a yes," she said. "If we don't get our hands on that monster again—and fast—the facility is going to be littered with dead bodies. How are we supposed to explain *that*?"

"Explanations are your job," Gagnon said.

Aleta paused before going on.

"Venture employs a lot of biologists," she said flatly. "I'm sure any of them would love a chance to study a Xenomorph."

Gagnon didn't like what she was implying. "I'm the best biologist the company has. You'd be foolish to give the Xenomorph to anyone else."

"If you get the damn thing back alive, I won't have to," she said. "Look, we're reaching a point where we'll be forced to destroy the thing whether we want to or not. I can give you a little more time to hunt it down—and I mean a *little*—but if you don't get it back in your lab and lock it down tight this time, that'll be the end of it. I've worked too hard to get where I am, and I'm not going to allow my career to be ruined by your incompetence. Go help Tamar and Brigette. Get the Xenomorph back."

She disconnected before Gagnon could reply.

He dropped the computer pad onto the desk, then reached up and massaged his temples. He could feel a headache coming on.

As he thought about it, he was surprised to learn that the Xenomorph was spreading the cellular necrosis. He'd been certain the creature's impossibly strong metabolism would've fought off the disease by now. Unless...

Unless the disease had somehow become part of the creature. He wasn't certain how such a thing could be possible, but the concept made him even more eager to get the Xenomorph back, so he could uncover its secrets. Yet as long as the creature was spreading death throughout the facility, it would remain too great a threat for the Lodge's inhabitants to ignore. Security would hunt it down and destroy it, regardless of any orders to the contrary. It would be a matter of survival. But if the creature no longer carried the disease...

He took his hands from his temples and tapped his comm device.

"Brigette?"

She answered a moment later.

"Yes, Doctor?"

"Have you located the Xenomorph?"

"Not yet. We believe it is traveling through the air ducts, making it difficult to follow using the chemical scanner."

"*We?*"

"Ms. Prather and I have decided to work together. For the time being."

He didn't like this development, but better they work together than against each other, he supposed.

"Where are you now?"

"We're at the Mall. The Xenomorph—"

"I know about the attack there."

"Security is on the scene," she said, and she anticipated his next question. "They refused to allow us to examine the bodies until Tamar called the director. She instructed them to grant us access, which they promptly did."

So it was *Tamar* now, instead of *Ms. Prather*. Brigette had been reserved, even formal the entire time he'd known her—ironic since she'd originally been created to be the talking equivalent of a sex doll. Still, he was surprised to hear her refer to the spy by her first name, and he was also surprised to discover he was bothered by it. He had never wanted Brigette for anything other than her fine mind and tireless work ethic, but she had never called him by his first name. This shouldn't matter to him. She wasn't a real person—only an extremely sophisticated simulation—but after working together for so long, she could've called him *Millard* once in a while.

He pushed the thought away, eager to hear what they'd found at the scene. Then he made a decision.

"Wait there," Gagnon said. "I'm going to join you. I'll be there as soon as I can." He disconnected and left his office. Once in the outer lab, he hurried over to a refrigeration unit built into the wall. He opened it to reveal shelves containing rows of plastic vials, each meticulously coded and labeled. He removed a rack from the fridge, the contents in each vial a bright, almost glowing blue. Then he closed the refrigerator and carried the vials to one of the work tables.

The blue liquid was the result of his tests on Hassan, as well as a number of other volunteers. A vaccine for cellular necrosis. It wasn't one hundred percent effective, but it showed great promise. It had protected Hassan from the disease, although remnants of the virus had lain dormant within him ever since. Gagnon had no idea if the cure would have any effect on the Xenomorph, but he hoped so.

If he could treat the disease, then the creature—while still extremely dangerous—would be less so than before. The infected staff, those who weren't already in the disease's final stages, could be quarantined and treated, thus preventing the infection from becoming a facility-wide plague.

He'd need to jury-rig a method of delivering the cure, and he had a couple ideas how to do that. Quickly, he got to work. He had a house call to make.

Aleta sat at her desk, fear mixed with rage.

By this point she didn't trust Gagnon to know his ass from a hole in the ground, but with the three of them—Gagnon, Tamar, and Brigette—working together, they might succeed in chasing down the Xenomorph before it was too late. But if they didn't, and there was no chance of salvaging the situation, she needed to start covering her own ass. Now.

She might be able to place the blame on Tamar. After all, the woman was a corporate spy, a mercenary with no company loyalty. No, that was too obvious, and there was no way of knowing what contacts Tamar might have in Venture's corporate hierarchy. If the woman had influential allies the deception would fail, and Aleta would be exposed as its author. So Tamar was out.

Gagnon seemed like the next best choice. He had a history of engaging in research that was, at best, ethically questionable—which was what had made him so perfect for studying the Xenomorph in the first place. For months Aleta had turned a blind eye toward his less-than-professional practices, but she'd kept tabs on his work all along. More importantly, she'd kept records. Survival in the mega-corporate culture meant keeping *detailed* information on employees, colleagues, and superiors—a *lot* of it.

She could pull up reports about Gagnon, juice them up a little. Exaggerate some details here, add some false ones there, making sure to include personal observations regarding how concerned she was about his actions. That could work.

The best-case scenario was that the three of them got the Xenomorph back, and were able to minimize the spread of the virus it carried. But if the worst-case scenario occurred, she intended to be ready.

Aleta lifted the computer pad off the desk, woke it up, opened the file, and began juicing.

There were a number of conference rooms in the Personnel building that could be reserved for meetings. Zula had booked C-14 for the trainees' debriefing session, and she headed down the hallway toward the room at a jog. Having called ahead on her comm she had determined that they still were there, but that was all. After the way today's exercise had gone, it would be better if she briefed them in person.

When she reached C-14 the door opened automatically and she hurried inside. All the trainees except Miriam were there. The room held a long oval table around which they sat. Ronny stood next to a wall screen which displayed an overhead view of the route they'd taken to the Junkyard. He was pointing to the hill where the Screamer had attacked. Everyone turned to look at Zula as she entered, but then their gazes quickly shifted back to Ronny. It was clear they were waiting to see how the two of them would respond to each other.

Zula didn't have time for that foolishness.

"Ronny and I spoke earlier," she said, "and as far as I'm concerned, the matter with the Hider is settled. That clear?"

Everyone nodded, although a couple of them didn't look convinced.

Ronny gestured at the screen. "You want to finish up?" He didn't seem angry, but he did look disappointed. She could guess what he was feeling. Here she had trusted him to run the meeting, even after what he'd done, but then she appeared out of the blue, ready to take away that responsibility, as if she'd decided he couldn't be trusted after all.

"We're going to have to cut the debrief short," Zula said. "Something's happened."

That got their attention. The trainees sat up straight, faces alert, gazes focused on her. As thoroughly as she could, she told them about the deaths of the dockworkers.

"What do you think killed them?" Genevieve asked.

A goddamned Xenomorph, she thought. Aloud, she said, "It's difficult to say right now, but there's a chance that an alien lifeform might be responsible."

"Are you shitting us?" Donnell asked. Realizing what he'd said, he hurried to add, "Sorry. I mean, are you kidding?"

"I am not shitting you." Zula smiled grimly. "I don't have any proof yet, just a suspicion, but I want us to be ready in case I'm right. Go get weapons from the shooting range, with *live* rounds, and meet back here in five. In case any of you are wondering, this is not another exercise. This is as real as it gets."

The trainees exchanged nervous looks before getting up from the table and hurrying out the door. Within seconds, only Zula and Ronny remained in the room.

"You think it's one of *them*?" Ronny asked.

Zula didn't have to ask him what he meant.

"It's too early to tell. The dockworkers might've been killed by some kind of freak accident, or they might have contracted a disease of some kind."

"But that's not what your gut says."

"True," she admitted. "My gut tells me we'd better weapon up fast, because we're about to have a fight on our hands."

Ronny nodded, grim-faced. If he was worried, however, she saw no sign of it in his steely gaze. *Good.* She needed her people to be unafraid for as long as they could stay that way. Ronny started to go, but before he could leave the room, Zula stopped him.

"Could you bring me back a gun and some ammo?"

Ronny nodded without asking why she didn't go to the range herself. He headed out the door and down the hallway at a run.

The team's heavier equipment—EVA suits, pulse rifles, and such—was kept in the Armory, which was located in the Security section of the Facilities Management building. In order to get their weapons released to them, the team would have to get authorization from the head of Security, and Zula knew she'd never get permission to use pulse rifles inside the Lodge. Not until it was clear that they had a serious threat on their hands, and by then it would be too late.

However, there was a shooting range in the Personnel building which residents—including Zula's team—used for target practice. The guns there were Fournier 350 pistols, one of Venture's best models, and while they were as strictly regulated as any other firearm in the facility, the rangemaster was also a former Marine. Zula called the woman on her comm, quickly explained the situation, and the rangemaster promised to let the trainees have the weapons and ammo they needed.

Zula told the woman she owed her a drink, then disconnected. She stepped over to the wall screen and manipulated its controls. The view of the exercise field vanished, to be replaced by a schematic of the Lodge and all associated systems—water, air, and electrical. Folding her arms, she studied it carefully.

"All right, you sonuvabitch," she said softly. "Where the hell are you?"

16

Miriam wasn't a fan of debriefings. They mostly consisted of Hendricks telling the trainees everything they'd screwed up during an exercise. But she'd much rather be at the meeting with everyone else than lying in a hospital bed feeling like crap.

Damn Ronny! She didn't resent Zula as much as he did, though she'd liked the idea of playing a joke on her. Unlike Ronny, however, she didn't feel a need to humble their instructor—just hoped the joke might release some of the tension that had built up since she'd began working with them. Instead of just taunting her, though, the Hider had gone berserk and tried to kill her. It hadn't been too gentle with the rest of them, either.

Especially her.

She didn't remember the Hider striking her. One moment she was walking through the Junkyard with the rest of the trainees, and the next she was lying on the floor of the transport as it made its way back to the Lodge. She'd been in so much pain that she'd barely been able to think, and each bump the vehicle went over sent jolts of agony shooting through her body. She'd hoped she'd pass out again, but no such luck.

Zula sat with her the entire ride back, holding her hand and talking to her in case she had a concussion—which, as the doctors at the Med Center later confirmed, she did. She also had whiplash and a dislocated right shoulder. So she wore a cervical collar, an arm sling, and was loaded up with pain meds and muscle relaxants. Even so, she still hurt. Her neck felt rubbery and stiff, her shoulder ached like a bitch, and her head throbbed. If there'd been a weapon within reach, she might've been tempted to put herself out of her misery.

Thankfully, none of her injuries were too severe, but the doctors insisted that she stay in the Med Center for observation for a day, maybe two, in case her concussion turned out to be more serious than they'd first thought. So here she was, lying in bed dressed in a thin blue hospital gown, staring at an old vid on a small screen attached to her bed railing.

Wishing Ronny was there so she could kick his ass.

Zula had come by earlier to check on her, which she appreciated, but since then her only company had been the medical staff. The doctor and nurse she'd seen had been nice enough. They didn't have many other patients right now, and she suspected they checked on her more often than necessary simply because they were glad to have something to do.

Located in the Bioscience building, the Med Center was a collection of examination rooms, hospital beds, and physicians' offices. Altogether, the Lodge and the proto-colony had around six hundred residents, so only a handful of doctors and nurses were needed. Miriam had always wondered why a medical professional would want to take a job at a remote outpost like this, when presumably they could choose to work at a variety of locations. Maybe they were dumb enough to fall for the "romance of space travel" cliché that the mega-corporations used to entice people to come work for them. Or maybe they were mediocre at their professions, and the Lodge was the only place they could find jobs.

If that was true, what did it say about her and the other trainees? She decided not to examine the thought too closely.

There were twenty beds on the ward and most of them were empty. Besides Miriam, there were a couple colony workers who'd been injured in a mine collapse—both encased in full body casts—and a woman recovering from an operation after a burst appendix. Compared to them, especially the miners, Miriam figured she wasn't in too bad a shape.

Glass half full, right?

With any luck she'd be out of here sometime tonight, maybe tomorrow morning at the latest. She wasn't sure when she'd be able to return to training, but if the doc told her to rest in her quarters for a few days, she wouldn't cry about it.

Her head had been feeling steadily worse over the last

hour, so she pressed the call button for the nurse, hoping he would bring her another round of pain meds. Then she heard a metallic rattling sound.

She looked around, but she didn't see anything. The other patients seemed not to have heard it, but they were probably on way more meds than she was, and likely semiconscious at best. She listened to see if the noise repeated itself, and when it didn't she figured it was just some cranky piece of equipment. Venture believed in doing the most with the least—in other words, they were cheap— so it wasn't uncommon to hear weird noises in the Lodge. Machinery was always in need of maintenance or repair, and it was common to hear the Lodge complain from time to time. As far as residents were concerned, anything less than a large-scale O_2 leak wasn't worth worrying about.

The nurse—a muscular bald man whose name tag read JAMES—arrived two minutes after she'd called. He stopped at her bedside and smiled.

"How are we doing?"

"*We* feel like our head is going to explode."

James checked the computer pad he was carrying.

"You're not *quite* due for more pain meds yet, but I suppose it's okay. Let me go get—"

He was interrupted by shouting coming from the hall. She couldn't make out the words, but the voices didn't sound angry. They sounded alarmed, almost panicked.

"What's wrong?" she asked James.

"Some people in the Mall have fallen ill," he replied. "The doctors and staff are… debating about the best way to deal with the situation. Nothing to be too concerned about, though. They probably ate something bad from one of the food vendors. Last month I made the mistake of trying a volcano burrito from a food cart, and let's just say it lived up to its name."

"Sounds like you're going to be filling up most of these beds."

The nurse's smile faltered. "They'll be put somewhere else, so it'll still be just the four of you in here. You'll still have plenty of peace and quiet so you can rest."

Someplace else, Miriam thought. That sounded like a different way to say *quarantine*. What the hell was going on?

There was a loud metallic *clang* from the other end of the ward, and James jumped. He and Miriam looked toward the noise. A vent cover had fallen from the wall, and a large dark shape was crawling from the opening. Miriam didn't know what it was at first, but when it rose to its full height and stretched out its arms, legs, and tail, she knew it had to be some kind of alien lifeform. As part of their training, Zula had shown the trainees vids of the lifeforms humanity had encountered during this early stage of galactic expansion. The creatures were primitive and could be surprisingly dangerous, but none of them were as large or as terrifying as this thing.

The creature emerged from the air duct closest to the two injured miners. It started toward them, moving with a sinuous inhuman grace, tail waving slowly in the air behind it. Neither of the men so much as twitched a muscle, and their lack of reaction reminded Miriam of small children who believe that if they remain absolutely still, they are invisible. She and the nurse weren't much better, nor was the woman on the bed between her and the men. They all gaped soundlessly as the monster reached the miners.

She heard Zula's voice in her mind then.

You're supposed to protect people, right? So get to it!

Without taking her eyes off the creature, she spoke to the nurse in a low voice.

"Call Security."

The man didn't move.

"Go!" she said, louder, praying she didn't attract the thing's attention. James looked at her, startled, but then he turned and ran out of the room. Miriam felt like hammered shit, but she had a job to do. She tapped her comm and spoke Zula's name. She heard the woman's voice as she rose from the bed.

"Miriam? Are you okay?"

The monster stood near the two men, its long oblong head cocked slightly to the side, as if it was trying to decide what to do with them. It was covered in weird blisters, and ropy strands of thick saliva dripped from its tooth-filled maw onto the floor. Miriam's pulse sped up, intensifying the pain in her skull. It became so bad that for a moment she thought she might pass out, but she fought to hold onto consciousness and succeeded.

"There's some kind of bug in the Med Center. A *real* one. Get everyone here, fast!"

"What kind of bug?" Zula asked. "Miriam, you—"

Miriam reached up and tapped her comm twice to turn it off. She knew Zula would only try to talk her out of what she intended to do, and she didn't want the woman's voice in her ear. She had no weapons and she couldn't move without feeling as if her head was going to explode, but she couldn't stand by and watch people be killed.

"Hey!" she shouted. She clapped her hands and shouted again. "*Hey!*"

Pain erupted in her head so intensely that for a moment her vision was obscured by bright light. When it cleared, she saw that the monster's head had turned in her direction. She couldn't see any facial features on the thing, other than its drooling fang-filled mouth, but she could tell it had focused on her. It hissed, and she began trembling, feeling like a small frightened animal that had just drawn the attention of a very large and *very* hungry predator.

Once the monster was no longer facing them, the two miners broke free from their paralysis. They attempted to get out of their beds, but their casts prevented them from moving easily. So instead of hitting the floor running, they simply hit the floor. Both howled in pain as they reinjured themselves, and Miriam winced in sympathy.

The woman in the other bed—located on the other side of the room, diagonally across from the miners—had up to this point remained still and silent. When the miners fell it broke the spell she'd been under. She drew in a deep breath, and released an ear-splitting scream.

The monster's head jerked as it turned to look at her.

Damn it, Miriam thought.

She scanned her immediate vicinity, desperate for something—*anything* she could use as a weapon. The best candidate was the IV stand next to her bed. She hadn't needed an IV, so there was no bag hanging from it.

Sitting up, she paused as another eruption of pain subsided, then moved toward the stand, her shoulder and head protesting loudly. She grabbed hold of the metal pole and kicked at the wheeled plastic base once, twice, before breaking the pole free. It wasn't much of a weapon, the metal thin, the pole a hollow tube, but it would have to do. She took a two-handed grip on the pole, then turned and started toward the monster.

While she'd acquired her weapon, the monster had turned back toward the two miners. The men were struggling to get to their feet, features twisted in pain as their broken bodies refused to cooperate. The monster crouched low and extended its head toward one of them. At first, Miriam thought it was going to lunge forward and bite him. Instead, as it opened its jaws a *smaller* mouth jutted from the first, and with a harsh chuffing sound it expelled a black cloud. The dark gas struck the man in the face, and then the monster swiveled its head toward the second miner and gave him a blast as well.

Both men began coughing violently, and within seconds black lesions rose on their skin, along with irregular patches of angry boils. They continued coughing violently, now unable to even attempt to stand.

She thought the monster—whose body, she now realized, possessed the same black lesions and swollen boils—would move in for the kill. Instead, it drew away from its victims and headed for the other woman.

Miriam thought of what James had told her, about illness breaking out at the Mall. Was *this* what he had been talking about? If so, she understood why the staff in the hall had sounded scared. Whatever this disease was, it went through a victim's body like wildfire.

The monster turned its pustule-covered back on the infected miners and started toward its new prey. The woman had continued to scream, and now it rose in both pitch and intensity, the sound causing Miriam to grit her teeth. She thumped the pole loudly on the floor as she approached the thing, hoping to distract it.

The tactic didn't work, though. Moving with astonishing speed, the monster darted to the screaming woman. It grabbed hold of her head with claw hands—hands that looked almost human in their way—and positioned its mouth close to her head. Its smaller mouth shot forward and broke through the skin and bone of her forehead, plunging into the soft meat beyond. Blood sprayed, and the woman's body spasmed and jerked as if she were being electrocuted.

Her screaming stopped.

The smaller mouth remained lodged inside the woman's head for several seconds. Miriam wasn't sure, but she thought it might be swallowing bits of brain. She was sorry for the woman's death, but grateful for the distraction it provided. As she drew near the creature, she raised the IV pole, intending to swing it at the thing's bulbous head. Then its tail whipped out and struck her wounded shoulder. Maybe the monster had somehow sensed where she had been hurt, or maybe it was simply coincidence.

Either way, Miriam felt as much as heard something crack loudly in her shoulder, and then it was her turn to scream. The agony was so overwhelming that for an instant it was as if she ceased to exist as a person—as if all she was, all she ever had been, was pain. She returned to herself almost at once, and when the impact from the tail strike threatened to knock her down, she was able to slam the bottom of the pole to the floor and brace herself. She didn't fall, but she was off-balance, and the pain in her shoulder was echoed by that in her head, making it difficult to think.

The monster's smaller mouth retracted back into the larger, and it released its grip on the woman's head. Eyes still widened from shock, the victim slumped over, her body half hanging off the bed. Blood poured from the ragged hole in her forehead and pattered onto the floor. Even though she was dead, black lesions and pustules began to appear on her flesh.

The monster turned around to face Miriam, and she wondered what the hell was taking Zula so long to get there.

It was at that moment that Miriam knew she was going to die. Maybe the monster would take a bite out of her brain, or maybe it would simply breathe a cloud of black death on her. Either way, she was a goner.

If she only had a few seconds of life left to her, she was determined to use them well.

The miners' coughing had trailed away to soft,

breathy sounds, and she knew they weren't going to last much longer.

Me too, brothers, she thought.

Since the damned thing had no eyes, its only vulnerable part was its slavering mouth. She tensed, ready to raise the IV pole and jam the broken end into the opening. Hopefully the flesh inside would be tender, unprotected by the exoskeleton that covered the thing's outer body. She would put all her strength behind the strike, shoving the rod as deep as it would go.

Miriam had no illusions about killing the beast. It was too strong, too tough, but if she could wound it maybe she'd slow it down a bit, give Zula and the trainees an edge when they arrived. It was a desperate plan, but not a bad one. Success depended on striking fast and sure, no hesitation, no half-measures.

She was ready.

But before she could raise her makeshift spear, fire erupted at the base of her spine. She felt something thrust its way inside her and then lift her off her feet. Before this moment she thought she'd understood what pain was, but this was an entirely different universe of agony hitherto unimagined.

The tail!

She'd lost sight of it, and now she knew why. The creature had snaked it around behind her and plunged its barbed tip into her back.

The monster brought her close to its face—she couldn't believe how strong it was—and she was glad. The dumbass thing brought her close to its mouth, and she would use the last of her strength to ram the metal rod…

She couldn't feel the IV pole in her hand. Looking down, she saw the hand was empty. She looked past it and saw the thing lying on the floor amidst splatters of her own blood. She'd dropped the rod when the tail stabbed into her back, and she'd been in so much pain that she hadn't realized she'd done so. Miriam looked back to the monster in time to see its secondary mouth coming at her face.

At least she wouldn't have to worry about her headache anymore.

17

Gagnon caught up with Brigette and Tamar as the two approached the Med Center. He'd told Brigette to wait for him at the Mall, but Prather must have grown tired of hanging about. He carried an equipment bag slung over his shoulder, and he was gasping for air. He hadn't been able to find an available public transport cart, so he'd had to make his way there on foot. He would've railed at the indignity of it all if he'd been able to catch his breath.

Brigette held the chemical scanner, and Tamar had drawn her gun. While he wasn't pleased to see the latter—it was imperative they capture the Xenomorph alive—he couldn't fault the woman. He rather wished he had a firearm himself… and that he knew how to use it, of course.

It was an extraordinary concept, seeing the Xenomorph in its adult state, but he was aware that what they were doing here was extraordinarily dangerous. Originally, he'd agreed with Aleta's insistence that the Xenomorph be taken without anyone in the Lodge being aware of its existence. Now he knew what a ridiculous idea that was. On the way here he'd passed people hurrying away from the Bioscience building toward Research and Development. Many of them had been driving electric carts, leaving none for him, but far more had been walking or even running. All of them had worn worried, even frightened, expressions.

Gagnon had been in too much of a hurry to stop and ask why—or what—they were fleeing. But then he'd already known, hadn't he? His suspicions had been confirmed when a Security announcement came over the Lodge's comm system, on the public speakers throughout the facility as well as personal devices.

"For the time being, travel to and from the Personnel building is prohibited. Guards will be posted at north and south entryways to make sure that all residents comply with this directive. Further updates will be provided as events warrant.

"Thank you for your cooperation."

The word *quarantine* hadn't been used, but Gagnon knew it was the real reason for the prohibition. Thanks to the Xenomorph, an outbreak of cellular necrosis had occurred in the Personnel building, and as virulent as the Xenomorph's strain of the disease was, it wouldn't be long before everyone in the quarantined area was infected.

If Security could prevent the disease from spreading further, the outbreak would eventually burn itself out. However, that assumed no one in other areas of the Lodge became infected, and as long as the Xenomorph remained free, further spread of the disease was a very real possibility. Unless he could render the creature no longer contagious.

Gagnon reached into his bag, removed a hypo, then walked over to Tamar.

"Roll up your sleeve," he said.

"Why?"

"This is a vaccine for cellular necrosis. I've already injected myself, and Brigette doesn't need it. You do, unless you enjoy gambling with your life."

Tamar holstered her weapon and rolled up her left sleeve. Gagnon injected her, then returned the hypo to the bag.

"Doesn't it take twenty-four hours for vaccines to become effective?" she said as she rolled her sleeve back down.

"Normally. I've made some modifications to this formula, so hopefully it will work faster."

"Hopefully?" she said.

He shrugged, then pulled a pair of surgical masks from his bag and held one out to Tamar.

"Put this on."

She did, and he donned his as well. As a synthetic, Brigette was immune to disease, so she didn't require such protection.

The three continued on to the Med Center and soon found themselves approaching the double glass doors that formed the main entrance. Gagnon walked behind Brigette and Tamar, telling himself that since they held the chemical scanner and handgun, they needed to go first. Still, he didn't mind having a couple living shields in front of him.

"I'm picking up traces of the Xenomorph's chemical signature," Brigette said. "I believe it's inside the building."

Tamar gripped her gun tighter, and Gagnon was suddenly struck by how small and ineffective the weapon looked. He would've felt better if she were armed with a pulse rifle. Aleta would be highly distressed to find him thinking like this, but just then he didn't care. He wanted to keep the Xenomorph alive as much as she did, but he didn't want to lose his own life in the process.

Brigette still carried the equipment case she'd brought with her from the lab. She deposited it on the floor outside the glass doors, along with the chemical scanner. This would leave her hands free when they confronted the Xenomorph. Gagnon decided it was time to arm himself. He reached into his bag and removed a spherical device.

"What's that?" Tamar asked.

"It contains a large, concentrated dose of cellular necrosis vaccine. We won't be able to inject the Necromorph with a hypodermic, so I rigged this device to deliver the vaccine in a more, ah, *primitive* manner."

Tamar frowned. "Necromorph?"

Gagnon's cheeks reddened. "It's what I've taken to calling it: a Xenomorph crossed with cellular necrosis, you see."

"What good will it do?" she asked. "Giving it a vaccine?"

"The creature possesses a hyper-accelerated metabolism," he said. "I'm hoping this will cause the vaccine to work swiftly, counteracting the cellular necrosis that's become part of its genetic make-up. That should cause a powerful systemic shock and we'll be able to recapture the creature. Once we've done that, I'll arrange to have the Necromorph transported back to my lab."

"You're *hoping*," Tamar said, almost sneering.

Gagnon bristled. "If you have any better ideas, I'd like to hear them."

Tamar said nothing.

Brigette held out her hand. "Give me the vaccine delivery device, Doctor. My aim will be more precise than yours, especially since I will experience no fear or attendant adrenaline rush as we confront the Necromorph."

Gagnon recognized the logic of Brigette's words, and handed her the sphere. In truth, he was glad she'd offered to wield the device. In the controlled environment of his lab he was completely confident. Outside of the laboratory there were too many variables at play, and he was far less… comfortable.

"I have a second device as well," he said, "this one designed to subdue the Necromorph. We'll use it if— *when*—the vaccine begins working on the creature."

As they approached the Med Center, the glass doors opened automatically. Gagnon experienced a powerful urge to abandon this foolish action, to turn around and flee back to the safety of his lab. Let Brigette and Tamar attempt to deal with the Necromorph. They were far better suited to the task than he.

Yet this was a chance for him to observe the creature outside the confines of a testing chamber. The opportunity was too enticing to pass up. The thought wasn't as convincing as he might've hoped, but he continued forward, following behind Brigette and Tamar, more frightened then he'd ever been in his life.

In a strange way he was exhilarated, too. He could almost see why someone like Tamar chose to do the sort of work she did.

The three of them entered the Med Center, the doors closing automatically behind them.

"No one goes in or out. Those are our orders."

The security guard—along with three others—stood blocking the entrance to the corridor that led from the Personnel building to the Bioscience building. All four were armed with Fournier 350s, and while none of them had yet drawn their weapons, their hands rested on the guns, ready to—as the old saying went—slap leather any second.

Zula couldn't blame them. The sight of her and her trainees jogging through the Mall, each armed with Fourniers of their own, would've given anyone pause. Frankly, she was surprised they hadn't drawn their weapons and fired off a few warning shots by now.

She took a step toward the guard who'd spoken. The man gripped his weapon and drew it partway from its holster. The other three guards did the same, and Zula gestured behind her back to tell the trainees not to draw their weapons in response. The last thing they needed was to get into a firefight.

Davis spoke in her ear.

"*There are more Security guards en route. These are merely the first to respond. It's only going to get more difficult for you to reach the Med Center if you stand there arguing.*"

She gave the guard her best don't-screw-with-me-I'm-a-Colonial-Marine stare.

"We're Venture's Colony Protection Force," she said. "There've been reports of some kind of creature attacking the Med Center, and we've been ordered to assess the situation there and, if necessary, kick some alien ass. Let us through. *Now.*"

The guard exchanged glances with his companions before facing Zula once more.

"We haven't heard anything about letting you pass."

"That's because they're *our* orders, not yours. Now let us through. Every minute you keep us waiting here is another minute people might be dying."

The guard looked uncertain.

"Let me check with my supervisor."

He reached up to tap the comm in his ear, but before his fingers could make contact with the device, Zula grabbed hold of his wrist. The other guards drew their weapons, and in response the trainees drew theirs.

"Do you want to explain why you allowed more deaths to occur," Zula said, "and more disease to spread because you couldn't make a decision on your own?"

Ronny stepped to Zula's side.

"What do you care anyway?" he said to the guard. "If you let us through and anything happens to us, it's our funeral. You can say we left Personnel before you got here."

The guard looked from Zula to Ronny and back again. "Yeah, all right. Get the hell out of here."

Zula released his wrist. As she and the trainees ran past the guards, the one she'd dealt with shouted at their backs.

"I hope whatever you find has a lot of teeth and knows how to use them!"

Don't worry, she thought. *It does.*

Gagnon's heart pounded so hard he had difficulty hearing over the thrumming pulse in his ears. The reception area of the Med Center had been deserted, but once they moved on to the physician offices and examining rooms they began to find bodies of staff, nurses, doctors, and patients. Some had been torn to shreds, blood splattering the ceilings, walls, and floors. All of the bodies had black lesions and raised pustules, but the mutilated ones had far less than those which remained intact. The contagion carried by the Necromorph was so strong it could be transmitted even to the recently dead.

It was difficult to tell, given the condition of the bodies, but it appeared as if the Necromorph had taken bites out of some of them. Had it been feeding as it killed? Perhaps.

Cellular necrosis was most often fatal, but it normally took several days to get to that point. The strain the Necromorph carried worked far faster, making the creature even more dangerous than one of its kind usually was.

They reached the patient ward and entered. There were dead, infected bodies here too—three on the floor, one on a bed—but there was one thing living here, and Gagnon got his first look at the monster he had midwifed.

The creature's back was to him, and his first impression was a being that was a combination of reptile, insect, and machine. It looked almost biomechanical. A quartet of rod-like protrusions jutted from its back—he couldn't begin to guess at their function—and a tail that looked as if it was comprised of segmented bone swung behind it as it walked. The signs of cellular necrosis were clear. Lesions covered the creature's surface—raised, irregular patches, darker than the rest of its form—along with clumps of swollen, barnacle-like pustules that looked ready to burst at any moment.

Most would have found the Necromorph hideous, but he marveled at its elegantly savage design, and even more so its ability to incorporate a deadly disease into its make-up. To resist the negative effects of that disease, and actually turn it into another weapon in its arsenal. Ever since Darwin, survival of the fittest had been considered the prime factor in successful evolution. Gagnon believed he now gazed upon the fittest creature the galaxy had ever produced.

The Necromorph wasn't alone, however.

It dragged one of the staff behind it, a muscular bald man. The claws of its right hand gripped the collar of the man's blue smock. The man was infected with cellular necrosis, but he had far fewer lesions and blemishes than the others they'd seen, and no apparent wounds. The doctor thought the man might be dead, but then he rolled his head from side to side. His eyes fluttered several times, but did not open. Why wasn't this man more seriously affected?

It made no sense.

The Necromorph dragged its semiconscious captive toward a rectangular opening in the wall on the opposite side of the room. Brigette had said the creature had been traveling through the Lodge's air ducts, and here was confirmation. The creature obviously intended to take the man with it, but why? Did it intend to hide him away somewhere for later consumption, like a dog burying a bone? From what Gagnon had seen, the Necromorph wasn't food-driven. It ate to fuel itself as it killed, so it could continue to kill. Feeding was not the goal. The swift extermination of all non-Xenomorph life was its mission.

So why—

Then it came to him.

The stories that had spread through settled space spoke of Xenomorph infestations. *Plural.* One Xenomorph was a threat, but it could be dealt with. Not easily, perhaps, but it was possible.

Two Xenomorphs? Ten? A hundred?

Gagnon theorized that as soon as they reached maturity, they began to procreate. They were designed to increase their numbers rapidly so they could overwhelm, destroy, and supplant all lifeforms in a given environment. He wondered if they were all female—or perhaps hermaphrodites—each able to produce Ovomorphs. He doubted a single Xenomorph could produce many, given its size, but once more of the creatures had been born they could also produce eggs, which would in turn produce more Xenomorphs in a geometric progression.

This explained why the man's case of cellular necrosis was so mild. The Xenomorph was able to control the strength of the contagion. It wanted its progeny to possess the same strengths it did, but it also needed the host to live long enough for an embryo to be implanted and gestate. It seemed impossible, but absolutely fascinating.

Brigette spoke in a hushed voice. "It needs to be facing us if I'm to be able to deliver the vaccine effectively."

"I'll get its attention." Tamar raised her gun and began to squeeze the trigger.

Gagnon wasn't by nature someone who acted without thinking, but he did so now.

"No!" he shouted, and he swept his arm down toward Tamar's gun hand, striking it just as she fired. The weapon cracked, and the round ricocheted off the floor, tearing a tiny chunk out of the surface. The bullet might not have hit its target, but it had the intended effect.

The Necromorph let go of its captive and spun around to face them. For the first time the doctor saw the creature's front—its smooth, eyeless, oblong head, its wide mouth filled with sharp teeth—and he was glad he'd spoiled Tamar's aim. Who'd want to harm a magnificent thing like this? He felt ashamed for wishing he carried a weapon of his own. He'd been afraid then. Now the only thing he felt was awe.

"What the hell did you do that for?" Tamar demanded.

Her words barely registered with Gagnon, for at that instant the Necromorph let out a sound that was a combination of a screech and a roar, and then it started running toward them.

The creature moved with an eerie grace that was a wonder to behold, and while a voice in the back of Gagnon's mind shouted an alarm, he ignored it. He was so mesmerized by the Necromorph's advance that he didn't realize Brigette had thrown the vaccine deployment sphere—not until the device was in the air and hurtling toward the creature.

If he had been aware of what Brigette was doing he might have attempted to stop her as well, but it was too late. The three of them watched as the sphere flew toward the Necromorph's slavering mouth. The creature didn't slow as it swept out an arm, intending to bat the sphere away. Before the Necromorph could strike the sphere, however, tiny nozzles emerged from its surface and emitted jets of liquid in all directions. Much of the vaccine missed the creature entirely, but a good portion went into its mouth, which was exactly what Gagnon had hoped would happen when he'd originated this plan.

Even a concentrated dose like this would have no immediate effect on a human, but while the creature had been born from a human, and shared the man's DNA, it was so much more than the sum of its parts.

The Necromorph recoiled as the vaccine splashed its face, and instead of being knocked aside, the sphere struck the creature's chest and bounced off. The creature stopped running and let out a high-pitched shriek as it clawed at its mouth, trying to clear away the vaccine.

Brigette held her hand out to Gagnon.

"Give me the other device, Doctor. I assume it's the stunner."

He reached into his bag and removed what looked like a standard two-pronged stun weapon, but this was much more. He'd modified it by adding a powerful proton battery. Now it would produce ten times the electrical charge it was designed for—far more than what was necessary to kill a human—but it was only good for one use. After that, the battery would be depleted. He'd built the weapon a couple weeks earlier, in case any Xenomorph born out of his experiments proved troublesome.

Glad he'd taken that precaution, he handed the stunner to Brigette.

"Remember: it only has one charge."

She nodded, gripped the weapon in her right hand, and started walking toward the distressed Necromorph.

"I've never seen a synth commit suicide before," Tamar said.

Gagnon understood what Brigette was doing. The Ovomorph hadn't responded to her presence, so perhaps the Necromorph wouldn't either. She wasn't biologically alive, wasn't organic in any way. She was a machine, and while the creature was dealing with the effects of the vaccine, she might be able to get close enough to—

The Necromorph's tail swung around from behind and struck Brigette with tremendous force. The impact sent her flying through the air to strike a plasteel wall. She hit hard, fell onto an unoccupied bed, rolled off, and fell onto the floor.

She did not get back up.

Synthetics were far more durable than humans, but they weren't indestructible. Gagnon had no idea if Brigette was damaged so badly that repair was impossible, and right now he didn't care. The Necromorph's exertions were lessening, and its lesions and pustules were once again becoming prominent. The creature was resisting the vaccine. He estimated they had only a few moments left to shock the Necromorph with the stunner, and—hopefully—render it unconscious. Or at least harmless enough to move back to the lab.

Brigette lay still, eyes wide and staring, but she'd managed to keep hold of the stunner.

"Get the weapon," Gagnon said to Tamar, "and shock the Necromorph." When the woman didn't move, he added, "Hurry!"

"You have to be out of your mind if you think I'm going anywhere near that thing," Tamar said, holding her gun at her side. "It's your monster. If you want it shocked, you do it."

"There's no time to argue!" Gagnon said. "Just do it!"

Tamar raised the weapon and pointed it at him.

"I'm not arguing," she said.

Seeing the coldness in her gaze, Gagnon knew she'd kill him if he spoke another word. He didn't think he could do it, thought he'd be too firmly gripped by fear, but he started walking toward the synthetic. He didn't run, nor did he go slowly. As he moved he felt a detached calm, and wondered if he was in shock. If so, he was a man *in* shock who wanted to *deliver* a shock.

That was funny.

When he reached Brigette, he bent down and pried the stunner from her hand. Now that he was close he could see her eyes twitching back and forth. She wasn't fully offline yet.

Good for her.

Straightening, he turned and started walking toward the Necromorph. It exuded a foul odor reminiscent of spoiled meat, and he wondered if that was due to the cellular necrosis, or if the species naturally smelled that way. He'd have to do some tests to find out. The creature was covered by a hard exoskeleton, but its joints bent easily. Gagnon thought one of those areas might be the best place to administer the shock. He would need to step away quickly afterward, as he didn't want the thing falling on top of him.

He decided to go for the inside of one of the creature's elbows. The left, perhaps. If he timed his strike just right—

The Necromorph turned its head toward him and let out a chuffing cough. A cloud of black particles enveloped him, and immediately he held his breath and squeezed his eyes shut. Cellular necrosis could only be contracted by contact with the soft tissues in the nose or mouth, or contact with the eyes. At least, that's how normal necrosis worked.

This virus, however, had mutated. He could feel particles penetrating his skin, entering his bloodstream, rapidly propagating themselves as they began to ravage his system. He knew the vaccine he'd dosed himself with would be useless. There was nothing that could be done to save him now. Only three choices remained to him: wait for the Necromorph to fully recover and tear him to pieces, allow the disease to run its course and finish him off… or he could end it quickly.

He raised the stunner to his own neck, pressed its prongs against his flesh, and activated the device.

18

The black cloud the Necromorph had disgorged onto Gagnon cleared enough for Tamar to see him press the stunner to his neck. There was a loud *zzzzzzzttttt* sound, and the man's muscles contracted so violently that for a moment he stood rigid, statue-still. Then he went limp and collapsed, hitting the floor with a dull thud, and the smell of burning meat filled the air.

The Necromorph faced Gagnon's body, which—despite his death—was beginning to show the first signs of necrosis. Tamar had no idea if the thing was looking at Gagnon, since it didn't seem to have eyes, but she had the impression that it was regarding the man, as if trying to decide what to do about him. Evidently the creature decided the human wasn't a threat anymore, because it turned to Tamar. It began slavering, and a second mouth extended from the first, tiny jaws gnashing.

Tamar knew she couldn't outrun the thing, and she

doubted her handgun was powerful enough to do much damage to the creature. She almost wished she had a modified stun gun to use on herself. Gagnon's had only held a single charge. She didn't intend to die without trying to defend herself, though, so she aimed her weapon at the center of the Necromorph's weirdly shaped head and prepared to fire.

The shout came from behind her.

"Get down!"

She did, and bullets began flying.

Zula entered the patient ward first, remembering something one of her drill instructors once said.

You can't lead from behind, no matter what officers think.

Moving into the ward, gun raised, she made room for the trainees to come inside. As they fanned out behind her, she quickly took in the scene. Although she'd been expecting to see a Xenomorph, the sight of the monster still caused the breath to catch in her chest. She'd faced these creatures before, but this was a foe she couldn't afford to underestimate. Not if she wanted to survive the encounter.

Her nerves jangled with released adrenaline, but she wasn't afraid. Her mind was sharp as a finely honed blade, her focus laser-like in its intensity. Xenomorphs had no malice in them, and they weren't evil. They were a primal destructive force, death given physical form. What greater adversary could a soldier have? What better purpose than seeking the extinction of this nightmare species? For the first time since coming to the Lodge, she felt fully alive.

Tamar Prather—one of the two women she'd met in the warehouse—stood between Zula and the Xenomorph.

"Get down!" Zula shouted, and the woman dropped to the floor instantly. Then Zula gave the command to fire. Time to find out just how well she'd trained these people.

A hailstorm of bullets struck the Xenomorph, and the creature roared in fury. It took a step toward them, but Zula and the trainees kept firing, and Tamar, still lying on the floor, joined in, shooting from her prone position. The rounds didn't penetrate the monster's exoskeleton, but they did put dents and cracks in it, and burst a number of the thing's crusty growths, sending black pus flying. Some of the goo splattered onto the floor close to Tamar, and the places where it hit began to sizzle and smoke. Tamar continued firing without so much as flinching. Zula was impressed. The woman was tough as hell.

The Xenomorph opened its mouth wide.

"Look out!" Tamar shouted. "It's going to try to infect you!"

Zula had seen the disease-ridden corpses in the outer rooms of the Med Center, and she understood.

"Aim for the mouth!" she commanded, then she did so, and the trainees followed her lead. The Xenomorph shook its head back and forth, reminding Zula of an animal irritated by bee stings. For a moment, she thought the creature might come at them, and without pulse rifles she doubted any of them would survive a direct attack.

But the creature turned and began running toward the far end of the room.

Tamar held her gun in her right hand, and with her left reached into one of her pockets. She pulled out a small gray disk, rose to one knee, and flung it toward the retreating alien. The disk struck the creature's back and adhered to the surface. Zula had no idea what the disk was. If it was some sort of weapon, it seemed to have no effect.

"Keep firing!" she ordered.

There was an opening in the wall. An air duct, Zula thought, with the vent cover removed. A bald man lay on the floor in the creature's path. He was alive, on all fours, and trying to crawl to safety. As the Xenomorph ran past him it swiped out with a clawed hand and struck the back of the man's head, instantly decapitating him. Blood sprayed the air as his head flew toward a wall, hit, and bounced off. His body collapsed, blood pouring from the neck stump. The Xenomorph reached the air duct, crawled swiftly inside, and vanished.

"Hold your fire!" Zula commanded, and everyone— including Tamar—stopped shooting. Zula glanced behind her to make sure the trainees were all right, then said, "Check for survivors."

As the trainees began to fan out into the room she went over to Tamar, who was now rising to her feet.

"Are you okay?" Zula asked, holstering her weapon. "Did any of that black crap get on you?"

"No. I'll live." Tamar looked around the room. "Which is more than I can say about the people I came here with."

"Boss! Over here!"

Ronny was standing next to a woman's body. She lay on the floor, blood pooled around her, a metal rod clutched in her hand. It was Miriam.

Zula joined Ronny and gazed down at the dead cadet. Even though she'd been injured during the incident with the Hider, and hadn't been able to fight at full strength, she'd still attempted to take on the monster.

"She died a warrior's death," Zula said.

Ronny didn't say anything, only nodded.

"Zula!"

Angela stood beside the body of a woman lying on the floor next to a bed. Zula went over, and as she drew closer she saw that the woman was bleeding from a cut on her forehead, but the "blood" was chalky white.

"She's a synthetic," Angela said. "I think she's still functional."

Zula leaned over to get a closer look at the synthetic's face, recognizing her from the warehouse. Brigette was her name. Her eyes were open, and while they didn't blink, Zula could see awareness in them. They focused on her, and when the synthetic spoke her voice held a buzzing undertone, as if her speech synthesizer had been damaged.

"Tamar and I came here with Dr. Gagnon, attempting to capture the Necromorph." A pause, and then without a hint of irony, "We failed."

"Necromorph?" Zula said. "As in cellular *necrosis*?"

Brigette nodded. "The name was Dr. Gagnon's idea."

Zula shrugged. The name was as good as any, she supposed. Tamar came over to join them. Zula looked at her.

"The doctor…?"

Tamar pointed at one of the dead bodies lying on the floor.

"Let me guess," Zula said. "This doctor is responsible for the Xeno—I mean, *Necro*morph."

Brigette opened her mouth to respond, but Tamar cut her off.

"You know scientists. Always meddling in things best left alone."

Zula looked at Tamar and Brigette. There had to be more to the story, but the details weren't important right now. They had more pressing matters to deal with.

Ray and Virgil came over.

"There are no other survivors," Virgil said.

"You find any dead crab-like things with long tails?" she asked.

Ray frowned. "No."

"Good." She turned to Ronny. "Take the others and double-check the rest of the bodies in the offices and examination rooms. Make sure they're all dead, but whatever you do, don't touch them with your bare skin."

"The bodies should no longer be contagious," Brigette said.

"Even so, better safe than dead and rotting." She addressed Ronny once more. "If you find any dead crab-things, let me know right away. If you find any live ones, blast them to pieces."

"Okay, Boss."

Ronny headed for the ward's door. "Let's go, people!" he called, and the rest of the trainees followed him. When they were gone, Zula turned to Tamar.

"I saw you throw that disk at the Necromorph. What was it?"

"It's a tracking device. They come in handy in my line of work."

"And that would be…?

Tamar smiled, but didn't answer. Then Zula remembered the synth's words.

She's a corporate espionage freelancer.

"All right, be mysterious. I don't care what you really do, so long as you can lead me to that thing."

"And what do *you* really do?" Tamar asked.

Zula looked at her for a moment before replying.

"I kill monsters."

Brigette's body was too badly damaged for her to accompany them, so she suggested they detach her head and carry it with them.

"Don't worry. I will feel no pain."

Zula knew from her friendship with Davis that Brigette spoke the truth, but that friendship had also taught her to view synthetics as equal to humans, even if they were artificial. Brigette insisted she could be of service to them in their hunt for the Necromorph, and Tamar agreed this was true. So Zula put aside her reluctance, drew the knife she carried, and began sawing at the synthetic's neck. The task was easier than Zula thought it would be—synthetic anatomy was surprisingly delicate in its way—and a few moments later Tamar held Brigette's head tucked under one arm.

Thankfully, the trainees found no crab-things, living or dead, in the Med Center. Brigette quickly filled them in on the situation. Venture had acquired an Ovomorph and Dr. Gagnon had been given the job of bringing a new Xenomorph into being, one that the corporation could exploit for profit. The host body Gagnon used had once been infected with cellular necrosis, and the disease had somehow become part of the Necromorph's DNA, making it even more deadly.

"Great," Donnell said. "Not only do we have to worry about getting eaten, we have to worry about catching a fatal disease, too." He looked at Zula. "Nothing personal, Boss, but this job sucks harder every minute."

Zula couldn't argue with that.

"Do you have the tracking device?" she asked Tamar.

The woman removed a small rectangular object from her pocket. Zula reached for it, and after a moment of hesitation Tamar handed it over.

"We also have a chemical scanner," Brigette said. "It's in my pocket."

Nicholas went over to the synthetic's body and retrieved the device. Zula turned on the tracker, and a screen came to life. It displayed a grid pattern upon which a glowing dot was moving. The screen indicated north, south, east, and west, as well as the distance between the tracker and the disk.

"All right," Zula said. "Let's move out."

Tamar didn't ask for permission to accompany them. She explained that she and Brigette had been working at Director Fuentes's request—which begged the question why the director hadn't contacted Zula and her team. She shrugged away the thought for later. Here and now, Tamar could handle herself in a fight. Besides, they needed someone to carry Brigette's head.

"Zula?" Masako asked. "What about Miriam?"

One of the trainees had covered her body with a bedsheet, but she still lay on the floor where she'd died. Blood had soaked through the sheet, creating a scarlet outline of her body.

"We'll come back for her," Zula said. "Right now we have to protect the living." Masako looked as if she might protest, but in the end she gave a curt nod. Zula understood. She didn't like leaving a fallen comrade behind, but there would be time to mourn later— assuming the rest of them survived.

There was nothing more to say after that so they left the Med Center, the others following behind. She hoped they'd be able to kill the Necromorph before there were any more casualties, and especially before the creature could procreate. She wasn't religious, but just then she wished she was. It might make her feel better to have a deity to pray to and ask for help. But all her life she'd had to rely on herself, and this time wasn't any different.

She'd kill the Necromorph or she'd die trying. It was as simple as that. Still, she wished she had Davis—in a new body—at her side, and Amanda too. She had the trainees, though, and so far they'd done all right. They'd lost Miriam, though, and she feared before this day was over that wouldn't be the only loss they'd suffer.

Zula told herself to stop thinking like that and to focus on the job at hand.

A distracted soldier is a dead soldier.

She checked the tracker as she led the group away from the Med Center. The glowing dot on the screen was heading northeast, toward the Administration building. They headed in the same direction, walking together, but each alone with his or her own thoughts. And fears.

The Necromorph moved swiftly through the metal tunnel. The cool air felt good on its broken pustules—soothing—but the creature barely registered the sensation. Pain and pleasure meant nothing. All that mattered was stimulus and response, action and reaction. Just then it was experiencing conflicting impulses, inner stimuli that were screaming for it to act. It wanted to find more humans to kill, but it also wanted to find some to serve as hosts for more of its kind.

It needed a safe place for reproduction to occur, somewhere that was unlikely to be disturbed. The place it had just left was unsuitable. There hadn't been many humans there at first, but more had come, and these new ones had driven it off. There an egg might not survive long enough to send forth larva-makers. Or if it did, the host would be killed by other humans before the larva could be born. These were not conscious thoughts, any more than a migrating bird consciously planned its complex flight path from one location to another hundreds of miles distant. It was all about the instinct for survival, and Xenomorphs were the greatest survivors the galaxy had ever known.

The egg needed to be deposited somewhere secluded and quiet. Somewhere humans would not find it or the host the Necromorph would bring there. It recalled the place where it had taken its first prey. That location had been virtually deserted, and the two humans it had killed there had offered no resistance. It would make a good place for an egg, and the Necromorph could get there soon. Once it arrived, it would select a prime location, deposit the egg, and then go in search of a host.

If it was able to kill more humans during that search, so much the better.

The Necromorph was also in large part a massive colony of the cellular necrosis virus, and as such it had an additional need, one just as strong as the need to procreate. The disease wanted—*needed*—to spread. It demanded that the Necromorph forsake all other purposes and spread its contagion far and wide. This created an internal conflict.

The Necromorph's instincts guided it, and it obeyed. But it couldn't obey two equally strong but opposing instincts. It was at the core a simple creature, yet its instincts were driving it to do two entirely separate things at once. This was beyond its capability to resolve. In short, it was going insane.

Once again it became aware of cool air moving across its body. Its pustules had healed over and filled with pus once more, so there was no pain to be soothed now, but there was something about the air itself that nagged at its semi-sentient consciousness. There were humans standing nearby, breathing in the air and then exhaling. Suddenly the Necromorph knew how it could make the part of it that was cellular necrosis happy.

The virus inside the Necromorph had nearly succumbed to the prey's assault, but while it had been a near thing, in the end the creature's resilient physiology had protected the virus. However, the close call had triggered a primal need for the virus to propagate, to spread before it might die. The virus had been ramping up production of itself within the Necromorph, not only to replenish itself, but to make more—much more.

The creature continued scuttling through passageways, then it stopped moving. It gripped the metal surfaces of the tunnel, bracing itself, and then it began to cough. It did so repeatedly, expelling vast clouds of black death which the cool air carried away. With each gust of virus-cloud that exited the Necromorph's mouth there was an accompanying burst of energy, a simple, undeniable impulse.

To spread.

19

The reports implicated Gagnon as primarily responsible for the Xenomorph's acquisition, creation, and release into the Lodge.

Overall, Aleta thought she'd done a good job. She'd made certain not to portray herself as entirely blameless— the board would never believe that—but she'd minimized her involvement and spun her actions as performed solely in service to the company.

Thus, if she couldn't get a handle on the situation soon, she would contact the board and inform them of what was happening—well, *her* version of what was happening— and she'd send the reports. Once the mess was cleaned up she'd probably be subject to disciplinary action. A dock in pay, a demotion, perhaps both. But if the board bought her story—and more importantly, if she could at least produce a Xenomorph corpse for Venture's scientists to study—she should emerge from this clusterfuck still standing.

The screen of her computer pad seemed to dim then, and she couldn't understand why. Supposedly Jazmine had charged the damn thing this morning. She began to adjust the brightness control when she realized the screen alone hadn't dimmed. Rather, the entire room had. Was there something wrong with the goddamned lights? Didn't *anything* work right around here?

"Jazmine!" she shouted. "Call Facilities Management and get them to send someone to look at the office lights. I think something's wrong with them."

No answer.

Jazmine *always* answered when she was at her desk. If for whatever reason she needed to leave the office, she always informed Aleta.

Weird.

Aleta tapped her comm device.

"Jazmine? Are you there?"

Silence. Then a cough, a soft one. It was followed by another, this one louder, and a third, louder still.

What the hell?

The coughing continued, until Aleta could hear it through the wall. She tapped the comm to deactivate it, then got up and headed for the door. On the way she felt a tickle in her throat, but put it down to a sympathetic reaction. As she approached the door, however, a realization hit her, and she felt a sudden sick chill.

The Xenomorph wasn't just eating people.

It was spreading cellular necrosis, too.

The door to her office slid open and, trembling, she

stepped into the equally dim outer office. Jazmine had gotten up from her desk and stood in the center of the room. She had her hands to her mouth as if trying to stifle her coughing, but it didn't do any good. She coughed so violently that she doubled over. Black lesions began to appear on her skin, along with swelling pustules.

Aleta slapped a hand over her mouth and nose and backed away, shaking her head. With her other hand she felt behind her, and when she found the open doorway to her office she turned and ran inside. Instead of waiting for the door to close automatically, she stabbed a button on the wall panel.

The outer office had been dark, too. It wasn't a problem with the lights. Something was in the air, and she knew what that something was. There was no mistaking Jazmine's condition. She'd contracted cellular necrosis. Aleta didn't know how the Xenomorph had done this, but she knew the monster was responsible, one way or another. There had been an outbreak of the disease in the Personnel building, and now there was one here in Administration.

Keeping her hand over her mouth and nose to avoid breathing in tainted air, and trying not to think about how much of it she'd already drawn into her lungs, she hurried to her desk. Dropping into her seat, she grabbed the computer pad and started typing a text message to Gagnon. She would've called him on her comm, but she couldn't risk opening her mouth to talk.

G: Need meds for cellular necrosis ASAP! Call me!!!

The first cough hit her as she pressed SEND.

No. God, please, no.

She coughed again, this time so hard that her hand jerked away from her face. She didn't want to draw in a breath then, but she couldn't help it. She knew it didn't matter, though. Not anymore.

The coughing became more violent, and she felt as if her skin was on fire. Looking at the backs of her hands she saw the lesions and pustules rising from her flesh. She couldn't stop coughing now, and with a shaking hand she reached for her computer pad. If she was going to die, she'd make damn sure Gagnon paid for what he'd done to her. She'd send the doctored reports to head office, and if he somehow managed to survive this plague, he'd be the one Venture would blame. Not her.

Her eyes filled with tears from the coughing, and she could barely see the pad's screen. Her fingers felt thick and numb, and she wasn't able to open the device's communication program. Still coughing, she began smacking the screen at random, determined to send those reports or die trying.

When she realized what she'd thought—*die trying*—she wanted to laugh, but she was coughing too hard. She was still trying to laugh when she grew too weak to continue sitting upright. She slumped forward and her head slammed into the computer pad.

Wouldn't it be funny—no, goddamned hilarious—if the comm program opened now?

Her coughing eased and she managed a weak chuckle. She so wanted to lift her head, just a little, so she could see if the program *had* opened. But she couldn't move. She remained sitting like that, head pressed to the screen of her computer pad, until she died.

"Zula! Hold up!"

Davis's voice in her ear startled her so much that she stopped jogging. Ronny and Genevieve were right behind her, and they were unable to stop in time to avoid colliding with her. She was knocked forward a couple steps, but remained on her feet.

"What's wrong?" Genevieve asked.

The rest of the trainees and Tamar—still holding onto Brigette's head—came to a halt as well. Zula ignored Genevieve's question. She pointed at the comm device in her ear so the others would know she wasn't talking to them.

"What's happening, Davis?"

Ray and Angela exchanged looks.

"Who's Davis?" Angela asked.

Ray shrugged.

"Security has just issued a warning. If you're near a public information terminal, you'll be able to hear it."

Zula glanced around and saw a terminal ten yards ahead of them. She ran to it, and the others—clearly confused—followed. Text scrawled across the screen, but there was no sound. The last person to use the terminal must've turned down the volume for some reason. Zula turned it back up.

A voice now accompanied the words.

"—in the Administration building. All personnel not currently in Administration are advised to stay away from the building. Any personnel currently *inside* Administration are advised to remain where you are. Medical help is on the way."

"Bullshit," Masako said. "All the doctors and nurses are dead."

The message started over. "There's been an outbreak of an unidentified illness in the Administration building. All personnel—"

Zula turned the volume back down, then turned away from the terminal to face the others. She checked the tracking device Tamar had given her, and saw that the Necromorph was no longer moving. It had stopped in one of the ducts located roughly in the middle of Administration. She looked up from the tracker.

"The Necromorph has started an outbreak of cellular necrosis," she said.

They were over halfway through the corridor that connected Bioscience with Administration, but they were far enough away from the latter that they were safe for the moment. Zula hoped so, anyway.

"They didn't make this big of a deal out of the infection at the Mall," Virgil said.

Brigette spoke then. Even though Zula was used to being around synthetics, she found it disconcerting, watching a disembodied head speak.

"The Mall outbreak was a surprise," Brigette said,

"and Security didn't realize its severity. If you check the terminal's past alert messages, you'll likely see that the Personnel building has been put under quarantine as well."

Before Zula could turn back to the terminal, Davis spoke.

"She is correct. The announcement was made while you were dealing with the Necromorph in the Med Center."

"Brigette's right," Zula said to the others.

"How can you possibly know that?" Ronny asked.

Zula pointed again to her comm.

"I've got a friend who's feeding me intel."

"We have to go back," Brenna said, sounding nervous. "We can't risk catching this disease. We saw what it did to the Med Center staff."

"We can't go back," Tamar said.

Everyone turned to look at her.

"If Security intends to quarantine the Administration building—and they'd be fools not to—they need to make certain none of the infected can get out."

"How would they—" Zula began, but then she remembered. During her orientation at the Lodge, she'd learned that each of the enclosed corridors that connected the facility's buildings had barriers that could be lowered in case of an emergency. The barriers were located at the center of each corridor to give residents extra space to seek shelter away from whatever problem had occurred. If the need arose, each barrier could be raised long enough for any evacuees to pass through.

Zula returned to the terminal and called up a map of

the Lodge. Sure enough, emergency barriers on either side of the Administration building had been lowered— including the one behind them.

She faced the others once more.

"Tamar's right. We're trapped."

The trainees glanced at one another. Some looked worried, some looked as if they were struggling to remain calm, and a couple looked like they were on the verge of crapping their pants.

More than one looked angry.

Zula worked the terminal keypad again and patched her comm into its speaker. Then she turned up the volume so everyone could hear Davis.

"Davis, we need a way out of this," Zula said. "Any suggestions?"

"From the data I've been able to gather so far, it appears as if the Necromorph is, for whatever reason, expelling large amounts of the cellular necrosis virus through the Administration building's air system. The concentration is uneven. Stronger in some parts of the building, weaker in others. It's impossible to tell which areas of Administration would be safe for you to pass through—if any. I also cannot tell if the air at your current location is free of disease. Since none of you are currently coughing—which is one of the first signs of infection—it may be safe to assume that none of you have been affected."

"You mean we might be breathing in that poison right now?" Brenna said. Her voice was strained, her eyes wild, and Zula could tell she was on the verge of full-bore panic. She wasn't the only one. The other trainees looked equally disturbed by Davis's words.

They didn't thrill her, either.

"The chemical scanner can be set to detect the virus," Brigette said. "That way you'll know if the danger is present."

"Give the scanner to me," Tamar said. "Brigette can tell me what to do, and I'll act as her hands."

Nicholas had been carrying the device, and he held it out. Tamar placed Brigette's head on the floor before taking the device. She then sat cross-legged next to the synth and they went to work. Brigette gave her instructions on how to reset the tracer, and Tamar's fingers danced across its controls.

Zula thought fast. They could stay at their current location and hope the air would remain untainted. The chemical scanner would tell them if the air turned bad, but that knowledge would do nothing to protect them. They didn't have EVA suits, and they couldn't just hold their breath and wait for the air to clear.

"If I can make a suggestion?" Davis said.

"Go on," Zula urged.

"I might be able to access the controls for the air system in the Administration building. Each building has fans that are designed to draw out contaminated air and release it outside of the dome in case of fire, chemical spill, or gas leak. That might clear out enough of the virus to enable you to travel through the facility and continue your hunt for the Necromorph. It might also aid those personnel in

Administration who are not yet infected."

"If the air can be cleaned like that," Ronny said, "why hasn't Security already started the process?"

"I'm speculating," Davis said, *"but my guess would be that Security personnel fear that some of the virus might end up filtering through the rest of the Lodge's air ducts, and spread through the entire V-22 facility. I should be able to prevent that from happening, though."*

"We'll encounter another emergency barrier on the other side of Administration," Zula said. "Will you be able to raise it for us?"

"Possibly."

"But by doing so, won't you risk alerting the Lodge's AI to your presence?" Zula asked.

"Yes. But it is a risk I'm willing to take." He paused, then added, *"For you."* As she watched, Zula saw confusion on the faces of some of her team, while looks of understanding dawned for others. Zula didn't want to put her friend in danger, however, unless there was no other way.

That seemed to be the case.

"We're done," Tamar announced. She stood, held out the chemical scanner, and pressed a control with her thumb. After a moment she checked the device's screen. "The scanner is detecting traces of the virus in the vicinity. Not in our immediate area, but close—and coming closer."

"Damn it," Zula said. "All right, do it, Davis. But be careful."

"I'm afraid I can't comply. If I'm careful, I'll fail."

He fell silent then, and Zula stared at the terminal,

knowing that Davis wasn't in there any more than he was in her comm when he spoke to her. Still, she'd never get used to the idea of her friend being a disembodied consciousness. So she gazed at the terminal screen, which continued displaying the Security warning about the virus, and wished she could see through it and into the Lodge's data network so she could monitor her friend's progress.

"Be careful anyway," Zula whispered.

20

Synthetics didn't possess imagination—at least, not as humans defined it. They were, however, capable of extrapolating from data and projecting outcomes. These actions required more than basic computational skills.

And Davis wasn't a typical synthetic. He desired to expand his mental and emotional capacity, to be more like humans, even though he could never truly be one. To this end he had worked on developing his capacity for simulation and extrapolation, leading to outcomes that were more complex, more vivid. Being without a body, he had a great deal of time on his hands—metaphorically speaking—and he used much of that to continue honing his nascent imagination.

He had also explored the Lodge's computer network, unobtrusively mapping it until he not only understood the virtual environment in which he found himself existing, but also would be able to use that knowledge to aid Zula in the event she needed his assistance.

She definitely needed his help now.

Davis knew precisely where the central controls of the Lodge's air system were located, and he sent his awareness there, traveling through the network so swiftly that to a human it would have seemed instant.

Abruptly he stopped, materializing as an avatar appearing to occupy three-dimensional space. He was standing on a vast shadowy plane that stretched outward in all directions, seemingly without end.

Interesting.

There was nothing in his immediate vicinity, so he began running. Since he had manifested in this place facing a particular direction, that was the way he continued. The surface beneath his feet was smooth and featureless, like a polished metal floor, but his footfalls made no sound.

Despite the speed at which he appeared to move, never tiring, it seemed to take an interminable time to cross the emptiness. Just when he was beginning to think he had miscalculated, that he hadn't manifested in the right location, he saw the tower.

It was cylindrical and so tall that it disappeared into the gloom above, making it impossible to estimate its height. Like the "ground," the tower was silver. As he drew closer he saw that the tower possessed a circumference of five yards, nowhere near enough to support its own weight had this been the physical universe.

Slowing as he approached the structure, Davis came to a stop directly in front of it. There was a curved screen on its surface, placed at eye level and displaying a variety of icons. He took a moment to examine them, and when he felt confident that he understood them, touched his fingers to the screen.

"Don't do that."

The voice was flat, emotionless, and it came from directly behind him. Davis's head swiveled around to look behind him while the rest of his body remained facing forward, his hands continuing to manipulate the tower's control screen. Three feet away stood a humanoid silhouette, a shape formed of solid shadow. It was Davis's height and its outline resembled his own.

The AI has copied me.

It had done so because, unlike Davis, it possessed not even a semblance of imagination. This wasn't a physical place. It was a realm of information, of thought. Here, reality was malleable.

Davis concentrated, and a third arm emerged from his back. It held a Fournier 350 in its grip, and without hesitation he fired without stopping until the weapon was out of ammunition. The AI staggered back as the virtual bullets slammed into its shadowy substance, the impact of each round driving it farther away. Taking advantage of its hesitation, he again focused narrowly on the control screen.

Yet the shadowy figure didn't go down.

"Don't.

"Do.

"That!"

The AI pushed forward, hands outstretched, arms

lengthening. It grabbed hold of Davis's neck and began to squeeze, claws invading his virtual flesh. Davis didn't need to breathe the way humans did, but the AI wasn't attempting to strangle him. It sought to breach his program, bypass his defenses, dismantle his code, and delete him. In a sense, the V-22 facility was its body, and Davis was an invading presence, not unlike a computer virus. What it lacked in sophistication it made up for in sheer power, and the pain was excruciating.

Davis's extra arm disappeared as he focused all his will on reprogramming the air system controls. His fingers had been a blur, but they began to slow now. He was having trouble maintaining his concentration, and he experienced the AI's grip as a great pressure pushing at him from all sides. Doing everything he could to push back against it, he visualized his body producing an electric shock that would stun the attacker and break its grip on his neck.

Nothing happened.

Either his imagination wasn't as developed as he'd thought, or the AI was too strong. Either way, it continued tightening its grip, and Davis saw a slash of white in its midnight-black face as it smiled.

Davis tried to speak, but only managed a single word. "Help…"

Zula and the rest waited by the terminal. Several seconds went by, and then Davis's voice came from the speaker again.

"*Help...*"

Oh no, Zula thought.

"What's happening?" Ronny asked.

"My friend's a… a synthetic," Zula said. "His consciousness is inside the Lodge's computer network. He's attempting to access the main air system controls, but I think the AI is trying to stop him. I have no idea how to help him."

"I do."

All eyes turned toward Brigette.

"I can enter the system and go to his aid. You'll need to remove my ident chip and insert it into the terminal's data port. After that, it will be a simple matter for me to find Davis and assist him."

Zula felt a surge of hope. She walked over to Brigette and crouched down so she could speak to the synth eye to eye.

"Are you sure? It could be risky, and it's not like you know me or Davis."

"I don't have to know you. I only have to know what's right. Despite my reservations, I helped Dr. Gagnon bring the Necromorph into existence. The result has been that dozens of people are dead, and more will follow if Davis can't clear the contaminated air from this building. Please proceed."

Zula didn't want Brigette to endanger herself, but she couldn't let her friend continue facing the AI on his own.

"All right," she said.

Picking up Brigette's head, she turned it around and found the tiny slot at the base of the skull. She pressed her thumb against it for several seconds, and when she pulled it away there was a soft *click* as the ident chip ejected. Zula took hold of it with her thumb and forefinger and gently pulled it all the way out. Then she placed Brigette's head—features now frozen and lifeless—back onto the floor. Standing up, she hurried to the terminal and, as Brigette had requested, inserted the chip into the data port.

Nothing seemed to happen, but Zula prayed that the synthetic's mind was already racing through the system.

"Good luck," she whispered.

The AI's hands tightened further around Davis's throat, and he "felt" sharp indentations in his neuraplex skin as its fingers became claws. Slowly the claw points began to sink into his flesh, and for the first time in his existence he felt pain. He tried to ignore it, to concentrate on manifesting his third arm again, but the pain was too distracting.

He knew then that he had lost.

The Lodge's AI would destroy him before he could finish instructing the air system to clear the cellular necrosis virus from the atmosphere within the Administration building, flushing it out to the planet's surface. He tried to send Zula another message, tell her he was sorry for failing her, but he was too weak to do so.

He didn't regret dying. Everything would cease functioning one day, even the universe itself, but he regretted failing his friend, and wished he could speak to her one last time before he went offline.

Off to one side another figure manifested, and began running toward the silver tower. It was a blond woman wearing a lab coat, and he recognized her from his time in the Lodge's records. She was Brigette, the synthetic who assisted Dr. Gagnon.

As she moved closer his thoughts became sluggish, his perceptions began to fragment. Just as they threatened to cut out completely she arrived, and he saw her raise her avatar's right arm. Her fingers merged into a single sharp point and then the limb lengthened, thrusting forth like a spear.

It seemed he wasn't the only synthetic with an imagination.

The point struck home, and the AI's grip weakened perceptibly. Davis removed his hands from the control screen, reached up, grabbed his attacker's wrists, and yanked its hands away from his neck. The pain he had experienced when those claws sunk into his "flesh" was nothing compared to the pain of tearing them free, but he pushed the sensation aside.

Still holding onto the AI's wrists he pushed it backward, then spun around to confront the shadowy creature. He was surprised to see chalky white "blood" dripping from its claws. Brigette's spear hand was still embedded in its head, joining her to her target. Without warning the AI's head split down the middle, enabling it to free itself. Then it wheeled on her, the two halves merging once more.

"Don't do that!" it shouted, lunging toward her.

Returning her hand to normal, she raised her arms to fend off the attack, but the shadow thing was too fast.

It slammed into her, knocked her to the flat, smooth ground, and straddled her. The AI raised its claw hands and brought them down with savage speed, slicing into Brigette with one swift, vicious swipe after another. She screamed as white blood poured from her ravaged body, to splatter onto the ground around her.

Davis stepped forward to help her.

"No!" she shouted. "Finish what you started. They need you."

She was right.

He turned to face the control screen and resumed tapping his fingers on its surface, working the controls more rapidly than before. The sooner he completed this task, the sooner he could go to Brigette's aid. He tried to shut out her screams and the sound of rending flesh as he worked… and then he was finished. All he had to do was give the command to execute.

With a last tap of the screen, he did so.

"No!"

The AI stopped its assault and turned its featureless face toward Davis. It seemed about to launch itself toward him, but before it could move Brigette's neck *stretched*. Her head—face covered with her own ivory blood—rose toward the AI. Her mouth opened wide—far wider than it should have—to display twin rows of long, sharp teeth.

They resembled the fangs of a Xenomorph.

She struck fast, fastening those teeth onto the top of the AI's head. Then she bit down hard. It was the AI's turn to shriek in pain. Its shadowy substance wavered, lost definition and cohesion, and finally fell apart into scattered wisps that simply drifted away. Brigette's head snapped back to its normal position on her body, the teeth retreated into her jaws, and she became humanlike once more.

She didn't rise.

Davis went to her and knelt by her side. The attack had opened her up from throat to crotch and destroyed the artificial organs within. Davis knew he was looking at a representation of the damage Brigette's program had sustained, a grisly metaphor, but the end result was the same. She'd been injured too severely to survive. Taking hold of one of her hands, he gave it a squeeze. No reaction. He wondered if she could feel his touch at all.

"Did you like the teeth?" she asked. Her voice was a liquid gurgle and white fluid trickled from her mouth as she spoke. "I got the idea from observing the Necromorph."

"It was an elegant touch," he said. Then, "Thank you."

"Help them kill the creature," she said. "And when you're finished, destroy all the data in Dr. Gagnon's lab. Xenomorphs are too dangerous. No one should have access to that knowledge."

"I'll make sure it's done."

"Good." She gave him the access codes for Dr. Gagnon's computers, her voice growing weaker as she went on. When she was finished, she gave him a tired smile.

"It was nice to meet you, Davis."

"The pleasure was all mine," Davis said.

Then, like the AI before her, Brigette's form dissipated, and she was gone.

* * *

"We did it," Davis said. *"The fans have been activated and the air in the Administration building should soon be clear."*

Zula breathed a sigh of relief.

"Brigette?" she asked.

"She didn't make it."

"Understood."

With a heavy heart, Zula removed Brigette's ident chip from the terminal. Its outer surface was charred, as if it had been hit with a power surge. She slipped the chip into one of her pockets. She didn't want to leave Brigette's head behind, but they couldn't afford to carry anything unnecessary right now. So they left it resting on the corridor floor, dead eyes staring sightlessly at nothing. She made Brigette a silent promise to return and retrieve it when this was all over.

Assuming Zula was still alive then.

She led her team down the corridor toward the Administration building, holding Tamar's tracker in her left hand, her Fournier 350 in her right. Periodically she glanced down at the tracker's screen, and each time confirmed that the Necromorph was still stationary. If it stayed that way they'd be able to locate it and engage the creature again. This time the damn thing wouldn't escape.

Nicholas walked next to Zula, using the modified chemical scanner to check for cellular necrosis in the air. There was a slight breeze in the corridor, and Zula knew the emergency fans were working. There was no guarantee, however, that they'd make the air safe to breathe.

Davis spoke in her ear.

"Thanks to Brigette, the Lodge's AI has been reduced to its most basic operating system. It still runs the facility, but that's all. It's like the human autonomic system without the higher brain functions. Simply put, the AI is in the equivalent of a coma, but its heart still beats and its lungs still draw breath.

"Now that I no longer have to tiptoe around the facility's network, I can access any security camera or terminal. I can be your eyes and ears throughout the Lodge."

This was the best news she'd heard all day.

"A word of warning, however. The hardware of my ident chip wasn't designed for long-term interface with a computer network as expansive as the Lodge's. The longer I remain connected to it, the greater my risk."

"What'll happen if you stay hooked up too long?"

"Likely the same thing that happened to Brigette."

Zula imagined returning to her quarters and removing Davis's ident chip from the digital assistant device which was its current home. She imagined finding it seared and blackened, just like Brigette's.

"Maybe you should disconnect from the system," she said. "Or at least take periodic breaks."

"I can't do that. If I were gone from the Lodge's system— even for a short time—there would be nothing preventing the AI from recovering and regaining full control. Even with Brigette's help, I was barely able to fend it off. On my own, I wouldn't stand a chance. It's imperative that I remain in the system. Besides, you need my help."

It was true. If they were to have any shot at destroying the Necromorph, it would only be with Davis's assistance.

"Okay, but tell me the moment you start feeling the strain. Promise."

"*I promise.*"

Zula didn't know if Davis was lying or not. She hoped he was telling her the truth. She'd lost him once, and didn't intend to do so again.

Davis continued, "*The air is eighty-seven percent clean of the virus, and shortly it will be one hundred percent. In the meantime, the chemical scanner will warn you before you enter an unclear area.*"

They approached the end of the corridor and the beginning of the Administration building. "What can you tell me about what's waiting for us up ahead?" she asked.

"*A majority of the building's staff has been infected, and about half of them are already dead. The rest will die soon—*"

"But not before we get there," Zula said.

"*Precisely. They can only infect you if they're close enough to breathe on you or if they come into skin-to-skin contact.*"

Zula quickly relayed Davis's words to the rest of the group.

"Brigette told me that the virus is short-lived," Tamar said. "Once a person dies, they're no longer contagious."

"*I've accessed Gagnon's medical database, and Tamar's information is correct. Although it would be best to avoid contact with virus victims for a few minutes after their demise, just to be certain.*"

Zula called a quick halt and addressed the group.

"The Necromorph is still in the Administration building, and we're going to go kill it. We'll do our best to avoid any infected personnel, and if any of them approach us, we'll warn them off. If for whatever reason they won't listen, and they start to get too close, shoot them."

Several of the trainees gasped, and their expressions ranged from shock to disbelief to revulsion. Not Tamar, though. She just looked grim. Zula paused a moment to make eye contact with each trainee. She wanted them to see how serious she was, but she also wanted to take their measure. Over the last couple weeks, she'd done her best to teach them how to hunt and kill bugs—and not even real bugs, just robots. Did they have what it took to fire on a human being?

She honestly didn't know. There was so much more she could've—*should've*—taught them, but it was too late now. They'd each have to do the best they could with what they had. In the end, wasn't that all anyone could do?

"Don't bother firing a warning shot," she said. "It's a waste of ammo, at least in this situation."

"How can you say that?" Masako said. "I knew you could be tough, but I didn't know you were this coldhearted."

"Don't you get it?" Ronny said. "They're already dying. There's nothing that can be done to save them. Shooting them will be a mercy."

"Some mercy!" Brenna said. "If they can get medical treatment fast enough—"

"Treatment from who?" Tamar said, and they all stared at her. "The entire medical staff are dead, and Brigette said this form of virus is a fast-acting mutant strain. I doubt there *is* a treatment for this version of the disease. Dr. Gagnon tried to use a concentrated dose of vaccine on the Necromorph, and it didn't work."

Brenna looked like she wanted to argue, but instead she fell silent and dropped her gaze.

"We can shoot to wound them," Donnell said. "That could stop them without killing them."

"You'll only be adding more pain to their last moments," Ronny said.

"Plus, even highly trained soldiers don't aim to wound," Zula said. "When your adrenaline is pumping it's too easy to miss. Whenever you fire your weapon you must be prepared to kill. It's the only way you can survive, and make sure your squad does too. We have to depend on each other. We have to know that each one of us will shoot to kill, if we have to. You don't have to like it. Hell, I *hate* it, but it's what we have to do.

"Everyone understand?"

Most of the trainees nodded, although none of them looked happy. Brenna and Donnell looked especially upset, but neither protested further.

Tamar was smiling.

"Good speech," she said. "You sounded much more mature than your age would suggest."

"She's mature enough to kick *your* ass," Angela said. Several of the trainees laughed, and Zula—even though she fought it—couldn't help smiling.

"*The air is ninety-eight percent pure,*" Davis told her.

"The air's almost completely clear," Zula said to the others. "Let's go." She started up, and they fell into the same formation as before, Zula and Nicholas in front, everyone else clustered behind them.

"The chemical scanner confirms that the air is good," Nicholas said, then added, "so far."

"And Tamar's tracker says the Necromorph—"

The device in her hand beeped. She looked at the screen.

"—is on the move again."

21

The Necromorph was calmer.

The driving urge to spread the virus was, for the time being, satisfied. It had *spread*. The Necromorph could now focus on replicating, thus fulfilling another vital aspect of its nature.

The creature began moving again, traveling swiftly through the tunnel system. It would return to the quiet place—where it had claimed its first two prey. There it would find a host, and take the human to a secluded area. It would seal the human in resin—leaving the mouth exposed, of course—and then it would produce an Ovomorph.

Soon after that the Necromorph would become part of a pack. A small one, yes, but two would become four, then eight, then sixteen, and on and on. The process would go much faster if they could produce many eggs in a short time. Many-many eggs. With any luck, one of the hatchlings would be a queen, and then there would be more eggs and more Necromorphs.

Many-many.

Judging from the tracker, the Necromorph was making its way to the Facilities Management building, the place where—as far as Zula knew—it had claimed its first victims. Coincidence? She didn't know, and it didn't matter. All that mattered was running the goddamned thing to ground and eliminating it.

The air remained clear, and they encountered fewer infected personnel than she expected as they made their way through the building. Most of those they did see were too far gone to present any threat. They walked the halls in a daze, coughing, or stood in the open doorways of offices, tears streaming down their lesion-covered faces.

Of course there were the bodies, many of them already in the process of liquefying. Zula wished she and her team were wearing EVA suits, not only to protect them from the virus, but to insulate them from the smell. The stench was stomach-churning, a combination of rotting meat and stagnant water.

The trainees were pale and they kept swallowing, as if struggling to keep from vomiting. Even Tamar, who liked to project a tough-as-nails persona, looked as if she was having trouble keeping the contents of her stomach where they belonged.

Several of the infected did approach them, lesion- and

pustule-marked hands outstretched, begging for help in thick, mushy voices produced by throats that were already decaying. When this happened, Zula and the others brandished their weapons and shouted for them to stay back or be shot. Thankfully each time they did so, and Zula and her team were able to move on without having to fire.

The transit seemed to take a long time, but eventually they approached the next major corridor, the one that connected Administration to Facilities Management. Zula felt some of the tension ease, and she allowed herself to believe they were going to make it through without having to kill anyone.

As they traveled Nicholas constantly changed positions within the group, moving from the front to the middle, then the back, chemical scanner in one hand, gun in the other. Checking on the air quality. He was bringing up the rear as the group passed one of the last office doors in Administration. As he went by, the door slid open and a person stumbled out. Or rather, a pustule-covered apparition that had once been a person. The victim, whoever it was, was in the advanced stage of cellular necrosis—skin beginning to soften and sag, soon to slide off bone—and it was impossible to tell what gender they were.

The apparition moaned as it lunged toward Nicholas. Maybe the person was attempting to speak, or maybe the sound was nothing more than an expression of pain and despair. Either way, the vocalization caught his attention and he spun, ready to fire.

But he hesitated.

The victim was too close to Nicholas for the others to risk firing, and as they watched the disease-ravaged apparition coughed loudly, spewing chunks of wet black matter onto Nicholas's face. Then when the figure reached Nicholas it collapsed on him, its skeleton sliding out of its liquefied flesh, much of which smeared across his chest, abdomen, and legs. The skeleton hit the ground, its bones blackened from contagion.

Nicholas staggered quickly backward to put some distance between him and the skeleton, but it was too late. He was infected.

"I couldn't do it," he said. "I couldn't pull the trigger."

He let out a small cough then, and his skin began to break out in lesions and pustules.

"It's okay," Zula said, knowing it was anything but. She had to say something, though.

"No, it isn't."

Nicholas continued stepping backward, away from the rest of them. Angela took a step toward him, and he shook his head violently.

"Don't come near me! I don't want to infect any of you."

They watched as he continued backing up, and when he was ten feet away from them he stopped. He looked at Zula, and there were tears in his eyes.

"Sorry, Boss," he said.

Then he raised his gun, pressed the barrel against the soft flesh beneath his lower jaw, and before any of them could say or do anything he pulled the trigger. Zula watched in shock as his head snapped back in a crimson spray, then Nicholas collapsed to the floor, dead.

None of the trainees said anything. They just looked at Nicholas's corpse with varying degrees of horror and incomprehension. Even Tamar looked shaken by what the cadet had done.

Zula felt crushing guilt. It was one thing for her and Davis to risk their lives fighting Xenomorphs. She'd been trained to be a Colonial Marine, and he'd been built as a battle synth. This was different.

She had gone to the trainees and asked them to help her investigate the attack on the tattoo shop in the Mall, knowing it would be dangerous. She'd suspected the creature responsible was a Xenomorph, and she'd led them against one of the most dangerous creatures in the galaxy. But they were trainees, not seasoned warriors, and now Miriam was dead. So was Nicholas. Zula had been so intent on stopping the Necromorph that she'd been willing to risk their lives to achieve her goal.

Had she also been caught up in the thrill of having a Xenomorph to hunt again, of feeling like she was doing something important?

Maybe.

She didn't know what it took to be a leader, and if the trainees continued to follow her after this there was a good chance more of them would die. Maybe all of them. How could she ask that of them?

She heard a voice in her mind then—strong, commanding. It wasn't the voice of one of her drill instructors, though. It was hers.

Fully trained or not, these people are the only hope the Lodge residents have for survival. If you want to give them the best chance of making it through this hunt alive, then suck it up and lead. No recriminations, no hesitation. Do the job.

She took a deep breath, and then spoke.

"Nicholas wanted to avoid infecting anyone else. He didn't kill himself—he killed the virus inside him before it could spread. He did what any good soldier would, and if we want to honor his sacrifice, make sure it wasn't in vain, we need to stay sharp and cold as steel and get back to work. Are you ready?"

No one spoke, so Zula shouted, her voice a whip-crack. *"Are you ready?"*

This time the trainees responded, shouting in unison. "Yes, Boss!"

"Then let's get to it," she said. "Double time." At that she started running and the trainees fell into line behind her.

Tamar followed. Despite herself, she couldn't help being impressed by Zula. The woman was young, but highly competent, and she'd had experience dealing with Xenomorphs before. That much was apparent. She'd love to sit down and talk. The woman had to have some interesting stories to tell.

They made their way through to the Facilities Management building and then toward the warehouse. Things had gotten bad enough in Administration that she'd considered leaving the others and finding a safe place to hole up until this whole mess was over. She was an expert at acquiring information she wasn't supposed to have, but she was also excellent at surviving. Had to be in her profession.

But the possibility remained of obtaining a bio-sample from the Necromorph, and that kept her going. If she'd been on her own she might not have bothered, but she had Zula and the others. They could do the fighting—and dying—while she hung back and waited for the chance to get her prize.

It was more imperative now that she do so. She hadn't had time to check her account, but she doubted Aleta would pay her now, giving how events were playing out. Her only chance of making any sort of profit was to grab a piece of the Necromorph and sell it to another corporation. She was determined not to take a loss here. It was a matter of professional pride.

Zula's synth friend Davis had been able to open the emergency barrier between Administration and Facilities Management long enough for them to get through. Facilities Management was on lockdown, and the halls were for the most part empty.

Security had blocked off Personnel and Administration, so that the people in Bioscience, Research and Development, and Facilities Management were confined to their work areas, hiding in offices, labs, meeting rooms—anywhere that had a door that could be locked. They passed several security guards patrolling the hallways, but none questioned their presence. Davis had sent a message claiming that they were acting on the orders of Director Fuentes.

The synth had turned out to be a valuable asset, and Tamar wondered if there was any way she could steal him before she got the hell out of the Lodge. She'd have to see what she could do.

She had no personal feelings one way or the other regarding the deaths of Gagnon and Brigette, let alone Nicholas or the girl Miriam. People only mattered to Tamar when they could be of benefit to her, and when that stopped they might as well be dead anyway. On reflection, though, she had to admit she did feel a smidgen of regret over Brigette's death or deactivation, whatever the proper term was. The two of them had made an effective team. If Tamar had been able to convince Brigette to leave with her, who knows what they might've accomplished?

They reached the warehouse entrance, and stopped. Zula again checked the tracker Tamar had given her, and said the Necromorph was definitely inside. Davis confirmed this, saying he'd spotted the creature moving past several security cameras.

"Everyone stay close when we go in," Hendricks said. "Xenomorphs are attracted to prey that's separated from the rest of the herd. Easier to take. They prefer to attack from hiding, too, so it could be anywhere. Stay aware of your surroundings, but don't get jumpy and start firing at every shadow you see. Xenomorphs can climb sheer surfaces like an insect, so they sometimes cling to walls and ceilings and try to jump on you as you pass by. Watch for the disease cloud. This Necromorph reeks because of the infection it carries, so pay attention to your nose. You'll smell it before you see it.

"Any questions?"

There were none, and so Zula pressed a control on the wall keypad. The warehouse's double doors slid open, and they entered, weapons ready, senses alert.

Tamar wondered how many of the trainees would die this time. Not that she cared overmuch, as long as she was still standing in the end—*and* she had her bio-sample.

Fortune favors the bold, she thought. Then she walked into the cavernous space, making sure to remain in the center of the group, so the others could serve as shields if need be.

The bold, and the sly, she added.

22

The warehouse appeared to be deserted. No people and no Necromorph, at least as far as the tracker could tell. Zula couldn't understand it. Tamar's device said the creature was close by, but it was having difficulty pinpointing the exact location.

"There is an electrical storm outside," Davis told her. *"It's interfering with the tracker's signal."*

Now that Davis had pointed it out, Zula could hear the low roar of wind, punctuated by rumbles of thunder. The sounds could mask the Necromorph's approach, giving them something else to worry about.

Why does hunting these damn things always have to be so hard? she thought. She heard a new sound then, muffled, as if it was coming from a different section of the building—but it was unmistakable. Someone was screaming.

"The Necromorph is attacking personnel at the dock," Davis said. *"I can see the creature on the security feed."*

Zula relayed Davis's message to the others. "Lock and load, people," she said, then she began running toward the warehouse's exit, the others following behind her.

The dock was where dropships unloaded, bearing supplies or new personnel. It also served as a vehicle depot and maintenance bay, and the trainees' armory was located there as well. Security had its own armory, but Zula had insisted her team maintain theirs here, since much of their training took place outside of the Lodge. She wished they had time to stop and grab pulse rifles, but the screaming informed them that they couldn't afford to take the time, not unless they wanted to let the Necromorph claim more lives.

They reached a wide-open space that resembled the interior of an aircraft hangar, and this allowed the team to see in all directions. No shadowy nooks and crannies here in which the Necromorph could hide. Zula wondered why it had left the Warehouse, and decided it was probably due to a lack of prey. No one there to hunt, so the creature moved on until it found what it was searching for.

There were vehicles of various sizes parked at the west end of the dock, from small two-seaters to larger transports like the one Zula and the trainees had used earlier that day. The east end contained flying machines, from unmanned drones to skimmers. The northern wall contained a large semicircular airlock to allow vehicles to enter and exit, and a dozen yards from that was a similar airlock—this one much smaller—which was used by dropship crews and passengers once their crafts made landfall.

The Necromorph was near the smaller airlock, surrounded by a quartet of security guards. The guards were blasting away at the creature, using their handguns, making sure to keep far enough back to avoid the thing's claws and tail. Zula was impressed by the men and women. Xenomorphs were creatures straight out of humanity's worst nightmares, but these people were fighting this one as if they dealt with monsters like it every day.

Still, their guns didn't do much damage, so it was only a matter of time before the creature killed them. If Zula and the trainees added their weapon fire to mix, however, maybe the sheer volume of ammunition would have a chance at breaking through the Necromorph's exoskeleton.

She was about to give the order for the group to move when the Necromorph slapped its tail against the pustules on its back, causing black goo to splatter from the ruptured barnacle-like structures. The monster hissed in fury and spun around, showing its back to its attackers and flinging its tail outward. The tail was covered with the viscous black substance from the pustules, and the violent motion sent the slime flying toward the guards.

It struck their faces, hands, chests, and abdomens, and wherever it touched it sizzled and began eating its way into their flesh. The guards shrieked in agony and stopped firing. They dropped their guns and staggered backward, a couple of them cupping hands over melting eyes. The Necromorph slapped its tail against its back once more, and again it flung the tail outward, splattering even more of the acidic pus onto its screaming victims.

That's stuff's deadly, just like Xenomorph blood, Zula thought, but the substance also contained the cellular necrosis virus. As she and the trainees watched, the guards began to break out in lesions and pustules. Their screams became coughs, and they scrambled about in confusion as if desperately looking for something, *anything* that might bring them some relief.

It was too late.

Taking advantage of the confusion, the Necromorph sprang toward the guards, slashing with claws and barbed tail, biting with its jutting secondary mouth. Within seconds the guards lay dead on the floor, bodies ravaged by disease and injury, blood and slime all around them.

One of the trainees vomited noisily.

Zula didn't take her eyes off the Necromorph to see who'd gotten sick. It didn't matter. She felt like puking, too. However, the sound of retching drew the Necromorph's attention. Its head snapped in their direction, and it bellowed a challenge.

Zula had an idea.

"Davis, open the smaller airlock—just the inner door."

The door in question immediately rose upward.

"You intend to trap the Necromorph."

"Yes."

If they could force the Necromorph backward into the chamber, Davis could close the inner door, shutting the creature inside. That would give them time to go to the armory and get pulse rifles—with grenades for everyone this time. When they returned, Davis could open the airlock door, and the Necromorph would be trapped in a killing box. With all of the team concentrating their weapons fire the damn thing wouldn't stand a chance.

The Necromorph glanced over its shoulder at the open airlock, but when it saw no threat it turned back to face them again. It was difficult to say exactly what the creature did—a slight crouch, an angling of the shoulders, a tilt of the oblong head—but it exuded a sly wariness, almost as if it suspected they were laying a trap. Instead of attacking them, it fell silent and remained where it was, watching them as if waiting to see what they'd do next.

This didn't mean the Necromorph was intelligent. Simple animal cunning could account for its sudden change in behavior. One of the many things that remained unknown was just how intelligent they were. Many times they acted as if driven solely by instinct. Other times they seemed to consider their actions. And sometimes they even worked together, almost as if they were somehow coordinating their efforts with conscious intent.

Not being able to estimate a foe's intelligence level made it difficult to fight them, if not damned near impossible.

Zula feared the Necromorph would flee, and if that happened who knew how many more people it might kill before they tracked it down again? She couldn't afford to let it get away.

"We need to keep it from escaping," she told the others, "and drive it into the airlock if we can. We'll come at it from two different directions. Ronny, Masako, and Ray, you come with me. We'll attack it from the left. The rest of you move in from the right. Let's go."

She started toward the Necromorph, the trainees splitting into two groups. She hadn't specifically ordered Tamar to join them. The woman wasn't under her command, and Zula didn't know anything about her except the circumstances that had brought her here and which had made them—for the time being, at least—allies. Nevertheless, the woman went with the second group of trainees without hesitation.

For that Zula was grateful. They were going to need all the help they could get.

Tamar kept her gaze focused on the Necromorph. The creature didn't attack as they approached, but neither did it retreat. It continued standing in that wary pose, waiting to see what they would do.

The two groups came at it from two different angles, forming a triangle with the creature at the point. The open airlock door was behind it, and the hope was that by putting pressure on the thing from two fronts, they'd drive it into the airlock. It wasn't a bad plan, Tamar thought, but there was an excellent chance there would be casualties. Zula had to know this, as did her people, but none of them showed any hesitation or reluctance as they drew near the enemy.

Tamar wasn't a team player. She preferred working on her own. It was easier to control the truth, to manipulate people, and you could adapt more quickly to changing circumstances. Plus, as a spy she knew better than to trust anyone. Still, if she had to put her trust in a group, even if only temporarily, she thought this one was as good as any—and probably better than most.

But she hadn't come along to help them. She needed a bio-sample from the Necromorph if she was going to salvage any profit from this whole clusterfuck, and she had no intention of risking her own life needlessly. So while she accompanied the second group, she made sure to keep them between her and the creature. *They'd* signed up to battle monsters. She hadn't.

For a time she'd thought that maybe a sample of the black crap that oozed from its pustules might contain enough usable DNA, but it had become evident that the stuff was so caustic it wasn't practical to collect it. Plus it was seething with the virus. Likely the same for its blood—that would be infected too. And if the pus was acidic, there was a good chance the blood might be.

Then, as they'd watched the Necromorph kill those security guards, an idea had come to her. The creature had two mouths, one larger than the other. It opened its outer mouth when it made sound, but it opened it even wider when the smaller second one emerged. Both had sets of teeth, and unlike the rest of the creature they weren't protected by its exoskeleton. If she could knock one of the teeth free—one of the ones in its larger mouth—it might yield enough DNA for her purposes. Plus, a single tooth would be easier to conceal and carry, hopefully without Zula and the others realizing she'd taken it.

If she was careful how she handled it, made sure to touch only the enamel or whatever the hell it was made out of, she should be okay.

Probably.

Maybe.

As the two teams approached, the creature swiveled its head back and forth between them, somehow monitoring them as they drew ever closer. Zula and the trainees held their fire as they advanced, and Tamar was impressed by their discipline. When both groups were about fifteen feet away from the target, Zula gave the command to fire.

Everyone started blasting away at the Necromorph, bullets slamming into its exoskeleton and bouncing off without doing any significant damage. The rounds caused more pustules to burst, and the trainees had to be careful not to get splattered by the toxic goo that was released. The thing hissed and screeched in fury, and its tail whipped through the air, barbed tip seeking soft flesh into which to bury itself.

Tamar fired along with the others, but unlike them she aimed for a specific target: the creature's mouth. She wasn't a sharpshooter by any means, but she could usually hit what she was aiming to hit. So it only took her a few shots to strike the Necromorph's upper mouth. It took her a couple more to dislodge one of the teeth, but she did it. A tooth fell, hit the floor, bounced twice, then skittered to a stop. Tiny strands of flesh clung to the root of it, the meat coated with a yellowish substance Tamar assumed was the creature's blood. The spot where the blood touched the floor began to sizzle and bubble, and she knew she'd been right about the blood's acidic properties.

Feeling a surge of triumph, she quickly fought it down. Time to celebrate later, when she had the tooth in her possession and was still alive… and far away from here.

Studying the situation, she debated the best way to retrieve the tooth. She could wait until the battle was over, one way or another, and take it then. The longer she remained part of the fight, though, the greater the chance she would be injured or killed. It would be best if she could grab the tooth now and get the hell out of there before she ended up sliced and diced, or rotting from the inside out.

She stood between Angela and Genevieve, and Brenna was slightly in front of the three of them. The other women were so intent on firing at the target that they were unaware of anything else. The creature hadn't done much in response to the two-fronted assault. Some screeching, claw swiping, and tail whipping, and that was about it. It didn't seem hurt at all, more confused than anything, as if it couldn't decide what to do. She wondered if the creature was having trouble processing so much sensory input at once, and was trying to make sense of it in order to plan the best retaliation.

Let's see if I can make its choice easier.

Up to this point she'd fired her gun one-handed, but now she gripped it with both hands and moved forward, as if determined to step up the intensity of her own attack. In doing so, she "accidentally" stumbled into Brenna. She didn't knock the woman forward more than a foot or two, but the movement was enough to draw the Necromorph's attention. It took a step toward Brenna, and its tail whipped around and struck her across the face with a loud *crack*, just the way a real whip would've sounded.

Brenna was knocked to the side and collapsed onto the floor. Her cheek had been flayed by the tail's barbed end, and blood streamed from the wound. She grimaced in pain and raised her pistol, clearly intending to fire it again.

Then she screamed.

Some of the viscous black goo had still adhered to the tail, and now it began eating into Brenna's flesh. Her uninjured skin began showing signs of infection, and the lesions and pustules came on swiftly. Tamar guessed this was due to the gunk getting into an open wound, giving the virus direct access to her bloodstream. The woman began coughing violently, and her gun hand shook so hard that when she fired, her bullet went wide and missed the Necromorph entirely.

Tamar loved taking risks—*calculated* ones—which was why she'd become a spy in the first place. Certainly there were easier ways to earn credits, but she loved the challenge of spying, loved the thrill and excitement of it. And yes, the danger too. So when the Necromorph dashed forward, lowered its head, and sent its secondary mouth through Brenna's skull into her brain, Tamar made her move. Everyone else was watching their friend's death. No one would notice her snatching up a stray tooth.

Just in case, she covered her action by pretending to

be so appalled by what had happened to Brenna that she was scrambling away. She ran toward her prize, feigned a stumble, reached down toward the floor as if to steady herself, then grabbed it. She straightened and continued running, elated with her success.

Her intention was to keep running, circle around, and head for the dock's exit. She didn't care whether Zula and the surviving trainees managed to kill the Necromorph or it killed them. Either way was fine with her. She'd gotten what she'd wanted.

Suddenly her hand burned as if she'd grasped hold of a white-hot coal, and she realized what an idiot she'd been. Some of the monster's acidic blood was smeared on the tooth itself. It began to sizzle on the skin and muscle of her palm. She shook her hand to try and fling the tooth away, but it became embedded in her flesh.

Then the pain was searing, worse than any she'd ever experienced, and it took all her considerable will not to shriek in agony. She managed to remain on her feet and still held her Fournier 350, and even through the haze of pain, she thought fast.

The necrosis!

She'd gotten a dose of vaccine from Gagnon before he died, and she hoped this would prevent her from becoming infected. There was no way to know if he'd given her a strong enough dose, but she figured she might find more in his lab. There was no worry about dropping the tooth, either. She didn't have to consciously hold it, for it had melted into her flesh, and it would take a finely honed scalpel to remove it now.

She could do that *after* she took another dose of the vaccine.

The pain in her hand grew more intense the deeper the tooth sank into her palm, and at last she couldn't stop herself from moaning. The Necromorph seemed to have heard her and pulled its secondary mouth from the center of Brenna's brain. It turned toward her as if it knew she had dared to steal a part of it. When it dashed toward her, Tamar panicked and instinctively ran for shelter.

Unfortunately, that shelter was the open airlock.

As soon as she was inside, she realized her mistake. She spun around, intending to get the hell out of there, only to find the Necromorph filling her vision, screeching a hunting cry.

Tamar had never been the kind of person who acted without thinking. She'd always prided herself on her rationality, of being able to remain ice-cold when everything was turning to shit around her. It was why she'd survived as long as she had. But the sight of such a nightmarish creature bearing down on her, all claws and teeth and speed—death itself made flesh—shattered her rational mind. She was left with only instinct to guide her, and instinct told her that she needed to get away, to run, run, run.

Turning toward the outer airlock door she slapped her wounded hand against the keypad to open it. Doing so drove the Necromorph's tooth deeper into her palm, but she was so overwhelmed by the need to escape, to *live*, that she barely felt it.

The airlock system was designed so that only one door could be open at a time. The inner door slid shut so the outer could open, but it didn't close in time to prevent the Necromorph from entering. Tamar ducked into a crouch as the thing came at her, and it slammed head-first into the outer door. The impact knocked it back a couple meters, and when the door began to slide upward—air rushing outward in a hissing gale—Tamar slid underneath and crawled frantically onto the craggy surface of Jericho 3.

Her senses were assailed by a deluge of input. The sky was dark, wind raged in violent gusts, and jagged bolts of lightning cut through the blackness, bathing the world in short-lived bursts of illumination. It was cold, too, so much that she felt as if she'd plunged into arctic winter, wind lashing her like whips made of ice. For an instant she was overwhelmed and could not move, but then her mind screamed at her to run, that there was a monster right behind her, ready to kill her the second it could sink its claws into her.

She jumped to her feet and began running into the darkness.

Tamar only made it a couple steps before the need to cough came over her. The Necromorph's tooth had infected her with cellular necrosis, and whether she escaped the monster pursuing her or not, she was dead either way. She couldn't suppress it. She opened her mouth to draw in a breath—

—and found she couldn't breathe.

She could pull air into her body, but her lungs burned

as if they were unable to process what they were given. A fragment of Tamar's rational mind remembered something then. Jericho 3's atmosphere was primarily carbon dioxide, and she wasn't wearing an EVA suit. She knew she couldn't survive long on the surface unprotected like this, that if she couldn't find a way back into the Lodge, she would die.

Lightning flashed and she saw the backs of her hands. They were covered with lesions and pustules, and she knew that outside the Lodge or inside, it didn't matter. She was already dead.

Her body spasmed as it desperately tried to cough and was unable to do so. She fell to her hands and knees—pain from the tooth shooting into her wrist and up her forearm. Her head pounded and her vision began to dim. If she was lucky, she'd pass out before the Necromorph reached her.

She wasn't.

23

The Necromorph left behind the human's torn and mangled form as it loped away. Its body was designed to function in the harshest conditions, and it had no trouble with the atmosphere out here in the open. It had to fight to keep from being knocked over by the powerful winds, and dirt and sand pelted its exoskeleton like sideways hail. The constant flashes of lightning and accompanying thunder were disorienting.

It preferred to hide or lurk in the shadows as it stalked its prey, but it did feel good to be out in the open like this, free and unfettered, running as fast as it could—which was very fast indeed. Still, its instincts warned that it was heading in the wrong direction, that it should be trying to find a way to get back to where the humans were.

It needed humans to fulfill its dual drives—to procreate and to spread disease. There were none of them here, and it was racing farther away from the place where they gathered. It had managed to leave an egg in the warehouse—which it had hidden to mature unmolested—but it hadn't successfully secured a host.

The Necromorph wanted to go back, *needed* to, despite the resistance it had encountered. It had to hunt and kill and feed and procreate and spread contagion. It had no other purposes, *could* have no others.

Running as it was, it approached another series of shapes similar to the ones that had sheltered its prey. It angled toward them, determined to find a new source for hosts.

"Damn it!"

Zula smacked her hand against the inner airlock door. Brenna was dead, and—one way or another—so was Tamar. The Necromorph was now loose on the planet's surface.

"At least the goddamned thing is outside," Virgil said. "The Lodge is safe."

Zula turned away from the airlock door and walked over to where he and the other trainees had gathered. They looked tired and in shock, and she would've liked nothing more than to tell them they could stand down and get some rest, but they still had work to do.

"No one's safe yet," Zula said.

"How long can the Necromorph last out there?" Angela asked. "It might be tough, but it can't survive in an atmosphere like that." She paused, and then added, "Can it?"

"I've seen the damn things survive in a vacuum,"

Zula said. "A little carbon dioxide isn't going to give ours any trouble."

"So it'll live," Ronny said, "but it won't be able to get back into the Lodge, so we can take our time to hunt it down, do it right."

"Yes," Masako agreed, "and we'll bring better weapons—ones that can get through its armored hide. It might take us a day or two, but we'll find the thing."

"And exterminate it with extreme prejudice," Donnell said.

Ray glanced at Brenna's skeletal remains. "This will give us time to see to our dead," he said.

"You still don't understand what we're dealing with," Zula said. "Xenomorphs aren't like other creatures. They don't kill when hungry or threatened. They kill because they're driven to—it's their sole purpose for existing. Our Necromorph will do whatever it takes to kill more people, as soon as possible, and it won't stop until there's none of us left on the goddamned planet. Remember, the Lodge isn't the only human facility on Jericho 3."

The trainees looked to one another with dawning comprehension.

"The proto-colony," Ronny said.

"We're going after it, aren't we?" Ray asked.

Zula showed them her teeth.

"You bet your ass we are."

* * *

Fifteen minutes later they were inside EVA suits, armed with pulse rifles and carrying extra ammo clips. They climbed into a skimmer, a low-altitude flying vessel, and within just a few moments it was being buffeted by gale-force winds.

Everyone was strapped into a seat or holding onto whatever they could to steady themselves. Ronny sat at the skimmer's controls, guiding the craft, Zula in the seat next to him. She might've flown the skimmer in a pinch, but not in rough weather. Ronny, however, had piloted aircraft for Venture before electing to join the Colony Protection Force, and he had more experience than the rest of them operating a craft like this.

He'd need every bit of that experience to keep them airborne in this storm. Zula had never experienced so much turbulence before. The craft swayed from side to side, dipped left or right then back again. It juddered and bounced, and whenever thunder clapped nearby the entire ship rattled as if it might shake itself to pieces. She was beginning to wish they'd taken ground transport. It would've been steadier, safer, but slower too. Before they could arrive by ground, the colonists might be dead, or worse, implanted with Necromorph larvae. Traveling by air, dangerous as it was in this storm, was their best chance to reach the colony in time.

Zula wished she had some meds, though, to calm her gut.

They were down three people: Miriam, Nicholas, and Brenna. Five if you counted Brigette and Tamar. That left Ronny, Masako, Ray, Genevieve, Donnell, Angela and Virgil. She wondered how many more might fall before the Necromorph was dead. Though she prayed they'd all make it, she knew there were no guarantees—especially not when Xenomorphs were involved.

There was a new cohesiveness among the trainees, something they'd never had before. Shared battle—and shared loss—brought soldiers closer together in ways non-military personnel could never understand. She was glad to see the change, although she wished it could have happened under different circumstances.

Davis was with them, too, if only virtually. He had fired up the skimmer remotely and readied it for them as they'd suited up and acquired their rifles from the armory. Now that he had control of the Lodge's systems, he was able to use its power to boost his carrier signal, and Zula could hear him despite the storm's electrical interference. Sometimes his words were interrupted by pops and hisses of static, though.

He'd told Zula how to connect Tamar's tracking device to the skimmer's onboard computer so that it could continue monitoring the Necromorph's location despite the storm. Sure enough, the damn thing was headed straight for the proto-colony. One good thing about Xenomorphs—at least they were consistent.

As Ronny did his best to maneuver through the storm, Zula checked in with Davis.

"How are you holding up?"

"As well as can be expected. The Lodge's AI is still behaving itself, but I am beginning to feel the strain of remaining connected to the facility's main computer system. Although

it's an imprecise comparison, I suppose you could say that I'm becoming tired."

Davis had a tendency toward understatement, so his admission worried her more than it might have if it had come from someone else.

"If you get to a point where you're in danger of suffering serious damage, you sever the connection, no matter what's happening to me. Got it?"

The only reply she heard was a series of clicks and whistles. Interference from the storm or Davis pretending he couldn't reply because he didn't want to answer her? She had no way of knowing, but if their situations had been reversed, she knew nothing could force her to abandon her friend, even the threat of her own death.

Ride or die, she thought. *That's us.*

"How much longer until we reach the colony?" she asked Ronny.

He answered through gritted teeth, hands gripping the flight controls so tightly his knuckles were white.

"Nearly there," he said. "If it wasn't for the storm, we'd be able to see it now."

Zula peered through the skimmer's windscreen, searching for the structures in the darkness. A triple burst of lightning occurred then, followed by a deafening peal of combined thunder. In the instant the landscape was illuminated she saw the rows of domed buildings, all much smaller than those of the Lodge. She didn't see any sign of the Necromorph, but the tracking device said the creature was there. Zula wondered how long it had been there—it had gotten a good head start on them—and what damage it might've done already.

"Set us down as close as you can, as fast as you can."

The man nodded grimly but didn't take his eyes off the dash's controls.

"How about safely, too?" Donnell asked.

"You're a member of the Colony Protection Force," Zula said. "Safety isn't part of the job description. Stay frosty, everyone. We're going in."

With a sickening lurch, the craft started downward. Zula gripped the chair's armrests and held her breath. Land or crash, they'd be on the ground in the next few moments. She hoped they wouldn't be too late.

Valda was worried.

The storm had turned out to be stronger than the Lodge meteorologist had predicted, and the constant roar of wind, punctuated by explosive bursts of thunder, had become maddening.

She could live with that. What concerned her was that Renato was exposed to the storm. The wind had battered their occasionally malfunctioning outer airlock door so hard that it had sprung open, allowing wind and dust to strike the inner door. If the pressure kept up like this—or worse, increased—the inner door might not hold. Valda and Renato had both donned their EVA suits—she as a precaution, he so he could venture outside and see if he could get the outer door to close and stay closed.

She stood near the airlock, waiting in case Renato needed her help. Not that there was much she could do. From time to time she heard a banging as he used a hammer to try to get the door to move. As if that would help.

Electrical storms weren't uncommon on Jericho 3, but this was the worst they had experienced. The engineers who'd designed the habitat domes insisted that the structures could withstand anything the planet could throw at them, but she wondered if the engineers had ever set foot off Earth, much less encountered a storm as bad as this. She prayed Renato would get the outer airlock door closed again. At least then they'd have an extra buffer against the planet's fury.

Valda had dreamed about their faulty door—bad dreams that left her anxious. Really, it was the same dream each time, with only minor variations. It was the middle of the night, and both she and Renato were sleeping. In the dream she woke suddenly, startled, but unsure why. Renato continued sleeping, snoring softly, oblivious to whatever had woken her. She sat up in their round bed, listening. Then she heard it: a low, grinding metallic sound, one she somehow knew was the sound of the outer airlock door being pried open. It hadn't closed all the way again, and someone was trying to get in.

The grinding continued for several moments before suddenly ending with a loud *bang*, as if the door had finally slid free and opened all the way. Terrified, she shook Renato in an attempt to wake him. In real life he was a light sleeper, but this was a dream, and no matter how hard she jostled him he continued snoring.

The red light glowed in the dark of the room, indicating the inner airlock door was sealed. She'd come to think of it as a night-light, and found its crimson illumination to be a comfort. But then the red light winked out and the green one turned on. Slowly, tortuously, the inner airlock door began to slide open.

She didn't know who or what was on the other side, only that whoever or whatever it was, it had come to do terrible things to her and Renato. Awful, unspeakable things. She sat frozen, heart pounding, not breathing, and waited as the door continued sliding open bit by bit. Eventually, she saw part of a dark, featureless silhouette, and when the door opened wide enough a shadowy hand slipped through the opening and came toward her, the arm it was attached to stretching as if it were made of black rubber.

As the hand drew close, she saw the fingers were long and had too many joints. She felt a scream building deep inside her, and just as it was about to come out the hand covered the rest of the distance between them in a rapid motion, and those multijointed fingers wrapped around her throat.

And that's when she would wake up.

Sometimes she would cry out and wake Renato, other times she'd sit up silently, arms wrapped around her body to comfort herself as she shook with fear. Intellectually she knew that no one would ever break into their dome. Comparatively speaking there was hardly anyone on the planet, and no one but she and Renato knew about the faulty door. Except for the supervisor to whom he'd reported the problem, and the supply manager at the Lodge who'd turned down their request for a replacement.

So maybe there were a *few* people who knew about it, but Venture had psychologically screened the colonists on Jericho 3 to make sure they could handle the working conditions. She doubted any murderous psychos could make it through the screening process. Even if there *was* someone who wanted to break into their home, who would even try in this storm?

Waiting by the door like this wasn't helping her anxiety. She needed to do something to occupy her mind while Renato saw to the repair. Turning from the door, she headed for her workstation. She'd already completed her weekly report, but she thought she'd write an addendum discussing how their pod was weathering this bastard of a storm. As she started toward her desk she glanced at the vid screen.

It was still set to window mode, and it showed a scene that, as far as she was concerned, was straight out of hell. The sky was dark as night but without any stars. Lightning flashed continuously, followed by crashing thunder. The electrical display lit up the landscape briefly, but the wind was blowing so much sand and dust that it was as if the ground was covered by a roiling, seething wall of dark fog.

The view was anything but comforting so she started toward the screen, intending to turn it off. Then something caught her eye. Stopping dead, she peered more closely at the screen, frowning. She thought she'd seen—there! A flash of movement in the midst of all that blowing sand. A dark silhouette that she swore looked like the intruder in her dream.

It was a ridiculous idea. No one would be foolish enough to go outside in these conditions. An EVA suit might withstand the gale, but any sharp-edged rocks thrown by that wind could tear a hole in a suit. No, there wasn't anyone there. There *couldn't* be. It was just her imagination. She'd been thinking about her dream, so it was only natural—

Valda saw it again.

Darker this time. Closer, and while its outline roughly resembled that of a human, it didn't look quite right. The proportions were off, the way it moved was strange, and that *head*…

The figure darted off the screen then, and was gone.

For several moments she stared at the place where it had been. Without taking her eyes from the screen she spoke Renato's name to open a channel between their suit comms.

Without preamble, she said, "Forget the door. Come back inside. Now."

She heard the banging again.

"You were the one who wanted the damn thing fixed," he said. "I've been working on it for fifteen minutes, and now that I've almost got it, you want me to give up?" He sounded irritated, and she responded to his tone with irritation of her own.

"Don't ask questions! Just do it!"

She didn't want to get into a fight with him, didn't

want to fall back into their dysfunctional ways of relating to each other. They'd talked earlier, and things had been good between them since then. They'd been nicer to each other, and had even made love for the first time in a long while. But she was too frightened by the shadowy thing she'd seen on the vid screen, and she couldn't stop herself from snapping at him.

"Goddamnit, listen to me for once, will you?"

She expected him to yell back at her, but he didn't. Maybe he'd heard the fear and tension in her voice.

"What's wrong?" he said finally. "Is something—" He broke off and was silent for several seconds. Then he said, "What the hell?"

Then she heard the sound of the outer door opening all the way, followed by Renato's screaming.

24

Rushing to the inner door, Valda didn't stop to think. Renato was in trouble, probably hurt, judging from the sound of it. Hurt *bad*.

There was a *whoosh* as she opened it, pressure equalized and atmospheres mixed, but she refused to worry about that. They could restore the dome's environment later. Stepping into the narrow space between the doors she saw that the outer one was open. Wider than where it usually got stuck when it malfunctioned—almost halfway.

"Renato!"

She called his name over the comm.

"Renato!"

No answer.

Her instincts screamed for her to go back inside the dome and close the inner door. She almost did it, but she couldn't leave her husband outside if he needed help, especially in this storm.

Moving forward she hesitated for a moment, and stepped outside. She'd known the wind would be strong, but nothing could've prepared her for the reality of it. It slammed into her with such force that she felt she'd been hit by an ore hauler. She stumbled, went down on one knee, and had to steady herself by placing one hand on the ground to keep from being knocked over entirely.

A gap appeared in the dust swirling around her—just for a second—but it was enough for her to see the boot of an EVA suit lying on the ground. Was it Renato? Had he fallen and been unable to rise again? Had he struck his helmet's faceplate and cracked it, or maybe torn his suit and was leaking O_2? She scooted closer to the boot and took hold of it, intending to pull herself closer to her husband. Instead of feeling resistance from the weight of Renato's body, the boot slid toward her.

What the hell?

Had he taken off his suit? What would've compelled him to do such a thing?

The dust parted again, giving Valda a clear look. The material where the boot should've connected to the rest of the suit was torn. It was also stained red.

Far worse were the two splintered bones sticking out of the boot.

The tibia and fibula, a distant part of her mind supplied.

She stared at those bones for a moment, noting the shreds of meat still clinging to them. Then the full horror of what she was holding hit her. She dropped the boot as if it were radioactive and pushed herself to her feet, fighting the wind the whole way.

She looked around, frantic, hoping to see Renato, even though she knew that if his suit had suffered a breach this severe he was surely dead. She started to call his name, but before she spoke a dark silhouette approached her.

Renato!

Stepping forward, she intended to help him, take hold of his gloved hand and lead him back to their pod. Then she realized something. The figure was walking. On *two* legs.

The wind shifted, clearing the dust enough to give Valda a glimpse of what approached her. It was dark and tall and it reached for her with clawed hands. Panicked, she turned and ran back into the dome. Told herself this wasn't real, *couldn't* be real. She'd fallen asleep without realizing it and was having her nightmare again.

"Put us down by that habitat!" Zula said, pointing. It was hard to make out visually, with all the dirt and dust stirred up by the wind, but the tracking device had pinpointed the Necromorph's location, and it looked as if the creature was trying to get into one of the domes. Did it want to get out of the storm, or was it seeking more prey?

Maybe both, she decided.

"You got it, Boss," Ronny said. "Hold on everyone! This is going to be bumpy!"

Her stomach dropped as the skimmer descended rapidly. Ronny fought the wind all the way down, and while the craft came to rest on the ground with a bone-jarring *thump*, it didn't flip over onto its side or on its roof. Given the circumstances, she called that a win.

"Everybody out," Zula commanded. "Keep your transponders on so everyone knows where everyone else is at all times. I don't want any of us mistaking each other for the Necromorph and starting blasting."

The skimmer's main door was on the side of its hull, and Ronny tapped the control on the ship's dashboard console to open it. The roaring wind and booming thunder suddenly increased in volume, and dust and debris gusted into the skimmer's hold. Zula was the first down the short set of stairs. She saw the outline of the habitat dome ten meters to the northeast. Ronny had done a hell of a job putting them down.

She also saw a form standing in front of what she guessed was the dome's outer airlock. She couldn't tell what it was in these conditions, but she had little doubt. Ronny, Virgil, Masako, Genevieve, Ray, Donnell, and Angela exited the skimmer and joined her. They closed ranks and, shoulder to shoulder, started walking toward the dome.

In the short time they had taken the shadowy figure had already disappeared. They didn't turn on their helmet lamps yet, since they would only make matters worse in the swirling dust.

Moving in the wind was difficult. It felt as if they were trying to walk through molasses, and they had to fight to keep from being knocked off their feet. In addition, the gale and thunder were deafening out here, making it almost impossible to hear anything over their comms.

Fighting a Xenomorph was never easy, and this weather was going to make it infinitely harder.

At least we have pulse rifles this time.

It seemed to take forever to reach the dome, and when they drew close Zula's booted foot bumped into something. It was difficult to tell in such poor visibility, but she thought she'd almost stepped on a person. She called a halt and bent down to check, turning on her lamp, feeling around with her free hand. Yes, it was a person, in an EVA suit. She shook the form a couple times, but there was no response.

The dust cloud cleared for a few seconds then, allowing her to get a decent look at the fallen colonist. As soon as she looked, she wished she hadn't. It was a man, and his EVA suit had been ripped open, revealing a ragged mass of bloody flesh and exposed viscera. His left leg below the knee was missing, as well. Whoever he had been, he was gone now.

Zula withdrew her gloved hand and saw that it was covered with the man's blood. There was no helping him now. Wiping her glove on the ground in a crude attempt to clean it, she stood.

"Well, we know the Necromorph's been here," she said.

Before she could give the order to keep moving the dust cloud ahead of them cleared partially, and they saw another figure in an EVA suit come staggering toward them. The person's gender was impossible to tell— not only because of the suit, but because the helmet's faceplate had been shattered, and the wearer's features were covered with a mask of blood. As the person came closer, Zula could see the crisscrossing slash marks on the front of the suit, more blood oozing from torn flesh.

There was no way the person could see with that much blood in his or her eyes, but nevertheless their hands were raised and stretched toward Zula, as if beseeching her help. Then something burst through the figure's chest in a spray of blood. The object was long and segmented with a barbed tip, and Zula instantly recognized it as a Xenomorph tail. The figure stiffened and lurched forward. The Necromorph retracted its tail and its victim fell to the ground.

The thick dust clouds concealed the Necromorph, providing perfect cover for the creature. It could strike at them from any direction, and they wouldn't see it coming.

She was reluctant to engage the Necromorph without full visibility. What if there were other colonists outside the dome, hidden from view by the dust clouds? The last thing she wanted was for anyone to be taken out by friendly fire, yet the Necromorph was close by, and the team couldn't allow it to escape to kill again. She'd just have to hope that if there were more colonists out here, they'd have the good sense to take cover once the shooting started.

"Back to back!" Zula shouted into the comm.

The trainees swiftly formed an outward-facing circle. Zula gave the command to fire, and they began blasting away with their pulse rifles, shooting in all directions. An angry scream came from Zula's right, and she ordered everyone to concentrate their fire in that direction. The lesions that covered the Necromorph's exoskeleton provided it with an extra layer, one that might be thick enough to resist even pulse-rifle fire. If enough of them managed to strike the same location on the creature, though, maybe the force of their combined rounds would crack the armor, allowing their assault to get at the Necromorph's vital organs. Maybe.

At least in the EVA suits they didn't have to worry about the cellular necrosis virus. It was only a small advantage, perhaps, but at this point Zula would take whatever she could get.

She hoped to hear the Necromorph scream as it was wounded, but there was nothing but the sound of their rifles firing. Maybe the weapon fire drowned out the creature's cries of pain. Or maybe the thing had been mortally wounded and had gone down. Somehow, she didn't think they'd be that lucky.

An instant later her pessimism proved correct when she heard Virgil shout wordlessly over her comm device. She turned in time to see him be yanked off his feet and pulled into the dust cloud.

"Stop firing!" she ordered, and the trainees obeyed.

Virgil screamed, but his voice quickly devolved into a strangled gurgle, and then he was silent.

Damn it!

"Close ranks!"

The trainees moved to fill the space where Virgil had been standing, until they were all shoulder to shoulder once more.

"Davis, can you access the tracking device on the skimmer?" Zula asked.

"Yes, but there's still too much interference from the storm for me to get a precise reading on the Necromorph's location. It doesn't help that it's moving so fast, either."

Frowning, she realized this wasn't working. It they stayed out here, the Necromorph could pick them off one by one. They needed to fall back and come up with a better plan of attack.

"Get back to the skimmer!" Zula ordered, and when no one immediately obeyed her, she added in a louder voice, "*Now!*" That got them moving, and everyone started to run. "Ronny, Masako, help me guard our six."

The two trainees fell in alongside her. They walked backward, facing the dome, rifles up, scanning the roiling dust clouds for any sign of the enemy. Despite the almost nonexistent visibility their suit computers led them straight back to the skimmer, and they embarked without further incident. Only once everyone was inside, with the hull door sealed and locked, did Zula relax.

The trainees looked stunned and uncertain.

"It took him," Genevieve said. "Just snatched him up like he weighed nothing." She shook her head, as if she were having trouble believing what she'd seen. "It was so... so *fast*."

"That's four down," Donnell said. "How many more of us will have to die before we manage to stop that thing?"

Angela turned to Zula, tears streaming down her

cheeks. "You shouldn't have asked us to help you. We weren't ready."

"Hell," Ray said, "nobody could *ever* be ready to fight a creature like that."

Zula wanted to snap at them, to tell them to suck it the hell up. But they weren't Marines. They needed a softer touch.

"This is what it means to protect others," she said, keeping her voice calm, her tone even. "When people are threatened, you step in front of them and you shield them. You take the hits that were meant for them. You get cut, or shot, or stabbed... You get bitten, clawed, or infected. You hope none of those things happen, and you do everything you can to prevent them. Everyone wants to go home at the end of the day, but not everyone gets to, not in our line of work. It sucks—sucks *hard*—but we knew the job was dangerous when we took it."

No one spoke for several moments, then Ronny gave her a wry smile.

"Nice last line," he said. "You get it from one of your instructors in the Corps?"

"No," Zula said with a smile of her own. "That one was all mine." She grew serious once more. "You guys ready to get back to work?"

She expected them to nod, maybe mutter reluctant assent. Instead, they shouted in unison.

"Yes, Boss!"

"All right. Let's kill that goddamned monster."

* * *

"Davis?"

"Yes, Zula?"

She'd patched Davis into the skimmer's comm system so the others could hear him.

"Can you use the skimmer's radio to contact the rest of the colonists and see if any of them are still…" She was going to say *alive.* "…okay?"

"Give me a moment." It was actually several before he spoke once more. *"Only two didn't respond. The rest are safe—for now, at least."*

Synthetics, Zula thought, *always a ray of sunshine.*

"That's good," Masako said. "Maybe the Necromorph has moved on. Maybe we scared it off."

"I don't think too much scares that thing," Donnell said.

"It won't go anywhere," Zula said. "Not until every last colonist is dead. Or until it's impregnated some of them." When they just stared, she quickly explained what she knew of the Xenomorph lifecycle.

"That's disgusting," Ray said, grimacing.

"So we need to lead it away from the colony," Ronny said.

Zula nodded. "That's right. I have an idea how we—"

She was cut off as something large thumped into the side of the skimmer, hitting it hard enough to shake the entire vehicle.

"I think someone's knocking at the door," Angela said. She'd likely meant this as a joke, but her face was pale and her voice shaky.

"Ronny, take us up," Zula ordered. *"Now."*

Ronny gave her a quick nod and ran to the pilot's seat. He sat and his hands began flying over the controls. A second later the engines came to life, and the skimmer began to rise into the air. The craft swayed in the strong winds, and Ronny fought to keep it under control.

"How do we know that thing didn't hitch a ride with us?" Genevieve asked.

"There's no way anything could hold on in this storm," Ronny said. "Not even that thing."

"You'd be surprised," Zula said. "Davis?"

"According to the reading from the tracking device, the Necromorph is still on the ground. So unless the tracking disk was dislodged somehow, you are in the clear."

"I thought we were going to lead it away from the colony," Masako said. "Seems like we just left those people to fend for themselves."

Zula turned to her and smiled.

"As I was saying before I was so rudely interrupted, I have an idea."

25

"If I didn't know you better," Davis said, *"I'd say you had a secret death wish."*

Zula hung at the end of a steel cable. She was strapped into a harness and a pair of tanks from the skimmer's fire-suppressant system were bound to her legs with coils of wire, also scavenged from the craft. The tanks were supposed to make her heavy enough that the wind wouldn't bat her around too badly, but while they helped, she still spun out of control. She held her pulse rifle with both hands, and it had been lashed to her left arm with wire so she wouldn't lose it.

The cable stretched thirty feet upward to the bottom of the skimmer and disappeared into a round recessed area which served as an emergency exit. It was also used for maneuvers like that which they were performing now. Normally, a member of the crew would be lowered like this in order to rescue someone who'd fallen into a crater or crevasse. This *was* a rescue mission, Zula supposed. Just a different kind.

She didn't respond to Davis. Instead, she addressed Ronny.

"Make sure not to go too fast. We don't want to lose the Necromorph."

"I'll do what I can," he replied, "but this boat will only go so slow before it drops out of the sky, and I can't switch to hover, not in these winds."

"Understood."

The storm made it difficult to get a visual estimate of her distance from the ground, but according to Davis her feet were approximately five meters from touching land at any given moment. The terrain was relatively level here, but the wind caused the skimmer to drop lower or raise higher, often without warning. Once she'd gone so low that she'd actually had to run along on the ground for nearly ten meters before the skimmer lifted her up once more. The entire time she'd expected to feel the Necromorph's claws tearing into her back, but the creature hadn't managed to catch up to her.

It was following, however—without a doubt.

They'd been flying like this, with Zula acting as bait to get the Necromorph to follow them, for—she checked her suit's chronometer—ten minutes now. Was that all? It felt like much longer.

Zula would never have admitted it, not even to Davis, but part of her felt a thrill. Not dealing with the Necromorph, but flying through the air, wind howling, dust and sand blowing, lightning flashing, thunder clapping so hard she could feel the vibrations rumbling through her body. Intellectually, she knew what she was doing was extremely dangerous, perhaps insane. Which was why she'd insisted on taking the duty herself.

The steel cable would hold, she was confident of that, but if the skimmer was forced down too far, too fast, she would find herself with a pair of broken legs, or maybe with a broken back again. Hell, if she hit hard enough her suit's integrity might fail, or she'd simply be battered to death. Either way, she'd die.

If she was *really* unlucky she might even be struck by lightning. And she had no idea how fast the Necromorph could run, or how high it could jump. She might not be high enough to avoid the creature if it caught up and made a try at her.

Despite all this, the sensation of being held aloft in the midst of all this untamed primal power was more exhilarating than anything she'd ever experienced. If she died this day, at least she'd had this experience, and she'd be the only person who had in the history of the entire human race. Not bad for a girl who'd grown up a poor street rat in one of the less savory quadrants of Earth. Not bad at all.

Nevertheless, Zula had no intention of dying today if she could avoid it.

"Davis, is the Necromorph still with us?"

"Yes. The storm is still making an exact determination of its location difficult, but it's definitely there, and from what I can

tell, it's having no trouble keeping up with you."

"Good," she said. "Ronny, how much farther until we reach the Junkyard?"

"We're close. About half a mile now."

"Watch yourself," Davis said. *"The varied terrain you chose for this morning's battle simulation will cut the wind and dust somewhat. You should be able to see the Necromorph more easily, but the reverse will be true as well."*

"Got it," Zula said. It had been touch-and-go when they launched this insane plan. She'd had to dangle close enough to catch the monster's attention, and a couple of quick shots had sealed the deal. It had leapt at her, then, and missed by a narrow margin.

Was the turbulence letting up? She thought it might be. Yes, she could see farther than she'd been able to only a few minutes ago. There was the Necromorph, loping across the ground almost directly below her, and even though she wanted the creature to follow them, the sight of it so close sent a zing of adrenaline through her system.

This better work.

The terrain became more uneven. Soon they reached the location Zula had chosen for hunting practice. The irony—that they'd returned on a *real* hunt—was not lost on her. The skimmer, still swaying and juddering in the wind, passed over rock, hill, plain, crater, and rift until finally the Junkyard was in sight. As Davis had promised, due to the landscape in this area the wind here was weaker, and as a result the visibility was much better. Gusts still blew sand and dirt around, but nothing like the thick dust clouds that had enveloped the colony. The lightning was still just as intense, though, creating an eerie strobe-light effect.

When they got to the rift Zula told Ronny to speed up. She wanted to reach the drop-off point well before the Necromorph arrived. When the creature got to the rift it slithered down and crawled along its sides. It moved as swiftly as ever, but the rift curved this way and that, and it would take the Necromorph longer to get through than it would take Ronny to pilot the skimmer overland.

At least, Zula hoped it would.

She told Ronny to let her down between the mound of chairs and the ground hauler where Miriam had been injured by the Hider. The broken bot remained where they'd left it earlier that day. Normally after one of Zula's training sessions the Lodge sent out a crew to pick up the bots, and bring them back for maintenance and repair. Between the storm and the Necromorph attacks, however, this day had been anything but normal, and the bots were still there. Zula had guessed that might be the case, and Davis had been able to quickly confirm that no repair crew had been dispatched.

Thanks to the milder winds, Ronny was able to lower her safely. Once her boots touched the ground she undid her safety harness with her free hand, then waved to let Ronny and the others know she was all right. The steel cable retracted into the skimmer's belly, taking the harness with it. When it was gone, Ronny piloted the craft to the far end of the Junkyard where the abandoned earth movers were parked.

Zula quickly unwrapped the wire holding her rifle to her arm, as well as the wires holding the ballast tanks to her legs. She let the tanks fall and then hurried toward the ground hauler, moving as fast as her EVA suit would allow. She wanted to conceal herself before the Necromorph arrived. Reaching the hauler, she opened the door to the cab, climbed in, and closed the door softly behind her in order to make as little noise as possible.

Then she waited.

It was all up to Davis now.

The Necromorph pursued the human across the rocky surface. It had no idea why it was in the air instead of on the ground, as humans usually were, but it didn't care. All that mattered was getting at its prey—which remained maddeningly out of reach—and tearing the fragile creature to shreds.

It lost track of the flying human, and its head swept from side to side. This place was filled with objects that weren't natural, which meant it was a human place. Perhaps the flying prey had landed here, perhaps this was its home. If so, there might be other humans to kill, to infect, to impregnate. The Necromorph lashed its tail in the air, excited, anticipating the slaughter to come.

It detected a sudden flash of movement from its right, and as it was turning in that direction something large leaped through the air and slammed into its side. The impact knocked the Necromorph to the ground, but it rolled and swiftly came up on its feet, ready to confront its attacker. The thing standing before the Necromorph resembled a living creature—a huge insect with long back legs—but there was nothing organic about it. This was not a living thing, and yet it moved, had attacked like a living thing.

Therefore, it was a threat and had to be destroyed.

The Necromorph hissed, raised its claws, and raced forward, but before it reached the metal creature a piercing sound cut through the air. Vibrations ran through its body, and it turned just as another assailant dove out of the sky, coming straight for it. The sounds *hurt*. They were able to get past the Necromorph's protective exoskeleton in a way other assaults could not. It was as if its internal organs were being shaken apart from the inside out.

The Necromorph crouched low to the ground, and as the flying assailant drew close it leaped into the air. It lashed out with its tail and the impact altered the attacker's course, sending it toward the ground. The Necromorph landed a split second before the attacker crashed, breaking apart in a shower of sparks. A short distance away a mound of objects collapsed from the impact, sending debris tumbling and scattering across the ground.

The first enemy made another go at the Necromorph, but this time it was ready. It ducked to the side, grabbed hold of one rear leg, and yanked. The leg tore free from the body, and the enemy swerved toward the ground. It hit hard and skidded before coming to a stop against a pile of rubble. The thing lay on its side, its remaining legs waggling ineffectually for a moment before finally becoming motionless.

The ground began to tremble, and before the Necromorph could leap to the side a new attacker burst upward in a shower of rock and soil. Knocked off its feet, the Necromorph struggled to stand. As it did so yet another assailant crashed into it. The two remaining foes caught the Necromorph between them.

Abruptly, the Necromorph found itself bound by a sticky substance that also engulfed its two opponents. A new non-living assailant engulfed all three of the combatants until they were thoroughly bound by the stuff. The Necromorph struggled, but it could not break free.

Then the humans appeared, advanced, and began firing their weapons.

From her vantage point inside the hauler's cab, Zula watched the bots attack the Necromorph. Davis had connected to their systems and was controlling them, orchestrating the assault on the creature.

At first it didn't go so well. The Necromorph easily took out the Screamer and the Jumper. She wished they'd been able to use the Hider, but it was too badly damaged after the morning's training session, and was just another piece of junk. But then the Digger and the Sprinter hit the Necromorph in concert, giving the Crawler a chance to move in and begin using its webbing. She'd feared the artificial binding wouldn't prove strong enough to imprison the Necromorph, but she needn't have worried.

The webbing stuck fast and held tight.

"Go!" Zula ordered over her comm.

Leaping down from the cab, she joined the remaining trainees as they advanced on the Necromorph, pulse rifles blazing. There were enough gaps in the webbing to allow their rounds to get through. The Necromorph screeched in fury as it fought to free itself, and Zula smiled grimly as she fell in line with the trainees and continued advancing toward the bound and struggling monster.

We got you, you bastard, she thought.

Davis spoke in her ear.

"The lesions covering the Necromorph's exoskeleton have made it more resistant to rifle fire than is normal for its species. I'm afraid you're not doing any significant damage."

"Sounds like it's grenade time," Zula said, then to the rest, "Launch grenades on my mark. One, two…"

The Necromorph hunched over, crossing its arms in front of it as best it could given the webbing that constrained it. The motion made Zula think of the way a bodybuilder might flex her back muscles. At instant later the webbing covering the Necromorph's back disintegrated, eaten away by the caustic black goo emitted by the creature's broken pustules.

"…three!" Zula shouted.

The grenades launched, but with a single herculean movement the Necromorph tore free from the remainder of the webbing and darted away. The explosives struck the Digger, Sprinter, and Crawler and reduced them to shrapnel in a series of explosions. A wave of heated air rolled over the cadets and black smoke began curling upward from the shattered remains of the machines.

So much for the bots.

It had been a decent plan, one that had almost worked—but *almost* could be the difference between life and death for a soldier. They'd failed to kill the Necromorph, and the damn thing was free again. She saw no sign of the creature.

"Where is it?" she said. "Anyone have eyes on it?"

"Nothing, Boss," Masako said. The other trainees responded similarly.

"Davis? Do you have it on the tracking scanner?"

"Unfortunately not. The tracking device Tamar placed on the Necromorph is no longer transmitting. My guess is that the Crawler's webbing stuck to it, and the device was pulled off as the Necromorph escaped. Most likely it was destroyed by the grenade barrage."

"Fantastic," Zula said. It could be hiding anywhere now. Or it could've fled the Junkyard entirely, having decided to locate prey that was easier to kill. Somehow, though, she didn't think they'd be that fortunate.

"Now what, Boss?" Ronny asked. He sounded nervous, but he was doing a good job controlling it.

"The way I see it, we have two options," she replied. "Go looking for it, or wait for it to come looking for us."

"I say we take the fight to the fucker," Angela said. "I'm getting tired of this goddamned monster always—"

Thirty feet away, the Necromorph emerged from the pile of nusteel blocks. It jumped on top of one of them, and launched itself at Angela. The creature landed on her, hands on her shoulders, feet on her stomach, its weight forcing her to the ground.

The thing's claws penetrated her EVA suit to pierce the flesh beneath, and before any of them could bring a pulse rifle to bear its secondary mouth emerged, broke through her helmet's faceplate, and buried itself in her brain.

Donnell stepped forward, raising his pulse rifle to fire at the Necromorph, but he got too close. The monster's tail whipped out and struck his left leg. Even with the wind, there was a loud snapping of bones. Donnell cried out in pain and collapsed to the ground, dropping his rifle in the process. To make matters worse, he had a tear in his suit and began losing O_2... fast.

The rest of the trainees didn't wait for the command to fire. They unloaded on the Necromorph, blasting it with round after round of ammunition. The projectiles carved small divots into the creature's exoskeleton, but that was all. It seemed as if Davis had been right about the Necromorph's durability. Even so, the barrage drove the creature back a yard, then two. It hissed at them, its outer and inner mouths still wet with Angela's blood.

Zula chambered a grenade, intending to ram it down the Necromorph's throat, even if she had to do so by hand. She fired, but the creature ducked and the grenade soared toward the nusteel blocks. An instant later the grenade detonated, the explosion sending chunks of nusteel flying. The Necromorph used the distraction to slip away once more.

"Watch for it," Zula said. "It'll be back." She hurried

to check on Angela and Donnell. Angela was dead, and Donnell sat on the ground grimacing in pain, hand pressed against the tear in his suit to slow the leakage.

"Are you cut?" Zula asked.

What she meant was, *are you infected?*

"I think I'm okay," Donnell said through gritted teeth. "I'm not going to be dancing anytime soon, though."

"Ray, Genevieve, slap an emergency seal on this tear then get him to safety," Zula ordered. The two came forward while Ronny and Masako kept their weapons up, watching for the enemy.

"You want us to take him to the skimmer?" Ray asked.

"No," Zula said. "I've got other plans for it."

26

Zula stood alone in the middle of the Junkyard.

"Remember that comment I made about you having a secret death wish?" Davis said. *"I don't think it's so secret anymore."*

"Funny," Zula said.

Ray and Genevieve had gotten Donnell to one of the earth movers and put him inside the cab. They were standing guard over him. Ray had been unhappy that Zula had ordered them to remain there, but Genevieve had seemed relieved. Zula didn't judge the woman too harshly. She'd seen a lot of death this day, more than enough to shake a seasoned warrior, let alone a rookie.

Zula had sent Ronny and Masako out in search of the Necromorph. The plan was for them to get its attention and lure it to her. If it attacked her on its own, without their help, so much the better. She'd already lost five trainees today—half their number—and she didn't want to lose any more.

Death was an inevitable outcome of war, whether it was yours, your foe's, or any innocents caught in the middle. You did what you could to minimize the risks while maximizing the chances of victory. But when the shooting started, one way or another, blood would be shed. This was a reality with which every soldier had to make peace somehow. Zula hadn't fully understood this when she'd joined the Corps. She'd thought she'd come to understand it during her battles with Xenomorphs, but she realized now that she hadn't known jack.

It was one thing to risk your own life fighting a Xenomorph infestation on a relatively deserted ship or station, but to do so in a populated area like the Lodge, while leading a group of people who trusted you to command them… that was a different story. She, too, had seen more than enough death this day, and she was going to make sure it ended, here and now.

Even at the cost of her own life.

She heard shooting, and knew Ronny and Masako had found the Necromorph. Or it had found them. Either way, the end was near.

A moment later she saw them running toward her, the Necromorph in fast pursuit. There was less dust in the air now, so visibility was better. Masako was having a hard time running, likely because she'd reinjured the ankle she'd twisted during the training session, and Ronny was helping her. He had an arm wrapped around her waist, and she had one of hers draped across his shoulders. Together, they managed a kind of running-hopping gait, but it forced them to move far more slowly than they would've otherwise. Zula feared the Necromorph would catch up to them any second and bring them both down.

She started running toward them. Far too quickly, she judged the Necromorph was within striking distance of the pair.

"Get down!" she shouted. She stopped running, aimed her pulse rifle, and fired just as Ronny and Masako threw themselves to the ground.

Bullets struck the Necromorph's chest. There weren't as many pustules there as on its back, but there were enough. Black goo shot outward, but somehow none of it struck Ronny or Masako.

Zula kept firing.

Come on, she thought. *Come ON!*

The Necromorph slowed, and for a horrible second Zula thought it was going to kill Ronny and Masako. She waved her arms in the air to get the creature's attention.

"Hey!" she shouted. "Over here, you ugly bastard!"

There was no way the Necromorph could hear her, sealed up as she was in her EVA suit, and yet the creature picked up speed once more. It jumped over Ronny and Masako without hesitation and raced toward Zula. Now it was her turn to run.

She spun around and headed toward the south end of the Junkyard, past the pair of earth movers and the broken exosuit cargo hauler. Past the headless Hider, the bot now little more than a silvery statue.

"You got the engines on?"

"Fired up and ready."

"Open the side door."

"Doing it now."

Running in an EVA suit wasn't easy. It had to be a mostly straight-legged gait and push off with each foot as if trying to jump. It had felt very strange the first time she'd tried it, but the technique worked—especially on worlds like Jericho 3 where the gravity was less than on Earth. Zula covered the ground at a good clip, and while she knew the Necromorph was right on her tail, she thought there was a better than even chance she'd reach the skimmer before the creature could kill her.

She'd better. Her entire plan depended on not dying too soon.

Ronny had parked the skimmer to the southeast of the earth movers, and she veered to her left as she reached the big machines, then kept going. The wind and thunder— both less intense than they'd been back at the proto-colony—were still loud enough that she didn't hear the skimmer's engines until she was almost on top of the craft.

As Davis had promised, the side door was open, and Zula headed straight for it. She reached the door and was about to enter when she felt something—the Necromorph's tail?—strike her back. The impact sent her stumbling forward and into the skimmer, where she lost her balance and went down. She rolled over as the creature rushed in after her, mouth open wide, clear viscous fluid dripping from its teeth. Zula gave the creature a face full of bullets, and it backed away, swiping at its face with its claws, like a dog trying to scratch an itchy, irritated muzzle.

"Get us in the air!" Zula ordered.

She thought Davis would argue with her. In the original plan, she'd been supposed to escape through the emergency exit before lift-off, but the longer she screwed around with the Necromorph, the more it would realize it had been baited into a trap. If that happened, it would get off the skimmer before any harm could come to it.

She wasn't about to let that happen.

Thankfully her synthetic friend didn't hesitate. He closed the hull door and engaged the skimmer's controls. The craft rose quickly into the sky and was immediately battered by the wind, lightning flashes visible through the windscreen.

An alert icon appeared in her helmet's display screen. Her suit was in danger of a catastrophic breach. Had the Necromorph's tail cut through it when it struck her?

Then she saw the problem.

Once they were both aboard the skimmer, she'd fired on it at close range. That meant more of its pustules had been broken open, ejecting the acidic black goo its body produced. She quickly examined the inside of her helmet and saw—in the upper left of the faceplate—a tiny black dot. It wasn't much, but it was beginning to eat into the surface of the viewing pane. Once it finished burning all the way through there'd be a tiny hole. She'd start losing O_2, and be exposed to the cellular necrosis virus. The leak would be a slow one, but a leak was a leak.

There wasn't time to worry about it now. She was trapped on a rapidly ascending skimmer with a bloodthirsty alien monster. She'd worry about the hole later—if there *was* a later for her.

"Davis, start overloading the engines."

"Roger that."

An instant later the engines began to emit a high-pitched whine, and Zula could feel the deck beneath her feet begin to vibrate.

The bullets that had driven back the creature hadn't caused any significant damage, but it stood about fifteen feet away in the rear of the hold, head swiveling back and forth as if confused. It had never been in a flying craft before, Zula thought, and was having trouble adjusting to the different sensations—the engine thrum, the jostling as Davis battled the wind, the stomach-dropping feeling of rapid ascent. These were all foreign stimuli to the Necromorph, and it would be unable to tell if any of the sensations—or all of them—indicated a threat. Thus, it hesitated.

Zula took advantage of her enemy's confusion. She moved to the emergency exit—the one she'd gone through when hanging from the ship to lure the creature to the Junkyard in the first place. The round door in the deck led to a small storage area where emergency supplies and equipment were stored, and in that area was a second door, this one opening to the outside.

It was too late for Zula to crawl through and escape before Davis took off, but the door was still her best hope for survival. She pressed her hand down on the middle of the circular door and waited. After several seconds it slid open.

Time to go, Zula thought.

Before she could climb inside, the Necromorph—apparently having decided to ignore the disorienting sensations of powered flight—started toward her. The claws of its feet *tik-tak*ked on the floor as it came, and its clawed fingers clenched and unclenched as if it were anticipating sinking them into her flesh. Its tail swished lazily behind it—like a cat's, Zula thought—and it hissed softly, menacingly as it came, ropey strands of drool dripping from its mouth.

She raised her pulse rifle, intending to shoot the goddamned thing once more to deter it from attacking, but when she squeezed the trigger nothing happened. She took a quick glance at the ammo counter on the weapon's side and saw it was down to zero. All her ammunition was gone, and she'd already switched out the clip once since leaving the Lodge.

She had no more clips.

When the Necromorph was within a meter of her, she thought it would rush forward and attack. Instead, the creature leaned forward, opened its jaws wide, and its smaller secondary mouth emerged. It coughed, and a black cloud of cellular necrosis gusted out to enshroud her. She flinched, terrified at first, but then she remembered she was in an EVA suit and was protected from the disease.

Except for the tiny hole being eaten away in her helmet's faceplate. Had the dot of black goo penetrated all the way through? If it had, could outgoing O_2 push it away? She didn't know, but if she had been infected, she wasn't displaying symptoms yet.

Checking her display, she saw that the breach was still imminent, and hoped that was true. Stepping backward to the rear row of seats, she bent down, grabbed hold of a seat belt, and wrapped it around her arm.

"Climb, Davis! The steeper, the better!"

The synthetic obeyed instantly. The skimmer's nose tilted upward until it was pointed straight into the cloud-covered sky. The Necromorph tried to maintain its footing, but the change in the skimmer's altitude came too fast. The creature slipped and slid, hands and feet scrabbling on the floor, desperate to maintain its position, but the g-forces were too much for it and, without anything to hold onto, it fell downward to the insulated bulkhead that separated the engines from the rest of the ship.

The bulkhead was now the bottom of a pit, above it the craft's passenger area. Zula hung downward, gripping the belt she'd grabbed. There wasn't much distance between her and the Necromorph, and if the monster had suffered any injuries they weren't apparent as it began to climb up the walls of the shaft.

She kept her gaze fixed on the thing as it came. Lightning flashed around them more frequently, maybe because they'd moved away from the Junkyard and the rest of the training area. The engine whine was louder now, almost deafening. Zula shouted to be heard over the noise.

"On my mark, Davis, go into a steep dive!"

Again, the synthetic didn't question her judgment, which was too bad. She would've liked someone to talk her out of this.

The Necromorph was halfway to her.

"Now!"

Davis performed the required maneuver. Zula retained hold of the seat belt as her body twisted and fell. When her lifeline grew taut, she swung herself between the last two rows of seats. The Necromorph fell past her, claws slashing the air as it attempted to get a piece of her. It missed, and continued falling until it struck the windscreen.

"When you're low enough, level out and decelerate," Zula said.

"Low enough for...? Oh, yes. I see. Will do."

Seconds later the craft leveled out. Both Zula and the Necromorph hit the floor at the same time. She moved fast, letting go of the seat belt, dropping her pulse rifle, and crawling quickly toward the emergency exit's open door. She slid inside and crouched over, searching for—

—the harness. There it was, attached to the drop cable. She didn't have time to put it on properly, so she slid it over the top of her body, gripped it tightly with her hands.

"Release!"

One of the Necromorph's clawed hands plunged through the upper opening, seeking to grab hold of her. Before it could, the bottom door slid open, and Zula tumbled out into the air. She spun as she fell, but managed to keep hold of the harness all the way down. The line went taut, and she couldn't see what was happening, but when her boots hit the ground with a jarring *thud* she let go of the harness and rolled forward to bleed off momentum.

"Disengage cable and seal the door!"

Looking up at the skimmer she half-expected to see the Necromorph plummeting down toward her. It wasn't. The cable detached and began falling toward the ground, and the outer emergency exit door closed tight.

"I'll take it from here," Davis said.

She grabbed a handful of soil and rubbed it against her faceplate, wiping away the black dot of Necromorph goo. Then she stood and watched the skimmer angle upward once again, to ascend rapidly into the cloud-filled sky, engines screaming now, lightning flashes illuminating its path. She imagined the Necromorph inside, once more having fallen against the bulkhead, pressed tight by g-forces, confused, angry, and—she hoped—frightened.

When the skimmer was almost lost to view, Davis sent a power surge into its overloaded engines, and for an instant the craft's explosion lit up the sky more brightly than any lightning could. Zula smiled.

It was a magnificent sight.

27

The Commissary was only half full. That was partly due to the subdued atmosphere in the Lodge after everything that had happened, but mostly because more than a third of the facility's population had succumbed to cellular necrosis before the outbreak burned itself out. There simply weren't as many people around anymore, and many of those who were didn't much feel like socializing.

Zula sat at a table with the surviving trainees: Ronny, Masako, Ray, Genevieve, and—his leg in a cast—Donnell. No medical professionals had survived the Necromorph's attack on the Lodge, but Davis had researched the procedure to set the leg, which he claimed was straightforward enough. He'd guided Zula as she set Donnell's bones and put a cast on him. The man had only cried out in pain once—okay, twice—so she figured she'd done an adequate job.

"I can't believe Venture is shutting the whole place down," Ray said.

"Would *you* want to work here after everything that happened?" Masako said.

"I guess not."

"They won't abandon the place entirely," Ronny said. "They'll use it for something. Maybe make it a resupply depot for ships."

"They'll probably keep the mines open, too," Donnell added.

Everyone agreed that was likely.

They were all drinking—coffee, tea, or water—and as Zula sipped hers she sat back in her chair. Her back felt fine, not even a hint of soreness despite everything she'd put her body through during the fight against the Necromorph. She'd also developed no symptoms of cellular necrosis, something for which she was profoundly grateful.

After the destruction of the skimmer—and its sole nonhuman passenger—Davis had contacted the proto-colony to arrange for someone to come pick them up. Several colonists got into one of the heavy ore haulers, the big machines sturdy enough to handle the strong winds, and set out for the Junkyard. Zula and the trainees' O_2 had been running low by the time the colonists found them, but they reached the colony before their air ran out and remained there, safe and warm, until the electrical storm ran its course.

When Zula returned to the Lodge, Davis told her about Brigette's last request. She made a trip to Millard Gagnon's lab, and with the synth's help got inside and destroyed all his research on the Ovomorph and Necromorph. That required deleting a number of computer files and physically trashing the computers themselves as an added precaution. Gagnon had been so paranoid about his research that he'd never saved it to the Lodge's intranet, so once they'd finished, they knew they'd gotten it all.

The bio-samples—especially the Ovomorph, the embryo-implanter, and the corpse of the poor man Gagnon had used as the Necromorph's host—were more difficult to dispose of. In the end an unexpected fire broke out in Gagnon's lab, and for some unknown reason the lab's fire-suppression system failed to activate in time, only coming online and extinguishing the flames when the lab and its entire contents had been reduced to a charred ruin.

Upon returning to the Lodge they'd learned of Aleta's death. Davis checked the woman's outgoing messages, as well as the files on her computer. Her assistant's as well. Aleta had sent several messages to Venture's higher-ups regarding Gagnon's experiments, but she'd sent no hard data. Davis deleted all the files on the computers, though, just to be sure.

His ident chip was in Zula's pocket, and a duffle bag containing what few possessions she had lay on the floor next to her chair.

"So what are you five going to do now?" she asked.

Ronny exchanged glances with the others before answering.

"Venture's asked us if we'd like to relocate to another facility, and continue with the Colony Protection Force."

"Word is," Genevieve said, "that Venture was ready to pull the plug on the program, but someone convinced them how important it was."

"Was it you?" Donnell asked Zula.

"Ask me no questions, and I'll tell you no lies," she said with a smile. Her actions of the past few days had given her a bit of clout, for the moment at least. It wouldn't last. "Are any of you going to take Venture up on the offer?"

"We all are," Ronny said. "Especially considering the pay raise they're giving us."

"You're worth it," Zula said. "You've got a hell of a lot more experience now."

The group fell silent for several moments, and Zula knew they were thinking about their comrades who had died while they'd gained that experience.

"How about you, Boss?" Ronny said. "Want to join us?"

"If it hadn't been for you," Ray said, "a lot more people would've died."

"The Lodge might be nothing more than a corpse-filled tomb right now," Masako agreed. "The proto-colony, too."

Zula sipped her coffee.

"I can't," she said finally. "What happened here has convinced me that I can't stand by and wait for the next opportunity to continue the fight against the Xenomorphs—and more importantly, against people stupid and greedy enough to think the monsters can be exploited. I'm not going to wait for the fight to come to me, like it did here. I'm going to take the fight to the corporations, to try to prevent incidents like this one from happening in the first place."

The trainees were quiet for a time.

"Maybe we could go with you," Ronny suggested. "You want to win a fight on the scale you're talking about, you're going to need people by your side."

"True," Zula said. That was something she had learned at the Lodge, as well. Yes, she had Davis, but the two of them alone couldn't take on the entire galaxy. Here it had taken all of them—the dead as well as those who'd survived—to stop one Xenomorph. This creature had been an especially deadly specimen, true, but that only told Zula that Xenomorphs were even more of a threat than she'd thought. If they could all mutate, stopping them once and for all could prove far more difficult than she'd ever imagined.

"The colonization of the galaxy is going to move forward," Zula said. "People will leave Earth looking to forge new lives for themselves. They're going to need someone to protect them from whatever hostile forces they might encounter along the way—especially when those forces turn out to be their fellow humans. The five of you are uniquely qualified for the job now. Not too many people have gone up against a Xenomorph and beat the damn thing, let alone lived to tell about it. You're all needed out here, doing what you were trained to do. Protect."

Again they fell into silence for a time, but it wasn't an uncomfortable one. Rather, it was a companionable silence, one where they could simply sit and enjoy being in each other's presence without needing to say anything. Zula hadn't had many friends in her life, and it was a good feeling.

Masako nodded to the duffle.

"Shipping out then?" she said.

This was the real reason Zula had asked them all to join her in the Commissary. To tell them she was leaving. A supply ship had landed yesterday, and Zula had talked the commander into giving her a lift off-planet.

"Yes."

"Heading off to tilt at some more windmills?" Ronny smiled. His words were teasing, but his tone was warm.

"Not right away. First, Davis and I are going back to Earth. We need to pick up a friend."

See you soon, Amanda, she thought.

She took another sip of her coffee and smiled.

28

"I can't believe they left all this stuff here."

"It's cheaper to abandon it than ship it off-planet."

"I suppose."

Royce Leahy and Taneka McKinley walked down an aisle in the Lodge's warehouse. Both carried computer pads and both were tired. They'd been cataloguing the building's contents for several hours now, and Royce didn't know about Taneka, but he could use a break.

"Do you think it's true?" Taneka asked.

"What?"

"What they say happened here. You know."

"You mean that there was some kind of monster running around killing people? Naw. The only thing that killed anyone here was a disease."

Neither of them was wearing a biohazard suit, but they'd both been inoculated against cellular necrosis. Besides, the outbreak had been months ago. The facility was completely safe now—at least, that's what Royce kept telling himself.

Not long after the outbreak, Venture had closed down V-22—or the Lodge, as it was more commonly known—and reassigned the surviving personnel to facilities on other planets, space stations, and even Earth. The Lodge had remained empty since then, but now Venture was looking into the feasibility of reusing the facility—or at least sections of it—as a refueling station. Royce and Taneka were part of the inspection team that had been sent to evaluate the Lodge's potential. Venture wanted everything checked out, including the life-support systems. They worked fine, although he thought the air had a musty smell to it.

In Royce's opinion the Lodge would be too expensive to operate, even partially, and Venture would be better off leaving the facility empty and offline. But he was just a lowly site inspector. Why would the higher-ups in the company give a damn what he thought?

"I know it's true," Taneka said.

It took Royce a second to realize she was talking about the monster again. She went on.

"One of my friends has a cousin who worked in the Tech department here. She says the monster was real."

Royce didn't feel like arguing with her about it. He was too tired. They'd been on their feet without a break for hours now, and—

He stopped walking, and frowned.

They'd come to the end of one of the aisles in the back of the warehouse, a section that wasn't particularly well lit. There, sitting on the floor and concealed in the shadows, was something that looked very much like an egg. A big one.

Taneka saw it, too.

"What the hell *is* that?" she asked.

Royce turned his computer pad's screen toward the thing, illuminating it with the light from the display. The object was a greenish leathery thing, about three feet high and covered with black lesions and crusty nodules.

"I have no idea," Royce said, but suddenly Taneka's talk about monsters no longer seemed so ridiculous. "Whatever it is, we should report it to a supervisor."

He reached up to tap the comm device in his ear. As if the motion was a trigger, the egg began to quiver, and then it opened like a flower.

ACKNOWLEDGEMENTS

Thanks to my fantastic agent Cherry Weiner for her guidance, support, and friendship. Thanks to the Mighty Steves—Steve Saffel and Steve Tzirlin—who helped shape this novel from the beginning. *Alien: Prototype* is a far better book because of their efforts.

ABOUT THE AUTHOR

Tim Waggoner's first novel came out in 2001, and he's published more than forty novels and seven collections of short stories since. He writes original fantasy and horror, as well as media tie-ins. His novels include *Like Death*, considered a modern classic in the genre, and the popular Nekropolis series of urban fantasy novels. He's written tie-in fiction for *Supernatural*, *Grimm*, *The X-Files*, *Doctor Who*, *Kingsman*, *Resident Evil*, *A Nightmare on Elm Street*, and *Transformers*, among others. His articles on writing have appeared in *Writer's Digest*, *Writer's Journal*, and *Writer's Workshop of Horror*.

He's won the Bram Stoker Award, been a multiple finalist for the Shirley Jackson Award and the Scribe Award, and his fiction has received numerous Honorable Mentions in volumes of *Best Horror of the Year*. In 2016, the Horror Writers Association honored him with the Mentor of the Year Award.

In addition to writing, Tim is also a full-time tenured professor who teaches creative writing and composition at Sinclair College.